Jemima Price has travelled extensively and combines this with her love of writing. She is currently a busy working mother and teacher in Cambridge.

To ‘the dudes’ T, J and S and the best days of our lives.

Jemima Price

Finding Ruby

Austin Macauley Publishers™
London • Cambridge • New York • Sharjah

This is a work of fiction. Names, characters, businesses, places, events, locales, and incidents are either the products of the author's imagination or used in a fictitious manner. Any resemblance to actual persons, living or dead, or actual events is purely coincidental.

A CIP catalogue record for this title is available from the British Library.

ISBN 9781528945738 (Paperback)
ISBN 9781528971461 (ePub e-book)

www.austinmacauley.com

First Published (2020)
Austin Macauley Publishers Ltd
25 Canada Square
Canary Wharf
London
E14 5LQ

Special thanks must go to Christianne for being my first reader and laughing – and crying! - in the right places. Thank you to Mum and Sally for reading this so long ago and believing in me, even if it took me a while to do something about it. Thank you to my little army of boys at home, for making me want to keep my feet on the ground. Thank you to Jennie and Simon for that day, long ago, when we sat down in a pub with a map and worked out the trip that was to change our lives forever.

Finally, thank you to Tony for giving me the cosy fire but also the cool refreshing breeze.

Prologue

With a heavy stomach, I watched the bank moving further away from me as the small wooden boat crossed the river sluggishly. I felt the eyes of the boat driver on me as he manoeuvred the rudder, wondering no doubt why I was alone, why I wasn't with a boyfriend or a group of girl travellers like most of the other passengers. I looked towards the oncoming shore avoiding his eye contact. Scraggy palms swayed in the breeze and people moved along the narrow beach like ants, loading passengers, animals and sacks of coconuts onto boats. Growing smaller and further away by the second, the riverbank behind retreated from me, and with it, my old life. Clutching onto my rucksack to stop it from slipping over the edge and into the murky brown water, I turned back to the advancing shore. The approaching land looked verdant and alien. I couldn't believe I was doing this. A few months ago, everything had been so normal. Now here I was on a boat, deep in the heart of the jungle, heading somewhere I had never been before, with no plan and no concrete destination in mind.

Go back. The thought kept running through my head like a mantra. But from somewhere deep within, a small, resolute voice answered: "There was no going back." There was nothing to go back to.

How had it come to this? I was on my own in a strange country, far from anyone or anything I had ever known and I was terrified. I fixed my eyes on the shadowy, leafy bank, trying to numb my heart and silence my mind.

Just get through today, I told myself. Tomorrow was too much to think about yet.

Part One
London

Chapter One

I stared in disbelief at the small rectangular piece of paper in my hands and felt the happiness of the sunny morning draining away. Richard grinned at me expectantly; his eyebrows were raised in question, waiting for my response.

"Happy birthday, sweetheart."

He was evidently very pleased with himself.

I forced a smile onto my face but I couldn't raise my eyes from the piece of paper.

"Rich, this is...fantastic, but..."

I re-read the ticket; a round-the-world ticket flying to Thailand, Singapore, Hong Kong, and Los Angeles before returning to London.

"Valid for a year," Richie said excitedly. "We fly into Bangkok, then we can travel around South East Asia as much as we want, before flying to Singapore for a bit of shopping, then onto Australia for a couple of months and a few days in LA on the way home. It should take us about nine months, but we can extend it if we like, which I imagine we will..."

I had switched off after the 'nine months' because I had noticed the date of the first flight. It was 1st October. Today was the 30th August.

"Rich, this must be wrong," I said turning the ticket to face him, "The date says 1st October."

He shook his head, grinning that impish smile that always won me over, no matter what he had done – and trust me; he had done a few things that needed a lot of winning over.

"No mistake. I thought we should strike while the iron's hot. Feel the fear and do it anyway and all that. I thought a month was plenty of time to get things in order, buy our rucksacks and stuff, get our jabs, get your sabbatical sorted, get someone into the flat..."

"Get someone into the flat?"

I sat up straighter in bed, nearly tipping over the orange juice that was balanced on the tray on my lap.

"Well, yeah," he shrugged. "We can't just leave it empty while we're away, can we? The mortgage has to get paid somehow."

I stared at him, my mouth hanging open. His smile faltered. This obviously wasn't the reaction he was hoping for. I snapped my mouth shut, reached out my hand and squeezed his knee.

"Look, Rich," I said forcing a smile onto my face, trying to mean what I was about to say, "This is a really lovely surprise, but...well, it *is* a surprise. I mean you only mentioned you would like to go travelling the other day..."

"A month ago, and I haven't stopped talking about it since. You just never listen to me," he sulked.

"OK, a month ago. But there's been quite a lot going on. You know, buying a flat, moving in, decorating; you can't blame me if I didn't take you seriously about this," I tried to catch his eyes as they studied the floor, no longer smiling and happy. I suddenly felt awful. I put on my biggest smile, masking my dismay.

"Rich, this is great. It really is; I was just surprised that's all. Thank you."

I kissed his unshaven cheek. The dimples that I adored appeared as a slow smile spread over his face, and before I knew it, he had jumped astride me on the bed, pushing the breakfast tray aside, knocking juice all over the duvet as he bounced up and down.

"Rich, the duvet..." I protested weakly.

"I *knew* you'd come round. It'll be great, Ruby. Just imagine: you and me on a beach in Thailand. And you never know," he pinned my wrists to the bed either side of my head, "it may just be the kind of place that would persuade someone to get engaged..."

My stomach lurched as he leaned down to kiss me. OK then, that persuaded me. As he bounced off the bed and skipped into the bathroom singing a Bob Marley tune, I couldn't stop the sinking feeling in my stomach. Backpacking. I just didn't *do* backpacking.

***

"*Backpacking*?" the voice screeched down the phone, "What the hell are you talking about, darling?"

"Well, putting a rucksack on your back and travelling round the world. That's what I am talking about, Mother."

"You?" I could see her throwing her perfectly coiffed red hair back over her shoulders as her tinkling laugh came down the phone. "Don't be absurd! Get a refund. Go to Barcelona instead. Or New York for Christmas. It's just wonderful."

"Yes, I know, Mother, and that *is* more my thing, and it *is* what I would prefer to do. But Rich wants to go backpacking, and there's nothing I can do about it."

"Rich wants, Rich wants," she mimicked. "When are you going to do what *you* want, darling?"

I knew she would be shaking her head, and I heard her taking a drag on her cigarette. "Whatever happened to women's lib? Waste of bloody time. Your generation is more of a push-over than ever before."

I sighed. Mum just didn't get it. Rich was impulsive and was wont to do this kind of crazy thing – which was part of why I loved him – but there was no room for compromise; it was his way or none at all – and although I knew deep down that it probably wasn't very healthy in a relationship, I also knew that to hold onto him, I had to go along with it. It usually wasn't all that bad. Like the skiing trip he booked last minute, last Christmas, even though I had never skied before and had never entertained the idea in my life. Never mind that I broke my wrist on the second day and had to watch him hurtling down the slopes for the next two weeks; I was quite happy sitting by the fire and waiting for him to come home in the evening for romantic cuddles and candlelit baths. Although there was actually only one candlelit bath, as Rich had made some new friends on the slopes – some lawyers from London – and he wanted to go to the resort bar most evenings. Anyway, I was happy to let Rich shine. He flew, and I was the rock he always landed on.

"Mum, I'm only twenty-seven. It's about time I got out and saw the world."

I cringed. That was a load of rubbish and I knew it. I actually saw enough of the world as far as I was concerned – well, I'd seen a lot of Corfu and Crete, I'd been up to Scotland, and I was from Cardiff so I'd seen a lot of South and West Wales. Never been up to North Wales though, but Rich and I could do all that when we were married. I pictured cosy, country pubs, and cottage hotel rooms with roaring fires…

"Ruby? Are you listening?"

"Yes, Mother," I said sighing, knowing full well that she knew I was lying.

"I'm not saying you shouldn't get out and see the world. But you should do it because *you* want to – not because Richard does."

"I do want to," I protested quietly.

I didn't even convince myself.

"Hm. Well, just think carefully about all this. And make sure you get all your jabs and malaria tablets. Oh God and you'll have to take tons of suntan lotion, you know how you burn…"

"Yes, Mum, look I've really got to go. I'm going to Boxercise with Steph. Bye!"

"Ruby…"

I hung up pretending I couldn't hear. I didn't need my mum telling me that I was crazy to do this. I already knew it.

***

"What…uh…the…hell…oomph…do…you…uh…mean…backpacking? Oomph!"

Steph managed to gasp out in between kicks and punches. She was holding the pads and I was doing the punching.

"And roundhouse! Come on girls! Imagine the pad is your cheating boyfriend. Give it all you've got!"

I glanced at the bleached blonde instructor with the fake American accent bouncing around in her shiny blue leotard at the front of the hall, kicking her skinny little legs in the air. I knew it was a fake accent because I had seen her having a fag outside the Leisure Centre in the car park, complaining to the cleaner about her boyfriend who really was cheating on her. And she was doing it all in a broad Geordie accent.

"Why doesn't anyone understand what I mean by it? Backpacking! You know, carrying a rucksack, staying in pokey, dinghy hostels, hanging round with hippy do-as-you-likies…heeyah!"

I kicked the pad full force, nearly knocking Steph off her feet.

"God," Steph looked horrified.

"Yeah I know. But Rich is all excited and he hinted that he might propose in Thailand so I've got to do it."

"OK girls, swap positions!"

I took the pad and Steph donned the gloves and started tapping away lightly at the pad. She wouldn't have knocked out a flea.

"How long will you be gone for?"

"Well, Rich is talking about nine months, but it may be even longer," I said despairingly.

"*Nine months!* That's like *forever!*"

I nodded miserably. Steph had stopped punching at all now and stood with her arms limply at her sides.

"What about your flat? What about Moggy? What about *me*?"

Big fat tears threatened to spill out of her round blue eyes.

"Oh don't be silly, Steph," I said trying to be brusque, "it's not that long. And you can look after Moggy. And we're going to rent out the flat."

"But I'm allergic to cats."

I smiled weakly and shrugged. She suddenly leaned back and with all her effort gave the pad an almighty kick sending me flying backwards.

***

I lay on the tiny bed staring up at the ceiling. I had never felt so alone, in my entire life. I heard a cockroach scuttle under the bed. The noise of the fan was soothing. I couldn't believe I was doing this. I couldn't believe I was on my own. Nobody knew where I was. Rich's smiling face flashed into my mind, and my stomach convulsed into a ball. I pushed the image out of my mind and wearily got to my feet. I peered out of the grimy window and down into the street below. Street sellers sat behind their carts selling various foodstuffs; a couple of girls with enormous rucksacks on their backs were climbing the steps to my hostel. I felt so envious of them because they had each other. I looked around the room, at my forlorn rucksack on the floor. What was I doing here?

I headed downstairs in search of some food. At the reception desk a tiny Thai woman sat on a little plastic chair watching a tiny black and white TV.

"Uh, excuse me," I stood on tiptoes so I could see her. "Is there a restaurant near here?"

She looked at me, smiling blankly. I mimicked eating with an imaginary knife and fork.

"There's a restaurant down the road," came a deep voice from behind me.

I turned to see a guy with dirty blonde dreads sitting on the sofa. I beamed at him, so glad to see a friendly face.

"It does OK food: cheap prawns and stuff."

He had a Canadian accent.

"Are, uh, you going there now?" I asked, trying not to sound too needy.

He shook his head and motioned towards his feet. It was only then that I noticed his bags. My heart sank.

"Catching a bus to Vang Vieng."

I nodded brightly.

"Right well. Thanks. Uh bye."

I stumbled out of the foyer. I couldn't believe how desperate I had sounded. A few weeks ago, I wouldn't have given someone like him the time of day. But I just hated being alone. I didn't do *alone.*

Chapter Two

"Backpacking? What the hell is that?" Lata shouted over the din before lighting her cigarette from the end of Tim's.

I rolled my eyes and leaned closer so she could hear.

"You know, travelling on a budget."

She screwed up her tiny nose.

"Oh my fucking God. You mean like wearing stupid floaty skirts and hideous shoes and staying in flea-ridden bunk-beds and stuff."

I nodded with a rueful look on my face and shrugged. I was dying for a cigarette and watched as she blew the blueish smoke out from between her glossy lips. Her fingers were long and elegant with dark purplish nail varnish on her nails. Tim, as usual, sat silently, his eyes hidden behind his sunglasses.

"Tim darling, do take your glasses off. You look like a prick. We're in a bar," Lata ordered. Tim removed his glasses looking slightly surprised. Because he *always* wore them, he sometimes forgot he was wearing them. Lata had told me he sometimes got into bed with them on until she told him to take them off. The thought of Tim, naked in bed in sunglasses, crossed my mind and I had to think quickly of something else.

Lata and Tim were possibly the sexiest people I knew. Neither of them was amazingly good-looking – Lata had a slight over-bite and Tim was slightly chubby – but they both just had *something* about them. Lata's mum was Indian, so she had beautiful honey-coloured skin, long, sleek glossy black hair and heavily lashed inky-black eyes. She always wore spiky stilettos – boots or shoes – unless she was on Tim's motorbike, when she donned huge black biker boots. Tim was pretty non-descript, quietly good-looking, shaved black hair and slightly scruffy; always in hoodies and trainers, and his ever-present sunglasses. But when he smiled, his face changed. One flash of that smile and you were doomed. But what made him even more disarming was that behind his sunglasses was a pair of the bluest eyes you would ever see – which always made me wonder why he kept them covered by his glasses. But men are weird like that. He had this way of squinting that would make other people look like they were short sighted, but that gave him a smouldering, brooding look. Lata and Tim were inseparable, intimidating and great friends. Lata would defend you to the death once you were on her side.

She sipped her Disaronno on the rocks – she was probably the only person I knew who drank it. And she looked like she had stepped straight out of the advert.

"Why on earth do you want to do that?"

"Well, *I* don't want to do it. It's Rich..."

Lata rolled her huge eyes.

"Oh come on, Lata, it was really thoughtful of him. It's a really interesting birthday present. And he so wants to do it. At least he wants me to do it with him..." I trailed off pathetically.

"And he's going to propose in Thailand," Steph piped up from behind her huge glass of white wine.

I shot her an exasperated look and she took a huge gulp of her drink. Lata shook her head slowly.

"Ruby, Ruby, Ruby…"

"He just said that as a joke," I mumbled, feeling my cheeks burning. I drained my drink feeling desperate. I looked around at the heaving pub; city boys lined up against the bar, their ties undone and eyes sparkling from their after work drinks; a group of impossibly good-looking people from the insanely expensive hairdressers opposite in quirky multi-coloured outfits and matching multi-coloured hair cut at aggressive angles; another group of women in their latest skirt-suits from Reiss. Friday night filled the air with the promise of the weekend and all that London had to offer. This was me, this was my life. I didn't want to leave it. Not for a million quid.

"This is where you belong, Ruby," Lata said as if reading my thoughts. "Let him go alone. As they say, if you really love someone, you'll let them go, and if they love you, they'll come back."

"And who's going to stop me from sleeping with people if you go?" Steph piped up from behind her empty glass.

Steph had been my best friend since University. She had been in the room next to mine in the Halls of Residence and I had had to listen to the squeaking of her headboard from almost the first night I arrived. I had been a little bit intimidated by her at first, this tall willowy girl with long red hair. She was popular immediately with the opposite sex and I always saw her in the centre of a crowd of people. I assumed she was fantastically confident and, I am ashamed to admit, full of herself. It's amazing how you can get people so wrong. We first met in a pottery class that I had decided to take in my spare time to beef up my CV as I didn't have any other extra-curricular activities. She was at the back of the room looking like a little lost girl and when she saw me walk in her face lit up in a big beautiful smile. I looked behind me but no, she really was smiling at me I realised in amazement. She waved.

"Hi, Ruby," she breathed as I neared her. I was stunned that she knew my name. She patted the seat beside her. And from that moment we were firm friends.

I discovered very quickly that she had the lowest self-esteem of anyone I had ever met. As a result, she would sleep with anyone who was interested in her whether she fancied them or not. Quite often, however, most of these guys would fall head over heels in love with her. One guy serenaded her all night, drunk out of his skull. One guy spirited her away on an all-expenses paid trip to London to see Cats (which she hated) and stay in a pokey two-star hotel. All she said when she came back was that she knew it was over when they were in the middle of having sex and all she could think about was what had happened in *Eastenders* the night before. She still didn't finish with him for three more months.

I looked at her now, her heart-shaped face surrounded by her red hair cut into a bob. She blinked at me. I felt a lump in my throat and swigged back the last of my vodka.

"Steph, it's time you stood on your own two feet now," I squeezed her knee. "You know all there is to know now. You can do it yourself. You know you can. You don't need me to tell you anymore."

I smiled reassuringly, feeling like a mum sending her little girl out into the big bad world. She smiled a little wobbly and nodded.

Lata snorted into her drink.

"For God's sake," she rolled her eyes, "sleep with whoever you want to sleep with, Steph."

"Well, that's all well and good," I said wryly, "but she sleeps with people she *doesn't* want to as well."

Steph banged her glass down on the table, making us all jump.

"But not anymore. I will be strong. I will only sleep with guys I want to, when I want to. Not when *they* want me to. And not to make me feel good. You'll see, Ruby, I'll do you proud."

"Here, here," Tim said raising his glass. I had been wondering if he was actually asleep with his eyes open so it was nice to know he was with us in spirit as well as body. Steph groaned and slid down in her chair, looking over my shoulder.

"Oh God," Lata muttered darkly. "Obnoxious twats alert."

I glanced behind me to see the laughing faces of Rich and his mates coming through the door. I glowered at Lata and she smiled languidly.

"Apart from Richard, of course, darling."

The reason for Steph's groan and disappearing-under-the-table act was because – surprise, surprise – she had slept with at least four of Richie's close friends. And all of them were, true to Lata's word, obnoxious twats.

I watched Rich as he shouldered his way through the crowds to the bar, unaware that I was in the corner. Lata was right. I should let him go alone. I couldn't leave my life here, and my job and flat and Moggy. And he could go and get the whole thing out of his system and I would be waiting for him patiently, like the perfect girlfriend. And then he would always owe me that and would probably be willing to settle down once and for all in return for my generosity and understanding… I craned my neck to see who he was talking to. It was a girl with long, straight, blonde hair, smart white shirt and tight black skirt… Had she come in with them? No. I recognised her friend standing beside her as one of the Reiss girls from earlier. They were all talking to Richie and his mates. She was smiling up at him, a sparkly, red-lipped smile. I stood up quickly.

"No, I'm going to go with him. I've got to do it, for him and for our relationship," I told a startled Lata, Tim and Steph, "and it will be a shared experience that will make us grow as a couple."

I skirted my way round the table and headed quickly towards Rich at the bar.

"Anyone want a drink?" I asked airily over my shoulder without waiting for their answers, pinning Rich to the bar with my eyes.

***

I heaved my rucksack onto the 'bus' and climbed on after it. I wasn't used to lifting it on and off buses by myself. I filed onto the bus with the other thirty people. It was a seventeen-seater. The narrow central aisle had been filled with small plastic chairs and once all the proper seats were filled, people had to sit in these, or perch on any other available surfaces such as the dashboard. I was squashed in next to the only other two Westerners on the bus. One of them, a short chubby girl with long white blonde hair, sat against the window next to me. On the other side, seated awkwardly on one of the plastic chairs was a tall athletic girl with thick brown hair in a ponytail.

"How are you?" the blonde asked me in a broad Australian accent as I sat down. They were the two girls I had seen coming into my hostel the night before. I beamed at them.

The next ten hours were the most excruciatingly uncomfortable ten hours of my life. The bus rattled and belched along dirt roads and through swelteringly hot sweaty jungle, sending us a foot into the air every time we went over a bump. We wrapped sarongs around our faces to stop the all-pervading red dust thrown up by the wheels from infiltrating our lungs. Trish, the tall one on the plastic chair, slid back and fore down the aisle. We took it in turns to hold onto her. At one point, as we took on a new load of passengers, a tiny, wrinkled, ancient woman sat on Trish's lap.

"Make yourself comfortable," Trish exclaimed loudly but cheerfully. The old lady grinned a toothless smile at her and proceeded to perch on her legs until the next 'stop'.

The bus broke down twelve times in the first three hours. At each breakdown, we would all climb out and sit on the roadside as the driver's ten-year-old son picked up pieces that had fallen out of the engine and tried to force them back in. When we encountered a hill, we would all have to climb out again and, watched by inquisitive monkeys, walk up the hill behind the bus, wheezing and chugging its way up. We spent more time walking behind the bus than sitting on it. The most worrying thing, however, was that the brakes consisted of the ten-year-old son jumping off the bus and shoving a wooden block in front of the wheels. It was sheer hell. And it was one of the best times I had had in my life.

Tammy and Trish had me in stitches for the entire time. By the end of the journey, they had invited me to come and stay with them in Australia once my trip was over. I fully intended to take them up on the offer. They were loud, sunny, funny and open. I thought of them as my guardian angels, appearing when I was at an all-time low to help me get through the impossible.

We arrived in the dark at Nong Khiaow, a tiny village of bamboo huts huddled in the middle of ethereal mountains along the banks of a river. We traipsed around together, checking out the few guesthouses – all consisting of basic thatched huts with one bed, a hole-riddled mosquito net, and an outdoor squat toilet. We chose the cheapest, dumped our bags and headed out amongst the trees looking for somewhere to eat.

"And more importantly something to drink," Tammy informed me heartily.

We sat at a rickety little restaurant, on a veranda overlooking the river, watching the men tying up their long wooden boats. It hit me that this was the remotest place I had ever been in my life. I ordered some noodles and as Trish chatted about their lives in sunny Port Douglas on the East coast of Australia, I looked at them both gratefully for being so welcoming, so easy and so positive. I felt a rush of excitement flood through me as I breathed in the cool evening air and looked around at the rustling leaves above me and the stars beginning to appear in the inky sky overhead. The dark shapes of the mountains lurked in the background – faintly menacing and strangely comforting at the same time – hiding me and protecting me from the past and the future. Thoughts of home and family clamoured to fill my mind but I pushed them firmly away. I looked at Trish and Tammy's laughing faces; all that mattered was here and now. I was surviving.

Chapter Three

The seagulls swooped down onto the boardwalk, complaining loudly and pecking at crumbs of food that had dropped from diners' plates. The rare sun was shining onto the waters of Cardiff bay. There was a chill in the October wind but we had sat outside anyway, making the most of the sunshine that we hardly ever saw. I had gone to Mum and Dad's for a birthday lunch but as my mum didn't cook, we were at a new stylish restaurant on the waterside. I was eating something very small and beautiful-looking, Dad was poking his sautéed vegetables around his plate looking perplexed and my mum was sitting back smoking, having eaten about one piece of cucumber. She was running her fingers through her hair and blowing the smoke out in a steady stream up into the air. A few people turned and gave her dirty looks as the smoke swirled around their heads, and I looked uncomfortably at my plate. She was totally at home here, cradling a huge glass of red wine, the sun glinting off her Chanel sunglasses. Dad on the other hand looked completely out of place – not uncomfortable, just sort of lost. He looked kind of untidy as he always did, even though he was in a suit. His once-blonde hair was now a halo of thinning grey around his head, and his watery blue eyes were glazed over. He looked a bit bemused, like he didn't really know what he was doing there.

One tended not to notice either of them, however, because of my twin sister, Jess. She was shovelling pasta into her mouth, sucking up the spaghetti noisily much to my mother's distaste. Without even looking around, I knew that all eyes would be on her, watching her long, tanned legs crossed under the table, her pink wedge shoe with a ribbon tied around her ankle, bobbing up and down. Although we are twins, and are technically identical, we couldn't be more different. Although neither of us needs glasses, Jess wears coloured contacts to make her hazel-coloured eyes a startling blue. While we both keep our hair long, mine is still its original light brown, straight and long. Jess's, while still in immaculate condition was white blonde and I didn't know how long she spent getting it to tumble into the Jessica Rabbit curls she sported swept over one shoulder. It had previously been red, auburn, black and once, when she went through a phase of sexual experimentation, a shocking shade of pink. We both had bigger than average boobs, but while I saw mine as a bit of embarrassment, Jess always sported a fabulous cleavage. Except for today because, as we were having a bit of an Indian summer and October was just mildly cold rather than the bitterly miserable month it usually was, she was wearing a tight pink t-shirt with her short Miss Sixty denim mini skirt, sporting the catchy phrase 'So many boys, so little time'. I, on the other hand, was wearing a camel and beige Gap uniform. Unfortunately, I knew that people looked at the two of us and thought to themselves that Jess had got the better genes and I had what was left over. It sounds like I am feeling sorry for myself, but it's just the truth. Jess was just that bit slimmer, her bum a bit smaller, her boobs slightly bigger and her face a tad more symmetrical and, therefore, a bit prettier. Still, this was what I had always known and it didn't bother me really. I mean imagine being Elle Macpherson's sister. That's got to be crap.

Jess sucked her vodka and coke through a straw noisily and pushed another piece of garlic bread into her mouth.

"Well, I think it's fuckin' fantastic," she mumbled through a mouthful of food. The Welsh accent that I had tried so consciously to lose in London was as strong as ever with Jess.

"Jess," my mum admonished, flicking her cigarette stub onto the floor.

Jess glared at her and shovelled more food in her mouth. Her table manners were an endless source of irritation to my mother.

"Imagine it, Rube, swanning round Thailand; all those lovely beaches and lush food. I can get you a really lovely bikini at work, left over from the summer sales."

The differences between us don't just end in our looks. I got straight As in school while Jess failed every exam she ever sat, except for her Geography GCSE because she snogged the smitten Geography teacher in his cupboard. It didn't faze her though; she left school and worked at Top Shop for a few years, eventually becoming supervisor. She was, at this moment, deputy manageress of Morgan in a huge department store; she still lived at home, so her money was all her own and she was happier than ever. I, however, had gone on to university and was now a Marketing Assistant, struggling to survive on almost the same wage as Jess anyway.

However, the main difference between us is that, basically I am a good girl, and Jess is the wild child. While she was sneaking out of our bedroom window to run off to nightclubs with her mates, I was tucked up in bed terrified Mum would come in and catch her. While she left her virginity well and truly behind when she was fourteen, I managed to hold onto mine until I was nearly eighteen. While I was contemplating marriage and settling down, she was still partying at every opportunity she could get.

"But the thing is, Jess," my mum piped up, tapping another cigarette out of the packet, "Ruby doesn't actually want to go travelling. She's only doing it because Richard wants to and she can't say no to him because he walks all over her..."

"Mum!" I glared at her crossly.

"He *is* fit though," Jess said, grinning lasciviously. "I'd want to hang onto him too."

I tried to keep the pleased smile off my face. Jess had always been the one with the fantastically gorgeous, albeit meat-head, boyfriends. It had been considered a bit of a bulls-eye when I had bagged Rich.

I turned to my dad who was gazing thoughtfully at his seared asparagus.

"How's the food, Dad?" I asked, desperate to change the subject.

He looked at me as if he hadn't realised I was there.

"Oh, Ruby love. Hm? What was that?"

I saw my mum tut and knew she was rolling her eyes behind her glasses.

"The food; is it OK?"

He looked down at his plate as if seeing it for the first time.

"Oh yes fine, you know. Not overly keen on this new-fangled fusion cooking. But it's lovely really."

My dad was really into his cooking as he was the only one in the house who could do it. At the moment, he was tailoring his food to be carbohydrate free after my mum had embarked on the Atkins diet. Dad jumped as mum's mobile buzzed on the glass table top. She looked at the screen and scowled before answering.

"Speak!" she barked.

There were a few moments before she stood up and moved away from the table to lean on the metal balustrade overlooking the water.

"Well, can't you sort it out, Steve? I mean you are on-call this weekend. It's not my problem. I'm having a family lunch for my daughters' twenty seventh birthday..."

My mum was a very high-powered manager in an IT company. She had worked her way up from the postal room, where she had started when she was sixteen, to one of the most powerful positions in the company. She was the breadwinner in the family. Dad worked for the council – I never really knew what as. He just put his suit on every day and disappeared off to his office, appearing again at 5:30 and nobody ever asked him what he did. I imagined it was fantastically boring. Mum, however, got to travel all over the country with her work, sometimes overseas. Her co-workers were terrified of her, as were most people. Dad meanwhile just lived to retire, and I knew he harboured a desire to move to Spain and set up a little bistro.

Mum flipped her phone shut and turned to click her fingers at the waitress. I cringed down into my seat. I hated when she did that.

"Bill please," she called before settling back down into her seat and rummaging in her bag for her wad of credit cards. "Sorry folks, got to go into the office. Stupid incapable idiot I've got working for me has managed to crash the whole system."

"S'alright," Jess said pinching one of mum's cigarettes. "We've got to get ready for tonight, Rube. Let me do your makeup. I'll make you look stunning."

I blinked at her.

"Tonight?" I had been picturing curling up on the sofa with Bumble, our ancient Labrador and watching *Pop Idol.*

"Yeah, 'course. We got a wild twenty-seventh birthday night out lined up. We're going down to Swansea with the girls. It's gonna be such a laugh."

"Oh," I smiled weakly – the last time we'd been out in Swansea, Jess had managed to get us thrown out of a pub for dancing on the tables and had passed out in a kebab shop – "lovely."

"Shwansea's great," I declared to the taxi driver and to the other three passengers.

"My God, Jess, she's hammered," said Taylor, Jess's buxom friend who was wearing a long jet-black wig.

"I'm going travellin' drive," I informed the driver who nodded in faux interest, "I mean proper travellin'."

My Welsh accent had come back in full force in my inebriated state. I fished around in my bag and pulled out a blunt lip liner.

"But I don't wanna go, do I, Jess? No." I shook my head emphatically, "I wanna stay here and party with my little sis."

I leaned forward and started to draw a heart on the back of the driver's bald head.

"Rube!"

"Don't worry about it," the driver said, "As long as she's not sick."

I looked at Jess, and she looked at me, before lunging for the handle of the window. Too late.

Chapter Four

I couldn't believe this day had finally come. I stood in line waiting to board the plane. Rich kept looking at me, grinning and squeezing my hand. I smiled at him, hoping it looked convincing.

"This is it, Rube," he breathed, "the first day of the rest of our lives."

His smiling eyes were dancing. He was so excited. I wished I felt the same.

The night before had been heart wrenching. We had had a huge leaving party and invited all our friends and family. We had hired out a venue in Clapham, a DJ and a huge cake. I wore a fantastic wrap-over dress, with a turquoise and brown ethnic pattern on it, showing off my boobs for once, and knee-high, chocolate-brown leather boots. I went all out seeing as I figured I would be in horrible practical clothes for the next half a year. I couldn't believe how many people came; Jess, Taylor and all their girls; Richie's sales mates (most of them wankers but they were there all the same); my cousins I hadn't seen for about two years; an old school friend I had been reunited with on Friends Reunited; friends from work; Lata and Tim and their glamorous mates who all terrified me, including scary Tamsin; my mum who was in London for a conference and who managed to out-scare scary Tamsin; Richie's mates from home; my house-mates from Uni, and of course Steph. Steph spent most of the night in the toilet crying. Lata swanned around like an arrogant snob as she was coked up. I hated her like that, but Tim told me it was her way of dealing with me going. Rich's banker friends who had supplied the coke also all swanned around like arrogant arseholes trying to pull Jess and her mates. Taylor danced on the bar. Jess tried to pull Tim and was promptly told where to go by Lata. Taylor tried to hit Lata and got chucked out by the bouncers. I had to beg them to let her back in. There was a cake fight, Jess snogged our cousin and Richie threw up over my Friends Reunited friend. I overheard scary Tamsin telling my mother in a loud, posh voice, "Oh my Gaad, last night I slept with this guy who had the smoothest cock in the whole waarld – it was so surreal."

All in all it was a good night. And I cried my eyes out when we got home, because I didn't want to leave them all, and I didn't want to leave my life.

"We'll be here when you get back, Rube," Steph had told me snivelling into my shoulder, trying to be the new strong Steph.

I nodded. Yes, I would just have to keep my head down and get through it, and in nine months we'd be back and we could pick it all up where we left off.

We left in the dark that morning. It was drizzling and I had a lump in my throat as I locked the door of my flat. Next week some stranger would be moving in and making it dirty. I hated the thought of it. My flat. With someone else in it. Moggy had gone to live with Lata and Tim. He'd have forgotten me by the time we got back.

We had driven to the airport in silence – me miserable as hell and hung over, and Richie still half asleep. He perked up once we had a coffee in the airport and he hadn't stopped chattering ever since. He had forbidden me from buying my weekly *Heat* magazine.

"We're budget travellers now, Rube," he'd scolded.

We finally got on the plane, and I found myself seated next to a twenty-stone man who smelled and had an irritating sniff. Rich was in the window seat so I was in the middle between the two of them, Rich babbling, and fatty sniffing. It was going to be a long flight.

The lights of London twinkled below us and faded into the clouds. It all felt so surreal. I was doing this. I was really doing this.

"Bye London," I said to myself, "See you soon."

Part Two

Thailand

Chapter Five

"You wan' t-shirt? You wan' taxi? You wan' sarong? You wan' jiggy jiggy?"

I withdrew in distaste from the pawing fingers clutching at my arm, unable to stop the sneer curling my lip. There were people everywhere, calling out to us, shoving things in front of our faces, clutching our arms, grinning at us. It was all just noise and smells; and not good smells – drains mixed with animal fat, and that sweet, cloying, vinegar smell of rubbish left out in the sun. My backpack was killing me; no matter how much I fiddled with it, as the enthusiastic young sales assistant had showed me in the shop a month ago, I just couldn't adjust it properly. Consequently, I scuttled along hunched over, looking like a demented turtle. Rich strode ahead of me, his rucksack fitting perfectly, of course, carrying half of the contents I had managed to cram into mine and, as a result, weighing half as much. He had shaken his head as I prodded in a silk sleeping bag liner, a universal bath plug, a portable washing line, and a medical kit the size of my head.

"Well, if we're going to do this, we may as well do it properly," I had argued as he threw in two t-shirts, one pair of shorts, his flip flops and three pairs of pants.

"I can get four days' wear out of each of them," he'd explained, "once the right way round, once back to front, once inside out, and once inside out and back to front."

Rich was holding his shiny new *Lonely Planet* in his hand, following the map of Khao San Road, the infamous backpackers' district of Bangkok and which, I had decided immediately, was a hell hole. It was dirty, stinky and heaving with people – Thai people selling shrivelled, fried food, sarongs and lurid t-shirts, and Western travellers with dreads wandering along the street stalls saying things like, "Dude, this is just the kind of leather bracelet I wanted. Can't believe I found it," before wrapping said leather bracelet onto their wrist along with ten other identical bracelets. People were spilling out of seedy-looking bars clutching beer bottles, still on the lash from the night before and we had to pick our way over piles of rubbish. Just as I was beginning to despair at the weight of my backpack, and rivers of sweat were pouring down my forehead, Rich stopped in his tracks at the entrance to a little dinghy alleyway.

"We're here."

I stepped over the legs of a couple that were locked at the mouth and dry humping each other on the sofa in the lobby of the dank little hostel we'd wandered into. I could see through the door into an adjoining bar where two bare-chested, tattooed skinheads were playing pool and swigging from their beer bottles. Music was still thumping from the speakers loudly.

"A dorm please," Rich casually informed the tiny Thai woman on the desk, as if he had been doing this all his life and wasn't normally safely ensconced behind his desk doing whatever it is investment bankers do. She smiled at him coyly and slid off her chair to fetch two pairs of keys. As she leaned over slowly to the key-rack, glancing over her shoulder at Rich, we had a nice view of her tiny bottom in a pair of tight cut-off jeans. She turned back to Rich. I clearly hadn't registered on her radar. She was very, very pretty with a tiny heart-shaped face, and long waist-length black silky hair. Rich was mesmerised. And then she opened her mouth.

"You jus' arrive?" she asked in a little girly voice.

We both gazed open-mouthed in horror. Her teeth were black. I was to find out later that many Thai women had this problem due to their addiction to betel nuts which, when chewed, slowly dyed their teeth a dark red or black colour. But at that moment, we just thought she had never brushed her teeth in her life and I felt immediately sorry for her. I wondered whether to fish out one of my spare toothbrushes (I had three) and my bumper tube of Colgate and offer them to her. We really didn't know how lucky we had it in the West. I kicked Rich and his mouth closed shut abruptly.

"Yes," I answered, suddenly feeling utterly exhausted and wanting to just get into our room. I grabbed the keys, muttered thank you and trudged up the stairs, after discovering the lift didn't work.

I had reluctantly agreed with Rich to give dormitories a chance as they were three quarters of the price of a double room. He had pointed out that a room was just to sleep in, after all; we'd hardly be in it as we'd have so much exploring to do he had pointed out excitedly. Dorms were to become the bane of my life.

This one, our first dorm, smelled of old, damp socks. There were clothes strewn everywhere. Our bunk in one corner was one of six, and all the others were being used. So naturally, ours was the worst. It was right next to the air conditioning unit that spewed out grey dust. Our mattresses were bare; black-toothed girl had bundled holey sheets and pillow cases into Rich's arms before we'd headed upstairs, and we had to make our beds ourselves. I really, really wished that the bed had already been made, because now I knew that my mattress had suspicious looking yellow stains all over it. I nearly gagged as I got a whiff of my pillow before pulling the pillow case on. I was to become very averse to that greasy head smell over the next few months, even opting to go pillow-less at times.

I scowled at Rich as we dressed our beds, and he purposefully ignored me, whistling cheerily to himself.

"For fook's sake man," a croaky voice mumbled from somewhere beneath a pile of manky blankets on the bed in the opposite corner, "Would you shoot oop?"

I looked round to see some bleary eyes peering from amidst a mop of tangled hair.

"Sorry mate," Rich mumbled, rolling his eyes dramatically at me and grinning as if we were in on some hilarious joke.

"What the hell…" grumpy bed-head guy mumbled, "May as well get oop now."

He threw the covers off and sat up, revealing a stained pair of boxer shorts and a scrawny body with a t-shirt suntan. He rubbed his eyes and looked at us. I forced myself to stop staring and turned back to unpacking my stuff from my rucksack, thinking better of it half way through as I couldn't find a clean surface to put anything on.

"Fook me," bed-head said, "Richard Dooby?"

I usually try to avoid the subject of Rich's last name because it usually only takes people a short while to realise that if we ever got married, my name would be Ruby

Dooby. Even a double-barrelled Ruby Jones-Dooby sounds ridiculous. Most people think that Ruby is a romantic name, but I was so-called because of the bright scarlet red colour I turned not long after I was born due to my intense screaming. Dad said I was his little red ruby and it stuck. So plain old Jane, as I had already been named, was dropped and Ruby it was. I used to think this was a good thing. Until I met Rich. Now I wished on a daily basis that I was still called Jane.

Richard spun around and focused on the skanky bloke who was emerging from the disgusting blankets.

"Bloody' hell! Dazzer?"

I froze. I had heard of the legendary Dazzer from Rich's uni days. He had been his housemate and was a complete head case – a Mancunian guy who had peed in every one of his housemate's bedrooms while drunk. There was much backslapping going on, and swearing and the like.

"What the fook are you doing here?"

"Me and my missus," (I cringed on hearing that. Rich only called me that to his mates and he *knew* how much I hated it), "are backpacking round Asia for a year. You?"

My mouth dropped open and I glared at Rich. *A year?* Since when had nine months become a year? I knew there was the chance it could happen, but I was hoping that we would speed around a few countries and, in about three months, Rich would get fed up and we'd come home early.

"Travellin' with me mates."

"Cool."

"Cool. Fookin' 'ell. Can't believe it's you like."

"Mad. Small world, yeah."

"Yeah, mad."

"Mad one."

They obviously had a lot in common then.

I still had my back to them, trying to pull clean knickers out of my bag without Dazzer seeing and without spilling all the other contents onto the floor. How the *hell* did people live out of these things? I was already sick to death of mine.

"Rube, come and meet Dazzer."

I plastered a fake smile on my face. I had always thought this guy sounded like a dick. I turned around and nodded at him.

"Alright?"

He nodded abruptly back avoiding eye contact and looking uncomfortable. He sniffed loudly.

"Hey listen, tonight, we're going to Patpong, heh heh!" He laughed dirtily and Rich chuckled along with him knowingly, "Come along. We're gonna catch a ping-pong show!"

I felt my insides crawl. Patpong is the infamous sex district of Bangkok, and it was a subject I had avoided with Rich ever since I'd read about it in the *Lonely Planet*. I had hoped that he hadn't read about it, and we could avoid going there altogether.

"Yeah defo man," Rich agreed enthusiastically. (Defo? When the hell had he started saying that?) My heart sank.

"Cool," Dazzer sniffed noisily again and then cleared his throat of phlegm, "Right well I'm gonna find the boys. They're still on the piss somewhere."

And with a faint whiff of BO and cigarettes, Dazzer left us on our own. The atmosphere was stilted as we undressed in silence; me behind a towel in case someone walked in.

"You don't mind going tonight, do you?" Rich asked eventually. He laughed light-heartedly, "I mean, you've got to experience the sex district while you're in Bangkok, haven't you? That's what it's all about isn't' it?"

I tried very hard to quell the anger rising up in my throat and again forced a strained smile on my face. I didn't want our first day in Thailand to be spoiled by a fight. And we could get Patpong out of the way and then we could head off to the beach and start having a romantic time on our own.

"Of course not, it'll be a laugh."

Even Rich agreed afterwards that it was the single most un-erotic thing he'd ever experienced in his life. Dazzer and his mates Tom and Tuna (who I was delighted to discover were the pool-playing skinheads from our hostel) led us on a tour through the seething streets of Patpong. Petite Thai girls hung out of doorways smiling and winking at any men that walked past or paraded in G-strings on top of bars that could be glimpsed enticingly through open doorways from the street or swung topless around poles. The streets were lined with stalls selling all kinds of food, clothes and hideous mementoes like those little rubber key ring figures that, when you squeeze them, huge willies pop out of. Lurid signs hung above us enticing us into various sex shows, or for buy-one-get-two-free drinks. Dazzer stopped outside the Pussycat Club.

"Now *this*," he said to Rich – I had not been graced with a single word from Dazzer all evening – "is the dog's bollocks."

Inside we were led up some dark stairs by a tall skinny Thai girl in enormous heels and a surprisingly subtle black dress. That was as far as the subtlety went. We sat along a long central stage and were all immediately surrounded by Thai girls in bikinis and high heels who started to massage us – even me. I glanced at Rich who laughed nervously. I grinned back, surprising him. There were five on Rich now, one doing each arm, one doing his back, one rubbing his legs, and one standing between his legs massaging his chest.

"Ow!" I squeaked. They were very forceful in their massaging. I began to suspect one of my girls was not a girl when I noticed a distinct lump in her throat. I looked over her shoulder and found Tuna's eyes on me. He winked over the head of his masseuse.

"OK?" he mouthed.

I nodded, surprising myself. I *was* OK, this was quite funny. I felt a giggle rising up my throat. A round, older lady with sharp eyes approached us, grinning a big gappy smile.

"This your woman?" she asked Rich loudly. He nodded. I glowed happily. The grin vanished from the woman's face and she snapped at the girls swarming around us and sent them on their way. They immediately latched onto some hapless guy with glasses who looked like Clark Kent. She flashed us her gappy grin again and then marched away barking orders at the girls.

We spent the next hour sipping our drinks awkwardly as the 'entertainment' came on stage. The light humour of the situation began to wear off as bored-looking girls simpered on stage and performed unusual feats with various items including ping-pong balls and bananas. I squirmed on my seat uncomfortably, aware of the seediness of the situation, aware that these girls survived on the 'amusement' of tourists, most of whom, like us, came along just to gawp from the outside like visitors at a zoo. Eventually, Rich and I caught each other's eye and he jerked his head towards the exit, raising his eyebrow. I nodded enthusiastically. We said quick goodbyes to Tom and Tuna who followed us outside making noises about going for a *pad-thai.* Dazzer had disappeared with one of the girls-who-weren't-girls to a dark corner table from where a lot of giggling could be heard. I almost wanted to stay to see what would happen when he found out.

As our *tuk-tuk* (a tiny motorised rickshaw) raced through the late night traffic back to Khao San Road, the wind blew through our hair and the lights of the city swirled around us. I felt a sudden wave of euphoria. Despite having dreaded this trip from the day Rich had bought me the ticket, I was actually having fun. Rich kissed my head and pulled me close into his chest.

"Glad you came, Rube?"

I nodded happily. I breathed in his smell happily and watched the lights fly by.

***

To: Rube99@hotmail.com
From: donnamjones@infosystems.com
Subject: Arrival

Ruby
Let me know if you arrived safely. Must go. Much work.
Mother

To: Rube99@hotmail.com
From: welshhottie@yahoo.co.uk
Subject: Mum is a bitch

So are you there yet then? Is it lush? Am so jealous. Bet you're on the beach right now with lots of fit men. So cool you're doing this Rube. Got me thinking about my life. Should do something different too. Hate work. Hate all the new clothes. They're so sluttish. Speaking of which, I got off with bouncer from Resolutions on weekend. Nightmare. Bit of a minger. Thought he was fit in the dark. You know that whole power trip thing bouncers are on and it seems sort of sexy when you're drunk? Have to go to Icons now instead for a few months.

Got in late and Mum was complete cow. Hate her. Looked at me like was complete scum and said house wasn't a hotel. I wish. Could make as much mess as I liked then. Instead have to tip toe round all her artsy crap statues and Japanese tea sets. She bought new paint for the lounge – red, to match her Japanese theme. Cow.

Let me know how lush it is there.

Jess xxxxxxxxx

PS Saw that bloke you flirted with when we went out in Swansea before you left – he's well fit but a real dick. Asked about you and then asked if we'd ever consider a threesome seeing as we're twins. Why do dicks always ask that?

To: Rube99@hotmail.com
From: babygirlsteph@hotmail.com
Subject: Miss you!

Dear Ruby

I miss you so much! I haven't slept with anyone yet though. I went out with Lata and her scary friend Tamsin who went on about sleeping with a guy with a really smooth cock. Gross. Had fun though but cried when I was drunk because I missed you so much. Feel like I must sleep with someone to cheer me up.

Love and hugs and kisses
Steph x

To: donnamjones@infosystems.com
From: Rube99@hotmail.com
Subject: Arrival

Dear Mother

Arrived safely and without incident. Bangkok is nice. Have been to lots of temples. Off to the beach now. Love to Dad.

Ruby

To: welshhottie@yahoo.co.uk
From: Rube99@hotmail.com
Subject: Hell

Dear Jess

Bangkok was hell. I hated every minute. We stayed in a scummy hostel and have ended up travelling with Rich's idiot mate from uni, Dazzer. Can't believe it. All hopes of romantic interludes are now out the window as we have to share a room with him and his two yobby mates Tom and Tuna. You'd probably fancy Tuna; he's quite fit and just your type – skinhead and tatts. Actually you'd probably like Khao San Road, lots of clothes you'd like and many bars and pissheads! Right up your street.

Can't believe you got off with that ginger bouncer! He refused me entry once for wearing a denim mini skirt – who still has no-denim rules?

Mum is just probably stressed with work. How's Dad?

Miss you all

Love Ruby

PS Don't EVER mention you know what or you know who again, in case Rich reads my emails. He is sitting next to me now in an internet café and could accidentally read something over my

To: welshhottie@yahoo.co.uk
From: Rube99@hotmail.com
Subject: Oops

Had to press send then as Rich looked over my shoulder. Case in point. So don't mention it again.

I wouldn't say all blokes that ask that are dicks. Some are just curious.

Rube x

To: babygirlsteph@hotmail.com
From: Rube99@hotmail.com
Subject: Miss you

Dear Steph

Miss you loads too Stephy! Can't believe I have only been away for one week, feels like forever. How is everything? What's happening in *Eastenders*? And who got evicted from Big Brother?! OMG can't believe I'm missing it! Give Lata and Tim big hugs and kisses from me – especially Tim! ;)

Tamsin is so scary. She once shouted angrily at me that did I know I was very sexy? I wasn't sure whether yes or no would be the right answer.

Anyway, Thailand is not what I thought. Bangkok was hellish – went to some horrid sex show. We are also stuck with Rich's mate from uni, Dazzer, who is now my nemesis. I don't think he has spoken one word to me yet. You can tell he wishes that I would just die and leave the boys alone to have fun.

Off to the beach next though, so hopefully it will get better. Wish, wish, wish that I was there having a bottle of wine and nachos with you.

Love you lots

Rube xx

Chapter Six

The wind whipped my hair around my head and into my mouth and eyes and I clung onto Rich for dear life. I could see Dazzer's moped zipping in and out of traffic ahead of us, and Rich was trying to catch up. I tried to relax and watch the groves of coconut trees swaying up the hillside but my heart was constantly in my mouth every time we hit a bump in the road or swerved to miss another moped or crazy pedestrian stepping out in front of us. Tom and Tuna were behind on their moped driving slightly slower than Dazzer, because they, like Rich, had never driven one before. Amidst my gut-wrenching fear of flying off the back of the bike, I registered that Ko Samui was a really beautiful place. I had wanted to go to Ko Chang further east than Bangkok, a small island that was apparently much less visited than notoriously busy and over-developed Ko Samui. I pictured hammocks and palm trees and solitary walks on long beaches alone with Rich. However, Dazzer had practically dragged us onto the bus to Ko Samui and thrown us onto the ferry to get here. Rich was all up for it anyway, after Dazzer told him about the wild bars, and the hordes of topless Swedish girls and the boat trip over to Ko Pha Ngan, the neighbouring island, for the world-famous Full Moon Parties.

I had to admit I was looking forward to a Full Moon Party; images of hippyish people sitting on the sand around bonfires, smoking weed and dancing till the sun came up made me warm to the idea. But when we first got to Ko Samui, I was sorely disappointed. The main beach Hat Chaweng, although staggeringly beautiful with snow-white sand, was horrendously built up with bars and restaurants all along the coast. There were at least 20 rows of people crammed in alongside each other right up to the shoreline. It went in layers: first there were the decks belonging to the bars and restaurants that were swarming with people, then there were the sun-beds hired out by the early birds, and then there were the people on towels. I had scanned the crowd and true to Dazzer's word, about 90% of the heads were blonde, 90% of them were female and 90% were topless. A pair of boobs covered by a bikini top stood out amongst the crowd. The girls who dared to wear actually got more attention because they caught your eye. Then there were the guys, invariably with bushy blonde hair-does and gravy-browning tans (Scandinavians – how *do* they go so brown? They surely don't see the sun for most of their lives, yet they all seem to have a very lived-in, deep even tan once they are on the beach) or blotchy pale with shaved heads and tats, still in their jeans even though it was 30 degrees Celsius (Brits). Music pumped relentlessly from the bars, and greasy burgers and chips were being devoured alongside the ubiquitous bottles of Chang beer. I spotted a girl strangely sipping from what looked like a child's bucket for making castles with. I was to find out what that was later on.

Once we had driven away from the main touristy area, however, even though it was built up, Ko Samui was truly beautiful. It was a relief to see that, while tourism had curled its dirty clutches around the coastline, the interior remained a palm-filled paradise.

Dazzer eventually turned in towards the coast, and we drove to a beach to see Grandfather and Grandmother Rocks. Once we had strolled past all the tourist stalls selling souvenirs and out onto the rocky beach, I realised what we had come to see.

"You're gonna love this," Dazzer said to Rich pointing at a huge rock protruding from a big pile. It was shaped like an enormous penis. Dazzer nearly choked himself from laughing too hard. Tom sniggered and snorted and Rich joined in. I wanted to hit him; he was being so pathetic around Dazzer. Only Tuna stood on the rocks gazing out to sea, apparently lost in his own thoughts. I dreaded seeing Grandmother Rock. Dazzer bounded over the rocks and stood pointing down below his feet, laughing hysterically. When we reached him, sure enough we saw that there was a huge crack in the rock, into which swirled white waves.

"Better watch out man," Dazzer said to Rich. "Your ol' lady'll look like this in a few years! Like a wizard's sleeve!"

He cackled away and Rich tittered nervously, glancing at me.

"Dazzer, man. Come on."

I turned in surprise to see Tuna looking at Dazzer with a frown on his face. He looked at me apologetically as Dazzer bounded away over the rocks. Rich took a picture of me standing over Grandmother Rock and then he bought a postcard with the two rocks on to send to his obnoxious mates back home.

On the way back, I had begun to relax slightly on the bike and to enjoy the feeling of freedom and watching people and scenery fly by. That was until another moped cut right across our path; Rich slammed on the brakes, we clipped the back wheel of the other moped and I came flying off in a little somersault onto the tarmac. I barely hit the floor before I had jumped to my feet.

"I'm fine! I'm OK! Everyone OK? Everyone alright?"

A young Italian couple on the other bike were looking worried and saying sorry over and over. Another moped hurtled past beeping a horn.

"No, no, it's fine, I'm fine. It was all our fault..." I babbled at nobody in particular.

"But we drove in front of you," the Italian boy insisted, "I am not sure of the driving rules here, I am very sorry..."

"No, no, honestly. It was our fault, honestly," I sounded like Eric Idle in *National Lampoon's European Vacation* when Chevy Chase keeps knocking him over. My voice was shrill and sounded weird even to my ears. Rich was busy studying the front of the moped.

"Probably won't get our deposit back," he muttered.

"Are you sure you are OK?" the Italian guy asked me looking concerned and pointing towards my foot, "You're bleeding."

"No, it's nothing! Really! Just a scratch."

I felt an arm around my shoulder and then I was being steered firmly towards another moped. It was Tuna.

"Come on, Ruby, get on my bike. I'll take you back to the hostel."

Rich jumped back on ours and called over his shoulder.

"Yeah, it'd be better if you go with Tuna, babe. I'm going to drive this thing up and down the road, see if it's running alright."

And with that he drove off. I climbed onto Tuna's moped, wrapped my arms around his bare and surprisingly skinny waist, waved maniacally at the Italians and we drove off. After a few minutes, I dared to look down at my ankle, which was throbbing. There was a deep graze, with gravel embedded in it, and there was also a bruise colouring my thigh. I let out a small whimper.

"I'm bleeding," I said in a small voice.

He pulled straight over to the side of the road and once I'd climbed off, he bent down to look at my ankle. I started to cry big, heaving sobs.

"You're OK, Ruby, it's only a graze. Really, you'll be fine, it looks worse than it is." He put his arm round me and led me down an alleyway to the beach. It was a surprisingly quiet part of the beach and I limped as he walked me gently to the sea.

"We'll just wash it in salt water to clean it. It'll sting a little," he splashed sea water onto the cut and I breathed in sharply.

"Sorry sweetheart," he said, looking up at me, "Just a little bit more to get the dirt out."

I nodded biting my lip and he rubbed the wound gently. He stood up and I saw his eye lingering on my thigh.

"Got yourself a mighty bruise there too."

I wiped my eyes feeling like an idiot. He smiled and shoved his hands into the pockets of his jeans which, as usual, were hanging off his hips. If he pushed any harder, I thought, they'll fall down. He jerked his head towards the road.

"Best get back. You got any antiseptic cream or anything?"

I laughed thinking of my jumbo-jet size medical kit.

"Just a bit."

Chapter Seven

"I haven't got anything to wear!" I groaned throwing my hideous walking sandals across the room. I couldn't believe that Rich had made me buy them. His only splurge before we left London had been a new pair of Merrel walking trainers. I had cowered at the sight of them.

"We're going to be doing lots of hiking, Rube; climbing mountains and hiking in the jungles and the like," he'd said in a warning voice, "You'd be better off getting a pair of these yourself and leaving behind your Jimmy Choos."

"I'm *not* taking my Jimmy Choos," I had been indignant as I held up a pair of strappy sandals, "These are just cheapy Top Shop ones!"

Rich managed to talk me into buying clumpy sandals – or shandy sandals as Lata had laughingly nicknamed them after the beardy shandy-drinkers that normally wear them – as they would be sensible to walk round in. These are basically outdoor, hard-wearing walking sandals, the ones that Velcro right across the most unattractive part of your ankle. They managed to make even my toothpick legs look like tree trunks. As it was, the high heels didn't make it to the final cut anyway. Any acquaintances that had gone backpacking previously had all told me to take clothes you hate, because they would get ruined and filthy anyway, and you could buy anything you needed in the amazingly cheap markets and shops. This, I realised very quickly, as I rummaged around in my rucksack, was complete crap.

"If I had my time over," I mumbled angrily, "I would stick in those strappy sandals and leave out the universal plug and all the other bollocsky stuff that I'll probably never even use. I would use the space wisely to fill my bag with clothes that I *love*. Because you wear the same outfits day after day, so you have to love them. I hate every damn ugly thing I've brought with me! And everybody else *does* care what you are wearing, everyone else is dressed oh-so-casually in their brand-new sarongs, and matching flip flops, and designer combats. It's a bloody backpacker fashion parade! And you *cannot* buy what you need when you're here. Because everything for sale is *crap*, and I bet it all falls apart after two wears anyway, and only comes in size minus 6 as all Thai girls are so bloody *tiny*!"

"Are you on?" Rich looked at me a bit warily.

I threw my hair straighteners at him and then immediately regretted it. These were my secret luxury item. They missed his head by an inch and landed on the bed behind him. He picked them up and then looked at me in disbelief.

"I cannot believe you…"

I shot him a warning glance with wild eyes.

"I'm going for a beer," he said, shaking his head in disbelief before leaving me to my misery and my pile of hated clothes.

***

From: welshhottie@yahoo.co.uk

To: Rube99@hotmail.com
Subject: ?

What do you mean I would like Koo San Road? Just cos I like going out with the girls and having a laugh, doesn't mean am just a piss-head. Is more to me than people think. Have decided to become more spiritual. Have been to Pilates twice. Taylor came once but got bored. Am also learning tarot cards. Practised on Mum but she had call on mobile and had to go to work. No change there then. Should be a card called High Bitch.

What's the beach like? Have you got tons of new bikinis?

Jess

PS Tell me more about Tuna. Sounds lush.
PPS Why is he called Tuna? Does he smell of fish?
PPPS Dad? Why are you asking about Dad? Is OK I think.
PPPPS Won't mention the guy you flirted with ever again. Saw him again though. Asked me about you *again*. Is fit. But still a twat.

From: lataandTom69@yahoo.com
To: Rube99@hotmail.com
Subject: Hello from London town

Hello darling

How is fabulous Thailand? Is it as awful as you expected? Or are you settling into the gypsy lifestyle? How was the shopping in Bangkok?

Tim and I are fine. He lost his sunglasses and wandered around lost for a few days. He was actually grieving. I have also put him on a diet. He is getting too fat. I've started calling him Tubby Tim, which he HATES. Ha ha. I am such a cow!

Oh, oh, big news! You know that guy that Tamsin was sleeping with, with the really smooth cock? Well, she's engaged to him! He's a doctor.

Must really do some work now I suppose.

Hugs

Lata

From: babygirlsteph@hotmail.com
To: Rube99@hotmail.com
Subject: I am bad

I slept with my boss. I am an awful person. He is married. He is sooooo fit though. And doesn't love his wife. I am a bitch. Do you hate me?

Hugs and kisses

Steph xxxxx

To: welshhottie@yahoo.co.uk
From: Rube99@hotmail.com
Subject: Accident!

I had a motorbike accident! DO NOT tell mum. I am OK but cut my leg and was bleeding and everything. Rich didn't even notice I came off the back! Think he was in shock or something. Tuna was really nice; he washed my cut and didn't make me feel stupid for crying.

Course I know there's more to you than going out on the piss. You like clothes as well! Only joking. You'd love Ko Samui, big party atmosphere, lots of people wearing hardly anything at all, lots of muscled Swedish blokes. Wasn't really what I had in mind but there you go.

PS Don't know why he's called Tuna but he doesn't smell of fish.

PPS I give you permission to snog that bloke we must not mention. As far as I am concerned, what happened didn't happen. So don't mention it again!

To: lataandTom69@yahoo.com
From: Rube99@hotmail.com
Subject: Tim is gorgeous and does not need to go on a diet!

You evil woman. Bangkok was horrid, all smelly and dirty. Went to some swanky malls though but felt like a hideous lump in my shandy sandals. Should have listened to you and packed my heels. Hate all my clothes and hate feeling like a minger.

Rich found my hair straighteners and won't let me live it down.

Went to a hideous sex show where women shot lots of weird things out of their bits.

Big news! Had a moped accident! Am fine, am fine, don't worry, just cut my ankle. But hopefully will have a war wound scar so people will feel sorry for me!

Only 8 months and 3 weeks to go.

Ruby

To: babygirlsteph@hotmail.com
From: Rube99@hotmail.com
Subject: You are not a bad person

But you should know better. Stop it. Right now. You will get hurt. And think of his wife. Even if he doesn't love her, she might love him.

Wish you were here to bitch about all the gorgeous topless blondes everywhere. Have never felt so conscious of my unsymmetrical boobs in my life – have to look at perfect, tanned, pert boobs all day, every day. So does Rich. Not fair. We don't get to look at perfect willies all day every day. Not that that would be very nice but we only think that because of our social conditioning etc.

Don't panic but I had a moped accident. Cut my ankle and felt very sorry for myself. Dazzer's mate Tuna looked after me so no longer think he's all that bad. Dazzer is still a tosser though. Hate him.

Love and hugs and kisses

Rube x

To: Rube99@hotmail.com
From: welshhottie@yahoo.co.uk
Subject: Phew!

That's a relief because I got off with him on Saturday. Knew you wouldn't mind.

Jess

Chapter Eight

Ko Pha Ngan, while not as developed as its neighbour Ko Samui, was certainly on its way there. It wasn't the chilled out, hippyish place I imagined it would be or at least the main town Hat Rin wasn't. I had wanted to stay at the quieter end of the island and travel to Hat Rin for the Full Moon Party, but no, Dazzer's word was God with Rich at the moment and Dazzer wanted to stay in Hat Rin. The town was more of the same with backpacker hostels, cafés and restaurants lining the streets serving all nationalities of food and playing all the latest Western films to try and attract the tourists. It was a bit more chilled than Ko Samui, without the same manic party atmosphere, until you hit the beach main beach. Not as many bars lined the beach but there were still plenty thumping out music day and night. The main beach itself was still overly populated with more of the same topless/muscled Scandinavians. You could, however, walk for twenty minutes and find quieter beaches.

Having already tired of pokey hostels, we felt we needed a treat. We all pooled in and splashed out on a split-level chalet up on a cliff with fabulous views overlooking the ocean. It was still cheap and basic by usual standards but to us it seemed like luxury. Rich and I were granted use of the big double bed with billowing (whole) mosquito nets, while Dazzer and Tom shared the pull-out sofa, and Tuna opted to sleep on the rooftop balcony in a hammock. I began to wonder after a couple of days if he had become entangled in it, because he never seemed to leave it.

On the first day on the island, eager to explore, we clambered up over the cliffs and found a wooden boardwalk leading around the rocky coastline. Once we rounded the headland, even Dazzer gasped in appreciation.

"Bloody hell," Tom muttered.

"Wow," I breathed. Before me was the most beautiful beach I had ever seen; milky blue water, blindingly white sand, palm trees being tickled by the breeze. We hurried down to the sand and as we strolled along, we realised that the clientele here was slightly different. This beach seemed to be appropriated by Israelis and Italians – while the main party beach was a sea of white blonde heads, this beach was scattered with brunettes, exuding a cool, disinterested confidence. This was more my style – especially as there were only a handful of boobs on show. I didn't feel quite so pressurised to get mine out.

We found a quiet spot on the sand, lay down our blankets and the boys quickly grabbed their Frisbee and ran down to the shoreline to chuck it around. I closed my eyes, lay back and breathed in the sea air deeply. This was more like it. I listened to the waves washing the shore gently, back and fore…

"You better put some of this on; you're looking a bit pink."

I jolted awake and shaded my eyes. They focused on a pair of long camouflage-print shorts sitting, as ever, ridiculously low around Tuna's hips. He was sitting up, his arms resting around his knees. He nodded towards a bottle tucked under his towel. I picked it up.

"Factor 30?" I scoffed, "I'm not an albino you know. Besides I've got plenty of this on."

I indicated my Factor 12 Ambre Solaire bottle. He shook his head, smiling to himself.

"You Brits."

"What about us Brits?" I asked defensively.

"You'll never learn. You always blast yourselves the minute you're in the sun and then spend weeks bright red and complaining. And then end up in 20 years with the 'C' word."

I rolled onto my side and propped my head on my elbow.

"So if you're not a Brit, what are you then? I have been wondering about that accent of yours."

"Half Irish, half Australian," he said leaning back on his elbows and stretching out his legs, "I grew up in Australia, but I've spent the last five years in Dublin – hence the weird hybrid accent. Been getting some money together before heading back home and enjoying a little trip round Asia on the way"

"Home, as in Australia?"

He nodded.

"I really miss it," he squinted in the sun as he looked out to sea, "and I can't wait to get back. My parents are divorced and my mum lives in Dublin, which is really beautiful and everything, but my dad owns a ranch in Queensland. I yearn to get back there, to those big open skies, and endless horizons."

I studied his shaved head, where light hairs were beginning to show through the skin. A tattoo curved across his shoulder blades and around his collar bone. There was a pointy stud in his eyebrow.

"I imagined all Aussies to have floppy blonde hair and to always wear board shorts."

I suddenly wished I hadn't said that; I realised that half the people I worked with in London were Australian and I'd never even thought about it. What a stupid thing to say.

"Oh I used to look like that. Long blonde dreads…"

"No!" I couldn't imagine it.

"And I used to only wear Hot Tuna surf clothes. Hence the nickname."

"Ahhhh," I nodded, "I have been trying to get close enough to smell you to see if it was because you smelled fishy."

He smiled wryly.

"Yeah, not my choice of nickname, but it stuck."

"So what's your real name?"

"Joe."

"Joe," I let it roll round my tongue, "You don't look like a Joe."

I wanted to say that he had looked like a Kevin when I first met him – like he was about to steal the hubcaps off your car while he was managing to woo you with his dancing Irish eyes, like Colin Farrell. Luckily, I managed to keep my blabber mouth shut for once.

Tom bounded up to us, out of breath. He threw himself down on the other side of me. Tom had grown on me in the last few days as well. He reminded me of a big overgrown puppy. I had assumed that the two of them were like skinhead versions of Dazzer, but they were actually nice guys. Dazzer was still proving to be an idiot though.

"How's the water?" I asked him.

"Fookin' lovely," he breathed, "but not as lovely as that."

I followed his gaze to the only blonde on the beach who was strolling along topless collecting shells and pretending not to notice everyone's eyes on her. Tuna smiled and shook his head at his friend. After a few moments of silent gazing, Tom came back to the present and turned onto his stomach.

"So how's your leg, Taff?" This had become his new nickname for me.

"Do all you guys have to give everyone nicknames beginning with T?"

"No," Tom shrugged, "Dazzer's is Dazzer."

I looked at Tuna and the corner of his mouth curled up into a wry smile. He shook his head slightly. Tom turned onto his back and watched Richard who I noticed with a dull feeling in my stomach was gazing up at the blonde shell collector from where he was at the shoreline.

"What could we call your man then?" he asked quietly, "Tit?"

Tuna thumped him on the arm quickly and glanced at me. I frowned and looked at Tom.

"What do you mean?"

He laughed heartily, but also not very convincingly.

"Nothing, Taff. Only joking."

Tuna met my eye again and smiled apologetically. He jumped to his feet brushing sand off his shorts and held out his hand towards me.

"Fancy a swim?"

I nodded and let him help me to my feet. We started to stroll towards the sea in companionable silence. I mulled over what Tom had said and felt protective of Rich suddenly. Why would Tom say that? Didn't they like him? Why on earth not? I shaded my eyes to watch Rich's dark figure. He spotted us and trotted up the sand towards us, his eyes gleaming like an excited puppy. He grabbed my hand and dragged me towards the water.

"Come on, Rube," he called over his shoulder, "It's amazing!"

I glanced back to see Tuna stop on the sand and watch us with a smile on his face as we splashed into the azure blue water.

Chapter Nine

On the night of the Full Moon Party, nine thousand people swamped Hat Rin beach from neighbouring islands and the mainland. Any images I had had of sitting around camp fires having Bob Marley sing-alongs were swiftly shattered. The whole place was one big seething, debauched dance party. Nothing hippyish and spiritual about this I thought as I sat on a plastic chair on the beach, watching the swelling crowd incredulously. People spilled out of bars and clubs all along the beach, dancing and drinking manically. The drink in favour was a whisky bucket – a whole quarter bottle of Sansom whisky (which legend has it is laced with amphetamines), Red Bull and coke poured into a child's sandcastle bucket. We all sipped out of one together and watched some fire dancers on the shore. About four buckets later, we were rolling around laughing at Tom attempting to fire dance, crazily swinging the ropes that had been doused in kerosene and set alight, and then setting his shorts on fire. He ran screaming into the sea, emerged dripping wet, reached for the nearest bucket and took a huge swig. He froze; his eyes widened and his cheeks bulged.

"My God," Tuna murmured, "He just drank the kerosene."

He jumped up and ran towards Tom.

"Spit it out! Spit it out!"

There was no need to tell Tom. He was racing back into the sea, spraying a mouthful of liquid out and splashing salt water in.

The night deteriorated after that. We had met a few people along the way in Thailand who had warned us not to touch the 'buckets'. What they neglected to tell us was that they turn everybody a bit nuts. Rich and I were the first to turn; I accused him of not caring when I came off the bike; he shouted back that I was just trying to pick a fight; I said that if he wasn't so busy staring at boobs all the time he may have noticed his girlfriend had been injured; he said he didn't exactly have a choice as there were boobs everywhere you looked; Dazzer murmured in agreement and I started on him, saying that he was just an ignorant pig and didn't even have the decency to speak to me; Rich told me not to pick on his mate; Tom said that I had a point about the bike; Dazzer told him not to get involved; Tom told Dazzer he was a wanker; Tuna told Tom to calm down; Tom tried to hit Tuna; Dazzer jumped on Tom's back and Rich shouted at me that it was all my fault. I left the boys rolling around in the sand thumping each other and decided to go and dance. I danced and drank buckets all night long. I wandered along the beach having a boogie here, a chat there. Everyone was so cool, I decided. I loved everyone. Except my hateful boyfriend and his horrible mates. I smiled at the beautiful Thai girl dancing opposite me and she hugged me. We danced on chairs on the sand and the stars sparkled in the sky above us.

The first remnants of sobriety began to kick in as the sun warmed my face. I opened my eyes. I was smiling and my arms were outstretched. I was in the sea up to my chest. There was a girl opposite me with a circle of flowers on her short hair. She was grinning too and her arms were raised to the sky like mine.

"...I mean, isn't this world just beautiful?!" She was saying. She looked at me, beaming. I thought she was lovely. I nodded happily.

I had a vague inkling in my head that I was acting very bizarrely but I didn't care. I realised that there was a group of about twelve of us in the sea. An Israeli guy with long dark curly hair and a beard swam alongside me and the hippy-girl.

"I have something on my leg," he said indicating under the water. He peered down at his leg, "I think it is a leech!"

He had a huge grin on his face and it made me laugh. And I couldn't stop.

"I have a leech!" he cried happily, "A leech on my leg!"

He reached down and pulled it out of the water – a long black leech-like creature which I was to later find out was a sea cucumber, and that when it is threatened, excretes its innards which have the consistency of a white thick fluid. He held the leech aloft and then looked at his hands covered in white sticky liquid.

He held his hands up to the sky.

"Why God? Why me?"

Hippy-girl and I laughed so hard I thought I might die and whenever I see in my mind's eye that Israeli guy holding that leech aloft with the dawn sun shining down on him it always makes me smile.

I decided I had better get out as my fingers were so wrinkly and it began to register that it was morning and although these people I was with were very nice, I didn't actually know them. I knew vaguely there was somewhere I should be, but I couldn't quite remember at that moment. As I stood on the shore, I realised that I wasn't wearing my denim skirt or my shoes. I combed the beach for them. Someone had dragged the sand and there was a huge pile of lost shoes in the middle of the beach. It was like a mountain. I searched for mine but couldn't find them, so I chose a rather nice pair of leather thongs. I found my skirt in a ball next to a bar stool on which was perched a young man. He looked like a rugby player, stocky and wearing a polo shirt with the collars up. He held out a beer to me.

"Thanks but no thanks," I said pulling my skirt on. Luckily, I had worn my bikini under my clothes that night in case some late-night swimming had been on the cards. I stumbled a little as I tried to get my leg inside the skirt.

"Go on," he said as a small Thai woman swept the floor around him. I looked at his friendly brown eyes and shrugged. It was a beautiful morning and I felt fantastic. And all these people were my friends.

I took the bottle and took a huge swig. I didn't even like beer but that morning it tasted great. I perched on the seat next to him and we swapped life stories. He was called Ben and was eighteen years old and had just finished sixth form in a public school and was about to go to Oxford to study law. Oh and he was in love with me.

"Those eyes," he kept murmuring.

"Yes, yes." I nodded, grimacing slightly. The beer didn't taste so good anymore.

Looking for an escape, I glanced over my shoulder to see a small wiry Thai man perched on the stool behind me. He too had bought me a beer and handed it to me. Ben looked irritated but I didn't care. Thai man was much more interesting. He was a Thai boxer. He couldn't say much else in English. Apart from the fact that he too was in love with me. They started to argue over who loved me more. I managed to slip off my stool and tiptoe away as they squared up to each other, Ben attempting some wobbly kicks as Thai-boxer jumped nimbly out of the way.

I wandered along the coast in the direction of our chalet but found at the end of the beach that the tide had come in up to the rocks. I waded in to swim around the rocks, putting my new leather sandals onto my hands so I wouldn't lose them. It was a lovely swim, I thought to myself feeling the sun on my face. What I didn't realise was that because I was swimming into the current I wasn't actually going anywhere. I opened my eyes. This was much further than it looked, I thought to myself. I closed my eyes again and enjoyed swimming on the spot. Some voices were breaking into my reverie and I frowned in irritation.

"...doing...Ruby...swimming..."

I opened my eyes again and followed the voices to a group of figures on the sand. One was waving. I waved back with my sandal.

"What are you doing?" the figure shouted.

"Swimming!" I shouted back thinking what a stupid question it was. What did it bloody look like I was doing?

"But why?"

The voice sounded familiar. It was a man.

"Because the tide is in, silly!" I shouted back.

"But it's shallow!"

I realised that the figures had their jeans rolled up and the water was lapping around their ankles.

"Stand up!" he shouted.

I stood and found that the water came up to my knees. I hadn't been moving because I had basically been on my belly. I waded towards them and as I got closer, I realised it was Tuna with two blonde girls. He was laughing at me as I came towards them.

"Ruby, why have you got your shoes on your hands?"

I shrugged.

"They're not my shoes."

He looked at the two girls who were smiling at me pityingly.

"I better get this girl home; her boyfriend will be worried sick about her."

They nodded. He leaned forward and kissed one on the cheek.

"See you tomorrow?"

She nodded and they strolled away along the shore.

I linked my arm through his and we walked the opposite way.

"Where on earth have you been?" he asked, "We've been looking for you all night."

"I've been dancing and laughing and swimming. I had a wonderful night. I made some great friends."

"You turned into Godzilla there for a while. You disappeared for a couple of hours and when we found you, Rich tried to drag you away from these people you had made friends with, but you screamed at him and then punched Dazzer in the face."

I looked at him, my eyes wide.

"No!"

He nodded, grinning. "He deserved it though. He called you a stupid cow."

"Damn. I wish I could remember!"

"Then you ran off cackling and we lost you in the crowd."

I sighed and leaned against his shoulder.

"Is Rich very angry?"

He nodded.

"Yep."

"Oh well," I smiled, "Isn't the world great?"

He chuckled softly.

"I bet you won't think so in a few hours."

"Oh I will," I said sincerely, "It's wonderful and I love everyone. I love you, Tuna."

He patted my arm.

"I know you do."

Chapter Ten

The rocking of the boat didn't help the nausea that threatened to overwhelm me. I lay prostrate on a bean bag and wished the boat would sink. It wasn't a boat exactly; it was a floating bar moored in a quiet bay, and it could only be reached by fishing boat. It had two levels, with deck chairs and beanbags. People lazed in the sun or dived into the sea off the edge. All the boys were drinking. I lay very, very still, with my bottle of water and hid behind my sunglasses. Rich wasn't talking to me, which was fine by me as I didn't want to talk to anyone anyway, and Dazzer wasn't talking to me but that was nothing new. Tom flopped on the bean bag next to me.

"OK, Taff? How're you holding up?"

"Bleurgh," I muttered.

"Yeah. I know how you feel. Those buckets man. They're crazy!"

"Mmhmm."

"Can't wait to get back on them."

"Oh God," I muttered and leaned over the edge of the platform. There couldn't possibly be anything left in me to throw up. I heaved a little but nothing came up.

"Made everyone a bit angry at first didn't it?" Tom didn't seem to have noticed that I was in the throes of vomiting.

I nodded weakly.

"But then later on I felt fantastically happy," he thought about this apparent phenomenon for a few moments. "Brilliant."

I caught Rich out of the corner of my eye talking to some girl wearing a bikini and baggy shorts. She looked a little like Mariah Carey. He glanced sideways at me, to make sure I was looking and then laughed very loudly at something Mariah had just said. She looked at him as if he was a bit odd. He was trying to piss me off after my performance the night before. And the weird thing was I really didn't care.

I dragged myself to my feet and went on a wobbly hunt for the toilet. I climbed some stairs, hanging onto the banister for dear life, and emerged onto the top level into brilliant sunshine.

"Hey!" a voice called, "It's Mike Tyson herself."

I squinted in the sun and focused on Tuna relaxing in a deckchair. The blonde that had been with him that morning was curled up on a bean bag next to him. I noticed her leg was draped over his. He beckoned me over and I sort of fell into the deckchair next to him. It had taken all my effort to get there.

"How are you holding up?" He looked at me closely.

"Not good," I whispered.

"That's the buckets for you. Best stay off those for a while. Turns everyone a bit crazy," he leaned back to include Blondie in the conversation.

"This is Karla by the way. You met this morning," he said grinning. I nodded in greeting and she smiled sweetly.

"You were very funny, yes?" she said.

"Yes." Please don't talk to me. Please don't talk to me.

Tuna obviously read my mind and he turned towards Karla and left me to wallow in my misery in the sun. I pretended to be sleeping but secretly I was checking out Karla from beneath my eyelashes. She was slightly chubby with *enormous* boobs and messy, sexy white blonde hair, like she had just got out of bed. She was also really pretty, with big blue eyes, round cheeks, freckles scattered over her snub nose and cute dimples when she flashed her ravishing smile. She was one of those girls that were a bit overweight, sort of scruffy and inexplicably sexy. Every now and then she got up and dived into the water, with her t-shirt still on. When she emerged, all eyes were on her, her wet t-shirt clinging to her curves. Tuna seemed quite taken with her.

I closed my eyes and drifted off into blissful sleep.

Once my hangover had worn off, the alcoholic remorse hit. I had never had it this bad before – probably because I had never behaved as badly before. Apart from the drunken night out with Jess before leaving where I flirted outrageously with that random man, I reminded myself, only to compound my misery even more. I wanted to punish myself. I had tried to cuddle into Rich's back that morning but he had lain stiff and unyielding. I had given myself stern talks about my behaviour and how I seemed to be deteriorating into a teenager on her first holiday away from home. This whole backpacking lark wasn't turning out how I had hoped – Rich and I on an enriching journey, designed to strengthen us spiritually, so that when we returned to our flat, we would feel fulfilled and grateful for what we had and ready to settle down for good.

Rich didn't talk to me for three whole days. He went off for drives on a moped with Dazzer. I spent a lot of my time sitting on the roof balcony, writing my journal and chatting to Tuna in his hammock. Every now and then Tom would join us and we would discuss such weighty issues as why and when did Kylie become sexy (obviously it was due to her Michael Hutchence dalliance). But when Tuna and I were alone, we talked about why we were here, what we had wanted out of travelling, what we had expected and whether things had lived up to expectations. I admitted that I hadn't wanted to come away but that seeing as I was, I had hoped for an enriching experience, and that although I was having fun (of sorts) it just seemed like one long party to me so far and not a lot else.

"There's so much more to South East Asia than Thailand, Ruby," he said rocking slowly back and fore, "And there's so much more to Thailand than Full Moon parties and sex shows."

This was Tuna's second trip around SE Asia – his first had been when he was eighteen, twelve years ago. He explained that for Australians it's so close, it's almost an obligatory trip.

"I'm just going along with what the boys want for now, because I explored Thailand pretty thoroughly my first time around. But if we carry on travelling with you and Rich, there's so much I'd love to show you."

I smiled and leaned back against the wooden railing, watching the sun melting into the horizon.

"I'd really like that, Tuna. But you may have to be an interpreter between Rich and I, because I don't think we'll be speaking any time soon."

Tuna opened his eye a fraction and looked at me sitting on the floor.

"I hope you don't mind me saying this Ruby, but you don't strike me as the type to be travelling in this way."

I smiled again.

"And why don't I strike you as the type to be 'travelling in this way'?"

Tuna shifted uncomfortably in his hammock.

"Well, I mean...you always look sort of...immaculate," he made a small gesture towards my clothes.

"I look disgusting!" I cried, looking down at my boring khaki shorts and white vest.

He smiled.

"But you always look clean, and sort of ironed. And you always have make up on. And you have at least four pairs of sunglasses – which I've seen anyway. And I am sure I can smell that distinct smell of fake tan?"

I felt my cheeks colouring.

"So what kind of travelling do you think I would normally do then? Pulling along my faux Luis Vuitton suitcase on wheels, tottering on my killer heels, wearing a huge pair of Jackie O' sunglasses and heading off on Easyjet to Kefalonia?"

How close to the truth! I smiled. Tuna shrugged, picking at the wooden floorboard beneath his hammock.

"Well, that *is* how I would class my travelling experiences to date," I relented, "and I didn't exactly *want* to come backpacking but..."

"But Rich did," Tuna finished for me.

Before I was about to launch into my usual self-defensive speech, he continued.

"But when you love someone, that's important, isn't it? Compromise."

"Yes!" I blurted, sitting up, "Why doesn't anyone else see that? They all just think I am being a doormat and letting Rich walk all over me by agreeing to come away with him. But it was something he wanted so badly and I want to make him happy."

Tuna nodded thoughtfully. Slowly it dawned on me.

"You've been there too, haven't you?"

He nodded gazing out to sea.

"I compromised for four years. It was the reason I stayed in Dublin and didn't go home to Australia sooner. But Niamh wouldn't do the same for me. She just would not entertain the thought of coming to Australia with me. Even for a trial," he shook his head, "In the end, I realised that I was miserable and if someone is right for you, you shouldn't be miserable, should you? So I made the decision to leave."

"And this little trip is to get her out of your system before heading home?" I asked.

He nodded.

"It's not really working at the moment," he smiled wryly, "Especially when I see you and Rich together, giggling, sharing private jokes and stuff."

I leaned over and patted his knee.

"You'll find someone new, Tuna, someone who loves...ranches and *Neighbours* and corkscrew hats."

He threw back his head and laughed.

"And surfing," he added.

I looked at him questioningly.

"When I get back to Australia, my dream is to open a surfing and diving school."

"I can't imagine that's what you were doing in Dublin too?"

He shook his head grimly.

"I was an ambulance driver."

"Wow!" I said, impressed.

"Oh dear. That backfired. It was a joke; I didn't think you'd believe me. And now my real job is going to sound really rubbish."

"It's got to beat Marketing Assistant aka dogsbody aka sit-and-read-the-internet-gossip-pages-all-day," I said, suddenly having a flash of the grey office back home and smiling smugly to myself.

"I was an outdoor pursuits instructor."

"Wow!" I said again.

He grinned.

"Not as heroic as an ambulance driver but it was a pretty exciting job."

I wrinkled my nose.

"What exactly are outdoor pursuits? It sounds like all the horrible stuff they used to make us do on school trips when I lived in Wales, like climbing into big wet holes in rocks and things."

Tuna chuckled.

"Well, it is sort of like that, but much more exciting. You know caving, hang-gliding, rock climbing, horse riding…that kind of thing."

"Can't have been much fun doing it in wet 'n' windy Ireland," I ruminated, wrinkling my nose again.

Tuna smiled and looked down at the floor where a small gecko was scampering its way across the floor.

"I loved it. Completely opposite to Australia obviously," he said grinning, "But it sort of adds even more excitement to it all, doing all that stuff in the wind and the rain. I love the rugged beaches, the craggy coastlines, the bleak grey skies. It's all very dramatic and romantic – very much like Wales I imagine."

I nodded, not finding the thought of horrible, British, winter weather very romantic at all. I could see why he would want to go back to Australia after a few years of hanging off cliffs in freezing cold rain. We sat in companionable silence for a while.

"So what's your dream then, Ruby?"

I shrugged.

"I had it really; steady boyfriend, great mates, a new flat, a job I didn't hate…"

He guffawed at that bit. I immediately felt defensive.

"Well, I know so many people who hate their jobs. I thought I was really lucky that I thought mine was OK. People seem to think that's bad."

Tuna shrugged.

"I suppose so, but wouldn't you want to *love* your job? Why settle for something that you think is OK?"

I shrugged.

"What would be your dream job?" he prompted.

"Well, aside from the obvious, you know, like a buyer of shoes for a famous star, I guess I'd love to have my own business, like a shop selling antiques, or furnishings and pottery. I love pottery. And maybe a little guesthouse, you know a quaint one with cottage style chalets and I'd make cream teas and cakes. Then I could be a stay-at-home mum at the same time because I could live in my business premises," I shrugged, "You know. Pie-in-the-sky sort of stuff."

"Why is it pie-in-the-sky?"

I shrugged.

"Well, it's a bit twee and unrealistic isn't it? I mean I live in *London*. It's hard enough to get a job like mine and scrape a living, let alone live in lala-land like Anne of Green Gables."

"So how did you afford this trip?"

"Rich had loads of money saved up. He earns a lot from commission. And..."

I felt awful admitting this.

"Well, I had a bit of a windfall about a year ago. A great aunty of mine died. And she left me about seven grand."

He raised his eyebrows.

"Nice. I mean not nice because your aunty died, but you know..."

I nodded.

"Well, half of it went on a deposit for the flat but the other half I was saving for..." I stopped myself short.

"For...?" he prompted.

Oh what the hell, I thought, I'd told him almost everything else. He made me feel strangely comfortable.

"My wedding."

"Ahh," he nodded, glancing at my empty ring finger, and wisely didn't say anything else at all.

With that, Tom bounded in and flopped down next to me. He grinned impishly. Now his dark hair was beginning to grow back, I realised he was really good looking. In a scruffy, needs-a-good-wash sort of way.

"Alright Taff? Your fella speakin' to ya yet?"

I shook my head sorrowfully.

"Give him a good ride tonight. That'll sort him out."

"Yeah, I'll be lucky with you guys around."

"We'll make ourselves scarce, won't we, Tuna?" Tom nodded his head enthusiastically at his friend and Tuna nodded back at me. I smiled.

"Thanks guys."

But that night I didn't get to go anywhere near Rich. He had horrendous sunburn all over his belly and his shoulders and back, so whichever way he sat or lay, he whined like a baby. I slathered after sun all over him.

"It hurts so much, Rube," he whimpered.

"Yeah," I said, suddenly feeling fed up of him being a hypochondriac, "And now you look like a big red baby instead of a white one."

He glared at me.

"What do you mean?"

What was wrong with me? I loved that Rich was slightly chubby. I didn't like these perfectly buffed, oiled gym freaks. I smiled gently.

"I'm only joking; you know I love you all cuddly."

But any headway I had been making was quickly destroyed and Rich went back to sulking and not talking to me.

Chapter Eleven

To: Rube99@hotmail.com
From: jeffmjones65@aol.co.uk
Subject: Hello

Hello

Ruby, it's Dad here. Not usedto this emaik thing. bear withme i wanted to writeto see hoo you are and to sayi really admire youfor doing this Not all ofus have the courageto follow our dreams and to leavetheir everydayg life behind. but you did and I am very proudof you for doing it your mother istoo she just doesn't know howto admit it

Take care and let me know your'e OK

I Love you

Dad

To: Rube99@hotmail.com
From: welshhottie@yahoo.co.uk
Subject: Accident

Rubes

Bloke-you-flirted-with (i.e. Damien. No that really is his name) was bastard. Caught him snogging girl who works on Clinique counter in Debenhams – you know, tarty one with loads of makeup. Bastard.

Anyway, am done with men. Am now a spiritually strong being and have decided to follow in sister's footsteps. You know that money Aunty Angharad left us? Decided am going to India with it. Thought I couldn't come to SE Asia as you've already done it. Got to be original. Taylor is coming too. She's already got a bindhi – one of them stick on ones from Claire's Accessories.

Mam thinks am talking rubbish and just having one of my '*phases*'. She won't think that when am in Delhi helping homeless kids will she?

So tips please. What did you pack?

Jess

PS Can't believe you had accident. So cool.

To: Rube9@hotmail.com
From: donnamjones@infosystems.com
Subject: Jessica

Ruby

Your sister has a ridiculous idea of going travelling to India. Please have a talk with her. She is just going through one of her phases and would not last a second over there, and will end up kidnapped or worse.

Must go, v. busy.

Mother

To: Rube99@hotmail.com
From: babygirlsteph@hotmail.com
Subject: Still a bad person

OMG! I can't believe you had an accident! Are you OK?! Please be careful, I need your guidance! You see I'm completely in love Rube. Mark (my new boss) has said he'll leave his wife for me when the time is right. But she's a bit vulnerable at the moment. I feel awful, but I love him so much. Sorry, I know I should have put a stop to it like you said, but I just couldn't.

Seriously though, are you OK? Did you hurt yourself? Am very worried about you. Why don't you come home?

Hugs and kisses

Steph x

To: jeffmjones65@aol.co.uk
From: Rube99@hotmail.com
Subject: Hello

Hi Dad

Lovely to hear from you. Having a great time. Thanks for the positive words, but I don't know if I was actually following my dreams. More like following Richie's. But don't tell Mum that!

I am sort of enjoying myself at the moment, but I can't imagine nine months of it. I miss London and my friends terribly. And all of you of course!

Love Ruby

x

To: welshhottie@yahoo.co.uk
From: Rube99@hotmail.com
Subject: Are you mad?

Jess, seriously, every single person I have met who has travelled in India has said it is a totally different experience than anywhere else. And not in a good way. It's meant to be crazy and filthy and people don't leave you alone, and there are limbless beggars everywhere and you get ill all the time. DON'T do it, you'd hate it. Just book a couple of weeks to Kavos with Taylor instead. Backpacking is not a lark; it's hard work, trudging around with a dead weight on your back and staying in shit-holes. You get to meet a lot of people, and laze on delicious beaches, and food and drink is ridiculously cheap, and it's like a permanent holiday. But it's mostly awful.

Ruby x

PS STOP mentioning the guy you shouldn't mention!

To: donnamjones@infosystems.com
From: Rube99@hotmail.com
Subject: Jessica

Mum

I have emailed Jess. Don't think it will do much good – once she has made up her mind about something that's it. You know Jess.

I'm really enjoying travelling, and am glad I made the decision to come for myself, not just for Rich.

Ruby

To: babygirlsteph@hotmail.com
From: Rube99@hotmail.com
Subject: Still a bad person

Steph, what are you getting yourself into? It's the oldest story in the book; of course he's not going to leave his wife for you. Don't cry, because I know you're about to… OK, had a little weep? Right, now get your sensible head on. You're a strong fabulous gorgeous woman who doesn't have to wait around for some bastard to break your heart; there are LOADS of lovely SINGLE guys out there.

Lecture over. (Is the sex good? I can't remember what sex is like as Rich and I are never alone anymore. Not that I mind that much because Tuna and Tom are good company. Still hate Dazzer and wish he would die though.)

Now my embarrassing confession – I got completely wasted at the Full Moon Party, had a row with everyone, danced all night with strangers, punched Dazzer (brilliant!), went swimming with more strangers in the sea until the sun came up and didn't get home until 10 am. Rich didn't speak to me for days. I am an awful girlfriend.

I felt debilitating alcoholic guilt for days as well and hated being here. I wish it was all bloody over and I was back home!

Love Rube x

Chapter Twelve

I managed to persuade Rich that we needed to spend some time alone to try and restore our relationship bliss. So when the boys suggested going off on the bikes for a day to Kanchanaburri to visit the bridge over the River Kwai, I persuaded him that we should head North to Chiang Mai so we could have some "us" time. He agreed, reluctantly – I think he was dying for sex to be honest – but only under the premise that we would meet up with the boys in Chiang Mai the following day. It was as if he could no longer function without them, like tranquilisers or an intravenous drip.

"OK," I had said soothingly, "Of course we'll meet them."

Twenty-four hours was better than nothing.

I gave Tuna and Tom both of our email addresses – I pointedly did not give mine to Dazzer, and as he never even looked me in the eye, I don't think he cared in the slightest. I saw Rich slip him a piece of paper with his address on when he thought I wasn't looking and I wondered what kind of grotesque Jackass videos or underage porn Dazzer would email him.

So I was feeling quite cheery as we drove North on the bus to Chiang Mai. The sun was shining (as usual), the bus was nice and comfy, the driver was a happy fellow, even though he drove like a loony, and I was in high spirits when we got to Chiang Mai. We stayed in a traditional style Thai house, a little out of town, with simple but clean rooms and owned by a Dutch couple who were erring on the hippy side and walked around their palm-filled garden carrying baskets filled with flowers or turnips or gardening gloves. We splashed out on a double room, anticipating our night of lust, but found that it only had two single rickety beds.

"We'll push them together later," I said meaningfully to Rich, but he was engrossed in studying the nets over the windows for holes. He was particularly susceptible to mosquito bites, and one night had picked up a record fifty-three bites on his back alone because there had been a tiny hole in his mosquito net. Along with his vivid sunburn, the angry bumps all over his body didn't make for a very attractive sight, but I was determined to have sex. I would just look at his face. Or the ceiling.

We headed straight out into Chiang Mai to explore and I was pleasantly surprised. It was such a lovely, laid-back, pretty town with a bohemian feel – lots of bookshops, cafés and bars with cushions on the floor, stalls selling bowls of fresh mango and sticky rice, and exotic interior design shops. We strolled around the streets and eventually I felt Rich's hand clasp my own. He was friends with me. I was elated, and felt slightly excited, thinking about later on.

I had read that Chiang Mai was *the* place to do a Thai cookery course and it was something I had looked forward to doing since we left home. True enough there were signs for different courses all over the place, and I persuaded Rich to book one for the next day.

"But the boys…" he protested.

"The boys won't get here till late, you know what they're like. We can meet them later on."

He saw the excitement on my face and kissed my forehead.

"OK honey. I'll do it with you."

I was so chuffed after I booked it that I couldn't stop talking for about an hour, until Rich told me to stop before my jaw fell off.

We went to a bustling night market once it got dark. The clothes for sale here were much nicer than in Bangkok; still flimsy, but there were some beautiful patterned dresses and skirts. I don't know what had got into Rich but he told me to treat myself. I bought a gorgeous strappy white sun dress which had a raggedy gypsy edge, (it's been my *dream* to have a white strappy sundress, but I've never got one because where on earth would I wear it for goodness' sake?), a floaty blue and white patterned skirt that was so fine it was like wearing tissue paper, and some lovely dangly silver earrings. He stopped me buying some strappy leather sandals even though this Thai man with dreads and a Rasta hat told me how he designed and hand made them himself, and completely won me over – but as Rich pointed out I still had the sandals I had appropriated for myself from the beach in Ko Pha Ngan. And they really were very pretty – I had chosen well in my inebriated state.

There was a huge food section in the market, where stall after stall sold shining fresh fish, succulent prawns, mouth-watering curries, sizzling stir-fries, and mounds of *pad thai*. Gorgeous smells filled the air. Rich had some squid and prawn kebabs, and I gobbled down a tangy *pad thai*. We drank cold bottles of Chang beer and sat in a bar with simpering lady-boy waitresses, who draped feather boas around Richie's neck and a cowboy hat on his head. He squirmed a little uncomfortably, but he broke out in a grin as they danced to the Macarena around our table.

We got back to the hostel and I fell into the shower, excitement making little fluttery butterfly movements in my stomach. I had a bit of a tan from the beach, and my hair felt lovely and clean and cool on my back when I climbed out. I put on a slick of mascara and walked to our room (communal showers unfortunately, even though we had splashed out on the double room) in my horrid travel towel (which is a bit like drying yourself with a chamois leather but does really dry very quickly and folds up into a very compact square). I opened the door expectantly, ready to see Rich naked on the bed waiting for me. But there was no sign; he must still be in the shower I reasoned. Good, getting himself nice and clean.

I arranged myself on the bed, first with the towel open. Then thought that was a bit too obvious and I still had red lines around the edge of where my bikini had been. So I lay on my side resting my head on my elbow, my towel falling open provocatively on my thigh.

I awoke with my head hanging off the edge of the bed and my towel tangled around my legs. It was pitch black and there were middle-of-the-night noises. And there was no sign of Rich; I checked my watch: 3:30 am.

I was puzzled and a little nervous now. I wrapped my towel around me and peered around the door. Then I tiptoed down the corridor to the showers. They were all empty. It was only as I was walking back to the room, feeling very worried by now, that I heard the groaning. It was coming from one of the toilets. I placed my ear against the door and listened. More groaning. I was sure it was Rich. Then a toilet flushed and the door next to me opened. A sleepy-looking guy walked out and stopped when he saw me, with my ear pressed against the toilet, in just my towel.

"Freak," he muttered before stomping off down the corridor.

I knocked tentatively at the door.

"Rich?" I said softly.

The door suddenly flew open and the smell that emitted nearly knocked me over. Rich was curled up on the floor, hugging the toilet bowl.

"Where the hell have you been?" he croaked.

"I was in bed. Waiting for you…"

I couldn't say much because I was shocked at the grey colour on his face. I kneeled down beside him.

"Poor baby, what's wrong?"

"I'm…bloody sick…that's what's wrong," he gasped, "I haven't stopped puking and having the runs for about the last 5 hours…bloody prawns…and you didn't even care…"

I smoothed back his hair from his sweating forehead.

"Rich, I didn't even know. I fell asleep…" I said lamely.

With that, he suddenly lifted himself up over the toilet bowl and heaved into it. Not much came up because I don't think he had much left in his stomach. He dry heaved for a while and then lay on the floor in a quivering wreck.

I made soothing noises and then went and got a wet flannel to mop his head and neck with. Eventually, he stopped throwing up and heaving and said he was well enough to try and hobble back to the room. I half carried him back down the corridor, his feet dragging, and his head hanging onto his chest, and he flopped onto the bed when we got there. I found a plastic bag and placed it by his bed 'just in case' and then tucked him in. He threw off the blankets in about twenty seconds though because he was too hot, and he tossed and turned and grunted for a while. I, on the other hand, climbed into bed, closed my eyes and fell into a deep dreamless sleep.

***

I awoke with the sunlight on my face, feeling refreshed. I stretched and opened my eyes slowly to see a sleeping Rich on the other bed looking flushed and with his hair plastered to his head. A rush of love overwhelmed me and I tiptoed over and pulled the sheet up over him. I went for breakfast on my own and chatted to the Dutch couple about how they had come to Thailand in their twenties (they were about forty now), had fallen in love with the place, and set up their guesthouse.

"So different then," Gerda said sadly, shaking her head, her long wheat-coloured plaits snaking back and forth.

"Yes. So different. Travellers then want to learn about culture," Hans said shaking his shaggy bearded head, "Now they just want to be drunk, and party."

He said party with an American accent.

"No one want to see the real Thailand," Gerda said, her blue eyes mournful in her tanned face.

"No," Hans shook his head, "No one care. They just want beer; Chang, Chang, Chang."

I nodded sympathetically as I chewed on my stale cornflakes and natural yoghurt (a strange combination offered in cafés all over Thailand due to the lack of milk, that I ate out of lack of choice at first but which I became strangely addicted to) and wondered to myself if Gerda had had to go back to Holland to buy those denim dungarees or if they actually sold them here.

When I returned to the room, Rich had woken up and was staring out of the window bleakly.

"Hey honey," I said softly, perching on the edge of his bed, "How are you doing?"

"Terrible. I think I'm going to die." I saw a wet patch on his pillow where he had been dribbling.

I cooed softly and helped him take off his t-shirt which was drenched with sweat. Then I went and asked Gerda for fresh sheets and changed his bed. He sat on the edge of mine looking all sorry for himself as he watched me.

"Are you well enough to come to the cookery course?" I asked him cheerily.

He looked at me and promptly threw up on my shandy sandals.

To: Rube99@hotmail.com
From: hottuna@yahoo.com
Subject: Where are you?

Hey Ruby! I sent an email to Rich as well but it got returned. So I thought I'd try you. Back from Kanchanaburri. Excellent day – you'd have loved it. Getting the bus to Chiang Mai now. Where are you and Rich staying? We'll meet you there.

T x

To: Rube99@hotmail.com
From: welshhottie@yahoo.co.uk
Subject: Up yours

Am not mad. Am going to India whether you (and mum) like it or not. Am new and improved person – don't even go out drinking anymore. Taylor and me go for drives into country instead and climb hills with carrier bags full of tins strapped to backs to prepare. Have bhindi as well now. What clothes should we take?

Jess

To: welshhottie@yahoo.co.uk
From: Rube99@hotmail.com
Subject: I give up

Well, OK, if you have made your mind up then there's nothing I can do. But don't say I didn't warn you. I think you're mad, but there we go. Maybe you should dye your hair brown and come over here and pretend to be me instead and then I can come home.

As for clothes – and I can't stress this enough – make sure you *love* everything you bring because you'll be wearing this stuff day in, day out. And contrary to what everyone says, you *can't* buy what you need when you're there (except I did buy a gorgeous white strappy sundress and floaty skirt. And dangly earrings. But usually you can't). And also contrary to what everyone says, backpackers *do* make an effort and most look nice and fashionable – except proper hippy types who are travelling to 'find themselves' or whatever. But also bear in mind you've got to carry this stuff and it's a lot harder than it looks, so don't take too much, just *like* what you take!

Oh and *Tampax, Tampax, Tampax*. It hasn't reached these shores yet.

Rube

To: hottuna@yahoo.com
From: Rube99@hotmail.com

Hi Tuna

We are staying at the Sa Wai Dii guesthouse. Cheap and friendly. Rich is very ill from some prawns! Glad you had a good time. I am booked onto a cooking course today – can't wait. Maybe I will cook for you guys when we meet up. So what was Kanchanaburri like? Well, I guess you can tell me when you get here! So there's not much point in me emailing you anymore is there? So guess I'll see you tomorrow!

Ruby x

Chapter Thirteen

I felt really nervous going out in Chiang Mai on my own but also strangely excited. I walked along tentatively looking around at all the shops, and cafés that I had seen the day before with Rich and seeing them through new eyes. I stopped at the internet café first to check my emails, and then headed to the hotel where we had booked our course. It was being held in the beautiful flower-filled garden of the hotel, with outdoor stoves and a table all set up ready for the students. I arrived ten minutes early and sat at one of the tables beneath the palms, which was laden with flowers, and I sipped a cocktail that was presented to me as part of the course. It was only 11:00 so I felt slightly naughty.

Eventually, the chef arrived, an extremely confident and arrogant Thai man, called Ni, who welcomed me abruptly and told me I was going to have a wonderful 'culinary experience'. *I* couldn't even speak as good English as he could.

We were interrupted by a flurry of activity as another student rushed through the garden to join us, exclaiming his apologies at his lateness due to a slow tuk-tuk driver and waving his hands around dramatically. A waiter held out his complimentary cocktail and he knocked it back in one. He plonked himself down beside me in a whirlwind and blinked in surprise when he saw me. He thrust a hand forward.

"I am Blanco. I am from Belgium."

I felt shy and naked without Rich to do the chatting and socialising.

"Uh. I'm Ruby. From London. Well, Wales originally. But London now. But I'm Welsh…"

Blanco got bored as I babbled and thrust his hand into his faded old satchel-style bag to fish out a packet of cigarettes. His hands shook as he held a cigarette between his lips and lit it with huge fingers. I studied him from the corner of my eye; he was receding and what hair he had was shaved almost bald, and he had a goatee beard. He was huge – about six foot six – and was wearing a tight black vest (which wasn't terribly flattering on his chunky build) with tight black jeans and black flip flops. Despite his size and bulk he was extremely effeminate, crossing his legs at the knees, and holding his cigarette over his shoulder.

"Blanco," Ni declared, fixing him with piercing dark eyes, "Don't get too comfortable, for we are going to the market now. I will show you how to shop for Thai food."

"Yes, Chef," Blanco gave him a salute and when Ni turned his back, Blanco winked at me, "At least in Thailand they are not so hung up about smoking, yes?"

I nodded, trying not to flap away the smoke that he blew into my face.

By the time we had walked to the market five streets away, Blanco had told me his life story – how he was running away from an abusive relationship and to escape the grief of his mother's death.

"She was my heart and soul," he declared wistfully, "life will not be same again."

He also managed to get out of me all about Rich and what we were doing in Thailand. Very quickly after I had told him the bare bones of the story, he informed me that Rich was taking me for granted and I was letting him walk all over me. I smiled weakly and shrugged, pointing out my name was Ruby not Rosy, but he ignored me, more interested in the lithe Thai boys wandering past.

Ni led us into a busy, colourful market that Rich and I had wandered through the day before, eyeing the clothes and Buddha statues. But just when I thought the stalls were coming to an end, Ni took an abrupt right, led us down a small alleyway and straight into the dark depths of a bustling, noisy food market. I wouldn't have even known it was there. And, in contrast to the main market set up for tourists, there wasn't another white face in sight.

"This is the place to come for fresh Thai food," Ni barked, pointing his finger at us angrily, "Not supermarket. Local market."

I nodded. I was terrified of him. Nobody hassled Blanco and I because we were with Ni. Had we been alone, we would no doubt have been bullied into buying twelve bags of chillies by now. Or I would have anyway. Stall holders eyed us longingly, but they were obviously as terrified of him as we were. Ni stopped suddenly by a stall and, grasping a handful of rice; he turned to us.

"I will show you all the different kinds of rice…"

And so the next hour passed in a whirlwind of spices, nuts, fruits, vegetables and herbs; multi-coloured vegetables and fruits filled boxes and sacks that had been placed in beautiful arrangements on top of and around each stall; Ni explained the difference between each vegetable, spice or herb and what to buy for what dish.

Then he led us back to the peaceful hotel gardens where we were fed more cocktails, and he strapped on his apron and set to work. He cooked the first dish for us, and then we got to eat it. After that we cooked with him, all the while sipping cocktails.

Blanco kept me entertained with stories of meals he had cooked for ex-boyfriends that had gone horribly wrong. I even saw a small smile creep onto Ni's face at one point, even though he was pretending not to listen, when Blanco told me about a previous boyfriend who had cheated on him, and Blanco had cut all the arms off all the tops in his wardrobe. Whenever Ni asked us haughtily if a dish was too hot for our tastes, I shook my head vehemently, tears streaming down my red cheeks.

By the time the course was finished, I was stuffed full of some of the most gorgeous food I've ever eaten and was feeling quite merry. Ni made an abrupt exit, after presenting us with recipe books and aprons, and Blanco and I stumbled out onto the street.

"My Gott," Blanco exclaimed, "He needs good seeing to."

I giggled.

"Where have you heard that phrase?"

"My last boyfriend, the abusive one, he was English. He was air steward. I was in love with him, but he was angry. He had emotional problems. He had wife who not know he is gay. He stay with me when he fly to Belgium. I go to Doi Suthep Temple now."

He stopped in his tracks and started to flag down a tuk-tuk.

"You coming?"

I looked at Blanco as he sucked on his cigarette deeply. I should really head home, I told myself, but I was having so much fun.

"Yes. I will come," I said decisively.

Blanco shook his head.

"Rich will be very angry," he said approvingly, pushing me inside the *tuk-tuk.*

***

Blanco puffed and panted as he climbed the three hundred steps leading up to the temple. People looked at him as he clutched his sarong up around his huge knees. We both had to be decked out in sarongs before we could head into the temple. That was fine for me, but Blanco looked a little bit like a mountain in a skirt.

"My old…boyfriend before my…last boyfriend…he is abusive too…"

Blanco kept up a steady run down of his relationship history all the way up in between panting. How old he was when he lost his virginity, when he came out, when he had been unfaithful, when he had experimented with girls – I got the whole history.

We walked through the grand golden entrance and into the main temple grounds.

"My Gott!" Blanco shouted, making me and about twelve other tourists jump out of our skins, "This is beautiful! Is it not, Rosy?"

I nodded in awe looking around at the gold pagodas sparkling in the sunshine, pink bougainvillea draped everywhere. We wandered around gazing at various statues of Buddha and watching monks in orange robes bowing before them. We eventually found ourselves on a huge, white, outdoor square with a pillared balustrade from which was a view of the whole town. We leaned on the balustrade drinking in the vista and Blanco was silent for once.

"How is your life-sex?" he asked suddenly.

Two elderly ladies standing near us moved away very quickly.

"Uh, I'm not sure…"

"You and Rich. You still make sex?"

I opened and closed my mouth like a fish and coloured slightly.

"Oh you British," Blanco said dismissively, "You so stiff and tight-up."

"Well, I…we…yes…sometimes…"

"Not enough though, yes?" Blanco asked slyly.

"Well, we've been together for three years," I argued.

"Sex is everything, Rosy," Blanco announced dramatically and loudly opening his arms wide towards the city, "Sex is everything."

People were staring at us openly now and edging around us in a circle.

"And I am going to make sex tonight!"

***

The *tuk-tuk* pulled up outside my hostel and Blanco air-kissed me on both cheeks before making me promise that we would be going out that night together 'to make fun and dance'.

"I will show you how to have good time!" he called over his shoulder as the *tuk-tuk* sped away.

I wandered through the gate grinning to myself. I had had such a fun day; after the temple, Blanco had made me wander round yet another street market with him. He had draped various fabrics over his ample torso; he wanted to have a shirt made for his abusive lover – even though he had sworn an hour earlier he would never see him again. We had gone for huge glorious ice creams and then Blanco had informed me we had to go home to get ready for our night out – something I had no choice about.

Walking around the corner of the hostel, I was greeted by shouts and splashes coming from the pool. Two guys were jumping into the pool madly, shouting and whooping at the top of their voices and another was sitting watching them on the poolside, laughing and sipping a beer. A head surfaced and focused on me.

"Fookin' hell, Ruby, you look fantastic!"

It was the first time Dazzer had ever spoken to me and I stood there in shock – *and* he seemed to have forgotten about me punching him. Tuna looked up from where he was sitting by the pool and grinned. I flushed with good will; it was like seeing old friends.

"Up for a night out, guys?"

Chapter Fourteen

Rich was still too ill to come out with us that night and was sound asleep when we left. I felt terrible leaving him, but Tom pointed out that I would probably just disturb him, and if I wanted to come home early, they'd come with me.

We wandered through the bustle of the night market, stopped at a food court for some noodles and then got a *tuk-tuk* to the bar that Blanco had arranged to meet us at. Tuna was busy telling me about their trip to Kanchanaburri as we walked through the doors of the open-air bar. Dazzer and Tom were ahead of us and Tuna spluttered with laughter when he saw the reaction they were causing as they walked through the bar. All eyes – and they all belonged to men – were on the two of them.

"Rube," he whispered, "this is a gay bar, isn't it?"

I thought about it for a second.

"Yeah, I guess," I said looking around at the beautiful Thai men and boys leaning against the bar, or playing pool, all watching each other surreptitiously, "Well, Blanco is gay so it makes sense. You don't mind, do you?"

He shook his head.

"Of course not, they're usually the best places for a night out. But Dazzer may have a problem with it," he nodded at Dazzer with his dirty blond hair sticking up all over the place, completely unaware of the attention he was attracting as he waited at the bar.

A wicked grin broke out over Tuna's face.

"Brilliant. Don't tell him," I said laughing.

A shrill shriek broke through the music making us jump and I saw a huge figure leap up from a booth, waving his arms frantically.

"ROSY!!!!!"

"That's Blanco," I said without needing to, as we made our way over to him.

"Mwa, mwa," Blanco air-kissed me and then turned to the skinny oriental boy sitting with him, "This is the beautiful Rosy I tell you all about."

The boy smiled at me shyly from under his floppy hair. He had the finest features of anyone I had ever seen, razor-sharp cheekbones, heavily lashed almond-shaped eyes, and was impossibly trendy, his jeans so low on his hips they were almost around his knees and wearing coloured sweat bands on his wrists.

"This my boyfriend Sun," Blanco told us to my surprise; he hadn't mentioned anyone but his abusive ex that morning, "We meet last night, that was reason I was late for cookery course."

He gave Sun a sly smile as he slid back into his seat alongside him.

"So this is Rich, yes?" he said to Tuna, shaking his hand.

"Uh..." Tuna looked at me.

"Rosy, you never say he so handsome," Blanco scolded me before waving his hand at the barman, "Four Caprinha's, Jacques!"

Tuna and I slid into the booth opposite Blanco and Sun.

"So Rich, you feel better?" Blanco asked without letting him answer.

"This isn't…" I began but Blanco talked over me.

"Rosy was so much fun today. We had good time, didn't we, Rosy?"

I gave up trying to explain about Tuna and nodded enthusiastically.

"So much delicious food and drink, and then temple…"

Blanco proceeded to tell Tuna about the temple visit, and then launched seamlessly into his relationship history. To his credit Tuna listened attentively, nodding when appropriate and making various noises of sympathy. Eventually, the barman flounced over balancing a tray containing four cocktails and placed them on the table with a flourish.

"Four Caprinha's, Blanco," he said in a very high voice and then turned to glare at me, looking me up and down critically. He was wearing a black and white stripy slash neck top and a red necktie, tied jauntily to one side.

"I like your skin and your hair," he informed me angrily.

Blanco waved his hand in our general direction.

"Jacques, this everyone; everyone, this Jacques. He is best barman in Thailand. You always come to him for drinks."

Jacques – although I seriously doubt that was his name – stood there looking like he was sucking a lemon, but I spotted a faint flicker of a pleasure around the corners of his lips. Then he flounced away suddenly, declaring that he was *so* busy.

We sat and chatted with Sun for a while, who turned out to be Chinese, and in Thailand on holiday. He was only twenty-one and was clearly completely in awe of Blanco.

"I come from Xian," he said softly, "Very different to Thailand. People not so open about sexuality. So I come here on holiday every year."

"He is coming to Belgium next year though," Blanco announced, apparently to Sun's surprise. Tuna excused himself to go to the bathroom and Jacques immediately appeared at the table.

"Rosy," he barked at me, "the other barman Kiet…"

He pointed to the bar and I looked over my shoulder to see a tiny, moody-looking boy behind the bar who was shooting me evil looks.

"He ask if your boyfriend have boyfriend, and he want his number. But I say no. He is yours. He not gay," he looked at me, with a small glimmer of hope in his eye, "he not gay?"

I shook my head.

"No but he's also not…"

"He the most good-looking man I ever see in my life," Jacques declared dramatically, placing a hand to his chest, "I cannot speak to him. He too good looking."

I laughed.

"He look like model."

I decided to play along with it.

"He is a model."

"NO!!!" Jacques almost staggered backwards.

I nodded.

"He modelled in London when we lived there."

Jacques put the back of his hand to his forehead and his chest heaved up and down.

"Now, I really cannot talk with him," he cried.

Tuna returned, unaware of the drama he was causing, and sat down next to me smiling politely. Jacques pointedly ignored him and studied his nails before flouncing away again. Blanco was engrossed with Sun so I gave Tuna a quick rundown of his new persona.

"You're my boyfriend, you're called Rich and you're a model. And Jacques is hopelessly in love with you," I whispered.

"A model?" he whispered back disbelieving.

I sniggered.

"I know! Ridiculous, isn't it?"

"Cheers, Rube."

He pretended to look hurt, so I grinned at him and nudged him with my elbow but as I took a sip of my drink, I glanced at him from the corner of my eye and he looked a little crestfallen. Tuna seemed so supremely comfortable with himself I didn't think he would have worried about what people thought of him. I tried to cheer him up by pointing out the men circling Tom and Dazzer who were playing pool.

"It's like sharks, circling their prey," I giggled.

Much of the rest of the evening passed in a blur. Once Dazzer realised it was a gay bar – after Jacques pinched his bum – he nagged us incessantly to go to another club.

"One with bloody girls," he muttered, looking around darkly at the other men in the bar.

"There is no completely straight clubs here my friend," Blanco informed him coldly – he had taken an instant dislike to him, as had I – "And you not worry about men in this bar, is your friend they like, not you."

But finally we left and Blanco took us to a very big, busy nightclub and we danced and drank the night away. Two Thai girls latched onto Tom and Tuna and dragged them to the bar; Blanco was dancing on the stage with Sun so that left me, to my dismay, alone with Dazzer for the first time.

We had been dancing but slowly shuffled to a halt when Tuna and Tom disappeared. He shoved his hands into his pockets and we ambled to the edge of the dance floor. There was an awkward silence (well as silent as it can be in a nightclub).

"So what was Rich....?"

"So how did you meet...?"

We both started to speak and then stopped and laughed awkwardly. I indicated that he should go first.

"How did you meet Rich?" he asked me, trying not to sound too grudging.

I laughed.

"Well, it was interesting..."

***

I had been walking through the supermarket one miserable grey Sunday afternoon. Steph was away so I was shopping on my own. I was wearing my comfy old grey tracksuit with holes and my hair was in a greasy ponytail. I was feeling depressed because a guy I had been seeing had just dumped me and Steph had met this glamorous business man who kept spiriting her away on dirty weekends. I had rented out various girly DVD's for the afternoon and was wandering the aisles of the supermarket looking for some suitable snacks and a cheap bottle of wine. So far I had nachos, sour cream and a salsa dip, a large bar of Cadbury's Fruit and Nut, and a tub of Belgian Chocolate Haagen Dazs. Now I was ambling my way towards the wine aisle – I hadn't grabbed a trolley because I hadn't planned to be buying as much, but my depression at seeing happy couples shopping together had doubled my appetite. I chose a suitably disgusting looking bottle of red and grabbed the neck with my little finger, trying to balance everything else under various limbs. As I swung around to head towards the till, a trolley rammed straight into the back of me, causing me to drop first the nachos, then the chocolate, then the Haagen Dazs, and then both dips – the sour cream stayed intact, but the salsa jar exploded on contact with the floor. Finally, in slow motion, I watched as the red wine bottle eased its way out of the precarious grip of my little finger, slipped to the floor and exploded even more spectacularly than the salsa. There was a pregnant pause as everyone in the aisle turned and stared at me aghast. I stared helplessly at the salsa/wine mess on the floor and only vaguely heard the heartfelt apologies coming from the trolley driver. I turned to look at him and all thoughts of salsa/wine splatter vanished as I took in the mischievous, dark eyes dancing before me, the heart-shaped face, the jaw lined with stubble, the messy jet-black hair. His lips were moving but I couldn't hear what he was saying. The eyes remained cheeky, even though he wasn't smiling. Then, in a rush, noise and real life flooded back into my brain.

"...so, so sorry... wasn't looking where I was going... let me pay..."

I just stood there gaping at this man that stood before me, having an effect on me that I had never experienced before. Then she appeared.

"Oh my God Rich, what the hell have you done?" She laughed a short sharp laugh, taking me in in my grey tracksuit with splatters of red wine up my legs.

She had long black hair, and very blue eyes, and sort of a sharp but beautiful face. And she was immaculate; a smart grey skirt suit, high sharp shoes, a crisp white shirt, long manicured talons, perfectly (and heavily if I'm going to be nasty) made-up face. Rich didn't respond to her. He just stared back at me. And I stared at him. She laughed again a little nervously.

"Come on Rich," she urged him, "Just give her some money."

He broke eye contact and fished in his pocket for his wallet. He shoved a few notes at me. I shook my head, trying to make my mouth form words.

"No...no..."

"Yes, really, honestly. It's my fault."

I didn't raise my hand to take the money, and so he pushed it into my slack fingers. The shock of electricity jolted us both and our eyes met again.

"Sorry," he murmured before she dragged him away, laughing as she went.

I was shaken back to reality when the loudspeaker came on.

"Spillage in aisle nine! Spillage in aisle nine!"

It was only when I got home, without knowing how I had driven back that I realised what a complete mess I had looked. I had to resign myself to never seeing him again, and even if I did, he would just remember me as skanky tracksuit supermarket girl.

I saw him again a month later. This time the Gods were smiling upon me and I was all dressed up for a night out. I felt fantastic, in a slinky deep purple dress and sexy knee-high boots, my hair had been in rollers all day and I'd spent at least an hour on my make-up. It was my return-to-normality night – the one we all have where *we know we're ready to pull again after a break-up. Steph, Lata and I swirled into the supermarket, to buy a bottle of vodka to take to the party we were going to, and heads turned as we laughed and strutted out way through. Well, actually, Lata strutted, and Steph and I sort of followed in her wake, basking in her glory. I was at the till when I saw him; he was standing at the till next to us and he was with her. His eyes were already locked on me when I looked up and saw him. I felt adrenalin rush through me. He sort of raised his hand and gave me a wave. She noticed and glared at me. He had already paid for his purchase, and as he walked past the end of our till lane, he caught my eye and winked. I flushed, my stomach churning and my heart leaping.*

After the party, during which I spent the whole night thinking about him, we went to a club. The minute I walked in, I saw him and warmth flooded through me. He was standing alone with a drink in his hand. Completely against my nature and emboldened by the fact that the effect he had on me was clearly reciprocal, I walked towards him.

"Hey supermarket girl."

"Hey."

We stood very close just looking at each other's faces.

"Where's your girlfriend?" I asked.

"Standing right in front of me."

From that night, we were inseparable. I did feel guilty about his ex, Sian, but they hadn't been together long and he confessed he'd been serially unfaithful to her. He also confessed that he had gone to the supermarket every day after ramming his trolley into me trying to find me again. I said I couldn't believe it after he'd seen me looking at my complete and utter worst. But he said that all he'd thought to himself when he'd seen me standing there looking completely bereft and covered in salsa and wine, was if I could look that good when I had obviously made no effort whatsoever, imagine how gorgeous I could be if I wanted to. I didn't believe him but I still liked to replay that conversation in my head when I was feeling low. Friends warned me that we hadn't entered into a relationship in strictly the best way – i.e. he had cheated on Sian and so wasn't I worried he would do the same to me? But I was in love.

***

"… and that was that. From that moment we were inseparable."

Dazzer nodded politely.

"That's nice," he said. I began to think to myself that maybe he wasn't so bad after all.

"In uni he was a real player," he continued, and then brayed like a donkey, "he shagged anything that moved."

I changed my mind again very quickly.

***

The next morning, Rich came down to the pool tentatively and we sat in the sun for a while, me nursing a hangover in silence because I didn't want to rub into Rich what a great night we had had. Blanco had burst into tears when we said good-bye because he was heading south to the beaches for a few weeks with Sun in tow. He had cried into my shoulder and clung to me as if we were best friends that had known each other for years. It struck me how being out of your familiar environment means that relationships develop much more quickly than they usually would.

At about lunchtime, Tom, Dazzer and Tuna appeared. Tom had one of the tiny Thai girls from the previous evening clinging onto his hand. He was looking hung over, but was wearing that lazy, happy smile of someone who has fallen in lust. They sat down next to us in the shade.

"Hey Rich," Tuna said straight away, "How are you feeling?"

Rich nodded.

"Much better, cheers mate," he looked a little embarrassed, "Gutted I missed out on last night's fun though." "Well, it's not over yet," Dazzer said groggily, "Where are you guys planning on going next?"

I looked at Rich expectantly. He had been the planner of the trip and I was just going along with his plans.

"Well, we thought we'd head straight to Laos from here and come back to Thailand later for a few weeks on the islands and beaches down South."

Dazzer grinned.

"No you're not. You're coming to Pai."

I had heard of hippy Pai, a relaxed laid-back place in the mountains and jungles of the North of Thailand. It was once a secret haunt of hippies and backpackers, but as always happens to these places, was becoming *de rigueur* for travellers, the 'new' undiscovered place. I had read that it was time to go there now before it became too saturated like everywhere else. Rich looked at me questioningly. I shrugged and nodded.

"Sounds good to me," I looked at Tom and Tuna, "Are you all going?"

Tuna nodded but Tom smiled shyly.

"Actually," he glanced at the Thai girl who smiled sweetly at him, "I thought I might stay here with Mali for a few days. She's going to show me the sights – you know the non-touristy ones."

Dazzer looked surprised.

"Alright, we'll stay too then."

Tom looked at him.

"Well…uh…"

Dazzer snorted like a pig.

"Only joking mate. I know the sort of sights you're going to be seeing!"

The Thai girl blushed and looked down at her feet.

"Shut up Dazzer," Tuna snapped. But Dazzer was leaning back in his seat with his eyes closed and was soon snoring. I was surprised at Tuna's reaction; I assumed they all thought Dazzer was hilarious and harmless, but he was obviously grating on other people's nerves too.

I leaned towards the Thai girl.

"I'm sorry; I haven't introduced you to my boyfriend, Rich."

Rich shook her hand smiling welcomingly.

"WHAT…IS…YOUR…NAME?" he said in a loud voice pronouncing each word slowly. I was mortified.

"MALI," she answered just as slowly and smiled at him as if he was simple.

I glared at Rich.

"Mali owns and runs her own restaurant, Rich. She did a degree in business management in America," I told him in a steely voice.

Rich raised his eyebrows in shock and spluttered a bit.

"That's…uh…cool. Well, I'm going for a swim."

He got up, peeled off his t-shirt and dived into the pool. I noticed he had lost a bit of weight after his bout of food poisoning. Tuna looked at me and gave me a small smile and I rolled my eyes and shook my head.

"Honestly," I said quietly to him so the others couldn't hear, "Sometimes I wonder what on earth I'm doing with him."

Tuna's smile slipped a little and he looked surprised.

"Really?"

I shook my head, instantly feeling awful. Poor Rich, he hadn't known any better, he hadn't met her the night before. I laughed lightly.

"Of course not. I love him to bits. So," I said eager to change the subject, "what happened to your lady friend last night?"

He smiled and shook his head, looking down at his lap.

"Nothing. She was a sweet girl, but I'm not interested in anything right now. You know."

I smiled sympathetically.

"I know. Apart from that Swiss girl in Ko Pha Ngan," I added lightly, giving him a sidelong glance.

Tuna laughed.

"You're terrible. She was Swedish. And she was a nice girl. And we got on well. And that was it."

"Sure," I said nodding, smirking at him.

Tuna suddenly jumped to his feet, grabbed my arm, yanked me towards the pool and before I knew what he was doing, picked me up and jumped in with me, fully dressed. I hate when people play practical jokes on me and I came up spluttering for air. I saw Rich's face, his eyes wide waiting to see me explode. I opened and closed my mouth like a fish, Tuna's head surfaced next to me grinning…and I burst out laughing. Within minutes, I had soaked Dazzer who then jumped in on top of me, Tom had thrown Mali in and it all turned into a big messy wet hilarious brawl.

Chapter Fifteen

The ride to Pai east of Chiang Mai is on one of the most breath-taking, gut-wrenching mountain passes imaginable. The bus was crammed full of both local people and travellers of various nationalities. My entire journey was spent buried in one or the other armpits of two Israeli guys who had scrambled on the bus in front and behind me. I was jammed between them, standing in the aisle, all of us hanging onto the overhead bar. Hence my head being about level with their armpits. And as backpackers usually do, they hadn't washed for a while, and had obviously been traipsing round with their backpacks on for a few hours before the journey so they didn't smell too fresh. They were, however, very sociable and interesting and I had an entire rundown of Israel's history and a list of all the countries that they had been thrown out of due to their nationality. I was also invited to come and stay in Tel Aviv whenever I wanted. Considering I had been dragged kicking and screaming to Thailand, I didn't think it was highly likely that I would take them up on the offer but it was considerate all the same. Rich kept shooting jealous glances over his shoulder from where he stood at the front of the bus but all I could do was shrug and smile apologetically. As a relief from being buried in Israeli armpits, I twisted my head at a tortuous angle in order to catch glimpses of the hazy green hills, thousands of feet high, as the bus screeched along, pistons screaming, engine groaning and scattering chickens into the gutters at either side of the road. Finally after straining up-hill for what seemed like hours, we found ourselves hurtling downhill, praying that the brakes would work, and rattling into Pai.

Wandering through Pai, we found cosy little winding streets, stalls selling various tie-dyed clothing, and local people making and selling beaded jewellery. Posters advertising sheesha bars and various adventure-filled treks into the mountains dotted the stone walls of the streets. Food stalls selling buckets of live beetles, stood alongside cafés selling curries and English breakfasts. Long-haired, ageing hippies strolled alongside Rastafarian Thais, whilst groups of European gap-year students and wrinkled old Thai men played checkers on the roadside. Incense wafted on the air and the sound of tinkling music floated out of shops selling ethnic shirts and sarongs. We strolled through the village to a wide river, where a few "guesthouses" stretched along the banks. These consisted of groups of huts of varying luxury dotted amongst the palms in wide grassy pastures. We opted for the cheaper option: quaint, tee-pee shaped rickety bamboo huts with a small veranda and containing a mattress and a mosquito net. There was a small window looking out of the back of the hut over the countryside. I loved it. The owners – Jake, an ageing, leathery hippy with a broad cockney accent and his wife, Suchin, a tiny middle-aged Thai lady who smiled permanently – gave us a pile of about twelve blankets.

"It gets *cold* at night," Jake warned us ominously.

I wandered around the grounds and found the communal toilets or 'jungle' toilets as they were named. The walls were made of wonky logs roped together and there was no roof; the toilet sat amongst huge leafy plants, pebbles and rocks and looked up at the blue sky above. The showers were similar; the shelves for your soap were rocks and logs. Open-air ablutions were not my cup of tea but after the first go where I kept looking behind me to check nobody was peeping through the log walls, I found it quite liberating looking up at the sky above me while I showered.

Freshly washed, Rich and I went for a wander through the little town; there were tiny bars and small restaurants, a relief after the proliferation of large, busy places in other tourist hot-spots. We stopped at a little roadside café and ordered a red Thai curry. Rich's appetite was back in full force and he gobbled it up. It was only half way through that we realised exactly how hot it was. Tears streamed down my face as I ploughed my way through it. The spiciest food I had ever had until I got to Thailand was chicken korma. The further North we travelled in Thailand, the hotter the food got. In hindsight, this was probably a bad thing with Rich's recent bout of food poisoning but we didn't think much of it at the time. After a stroll holding hands along the rocky streets, stopping now and again to check out various adverts and posters for day trips and tours offered in the area, we spotted a camper van parked on the roadside with a crowd of people standing around it. When we got closer, we realised that it had been turned into a bar – people were serving cocktails from the open side windows, and customers were perched on bar stools alongside it. We managed to edge our way onto some seats and drank cocktails, lapping up the laid-back atmosphere happily.

On our way back along the river, we came across Dazzer and Tuna sitting at a small relaxed riverside bar. It had bamboo platforms jutting out over the river, mounds of cushions for people to lounge on and a crowd of people was sitting around a huge fire. Dazzer spotted us first and waved languorously as we strolled past.

"Oi! Arseholes! Over here!"

Some guys sitting next to them, who turned out to be American, found this hilarious. I realised as we sat down that it was probably due to the massive reefer they were smoking.

Tuna smiled at us from where he lounged by the fire. I felt glad that we had friends there (or a friend not counting Dazzer) to relax with and I felt warm and fuzzy with the firelight on my face. Dazzer introduced us to the two American guys, Stevo and Marty, then the two Thai guys who owned the bar, one with long hair in a ponytail and one wearing a bandana, called Jonny and Tam, a Canadian couple Kim and Rob who were on their honeymoon and a rather miserable-looking French guy called Patrice. They were all pretty stoned and un-talkative which I was glad about as I just wanted to sit and stare at the fire. I snuggled in against Rich and smiled to myself. This travelling lark wasn't too bad at all.

Through the smoky haze I saw a figure approaching the fire carrying a tray of drinks. As she crouched down and placed the drinks in front of their respective owners, people smiled and nodded at her and made various friendly remarks that made me realise she was very much in the inner sanctum of this crowd. She had very long curly dark brown hair, slanted heavily lashed eyes and a petite heart-shaped face. She was also very, very skinny, that sort of model-thin where their hipbones hold up their trousers. She carried herself with effortless grace that reminded me of something I couldn't quite place. The drinks given out, she parked herself next to one of the brooding looking Thai guys – Tam, the one with the bandana – and he placed his arm around her. I noticed Patrice glare at them before downing his drink.

"Rich, Ruby, thish ish Nicole. She worksh here," Dazzer slurred. "She's with Tam. He ownsh the bar."

She glanced casually at us across the fire and smiled politely but coolly.

"Pleased to meet you," she said and as soon as I heard her accent, I realised what she had reminded me of. She had the effortless grace of every French girl I had ever met. I began to put the pieces together and started to ponder the situation with Patrice who was boring holes into her and Tam with his eyes. He caught my eye and looked away quickly.

Nicole took the reefer from Kim and took a long slow sultry drag. I watched the smoke snake from between her lips, and then my eyes were dragged towards the fire; the flames danced before my eyes, and they slowly began to close.

I awoke to the sound of giggles. I wriggled around trying to get comfortable. But there were those giggles again. I opened my eyes a crack and saw laughing faces watching me. Dazzer was snorting louder than most and I realised that there was something stuck to my lip. I pulled it off. It was a reefer butt. There was also one stuck in my nostril. Everyone was laughing, including Rich. I looked around. Kim, Rob, Patrice, Tuna and Jonny were gone, but there were some more people I didn't recognise, as well as Stevo, Marty, Nicole and Tam. And they were all looking at me and laughing. I pulled my skirt down because it had ridden up and sat up smoothing my hair, feeling my cheeks burning. I looked at Rich and he was weak with laughter, tears running down his face. I could see they were all completely stoned but it didn't lessen the humiliation. I tried to smile and laugh it off, and eventually they all went back to contemplating the stars or the meaning of life, or how cool Beavis and Butthead were. I looked at Rich, shaking with anger, barely able to control it.

"I'm going," I hissed, "Coming?"

He shook his head, beaming from ear to ear.

"I'm gonna stay here with my mate," he said ruffling Dazzer's greasy hair.

"Fine," I muttered and stalked off. I walked quickly along the riverbank. I couldn't believe he had done that to me. All the others were just stoned and drunk and didn't know me from Adam but Rich knew how much that would humiliate me. I began to trot, eager to get back to the hut, and angry tears started to sting my eyes, making everything blurry. I stumbled over a rock and went sprawling on my face into the grass.

"Ruby?" a familiar voice came from the darkness, "Bloody hell. Are you OK?"

I felt a hand grip my arm and pull me to my feet. I hurriedly wiped away the tears and saw Tuna's worried face in front of me. Seeing someone I knew, someone familiar, made it all come rushing out incoherently.

He led me up the steps onto the veranda of his hut. He sat me on the wooden bench.

"Who did it?" His voice was quiet.

"Dazzer I think. But they were all laughing including Rich. It was so embarrassing."

"He stuck a spliff up your nose. And you didn't notice?"

I smiled at the image and shrugged.

"Well, I was asleep."

I looked at him feeling really stupid and was surprised to see how angry he looked. He was shaking his head and looking at the ground.

"I've really had it with Dazzer. He is such a bloody idiot. I don't know why I am still travelling with him. He was just a mate from work at home and he seemed like a decent guy but…"

He bit his lip.

"I'm sorry, Ruby. If I had been there, I would have stopped them."

I nodded, suddenly feeling a bit foolish for over-reacting. What if I had ruined a friendship?

"It was just a joke," I defended Dazzer feebly.

"Not a very funny one."

We sat back on the bench and looked up at the stars, not speaking for a while. I shivered in the cold and pulled my cardigan closer around me. The smell of the river wafted on the air.

"It's funny how people are different when they are away from home, isn't it?" Tuna eventually said.

I thought about it and nodded.

"Are you different then?" I asked him.

He shrugged.

"I guess. I am different to the way I was. I have grown up I think. I don't see the point anymore in my life revolving around the next time I'm going to get drunk. Or the next time I'm going to get laid."

I nodded.

"What about you?"

"I'm more uptight at home. I think I'm more worried about what people think of me,"

I laughed, "But then I clearly am still worried or I wouldn't have performed like that back there, would I?"

"I don't blame you."

I thought for a few seconds about the Ruby I was now and the Ruby I was at home.

"I always thought of myself as a homebody. I want a simple life. Or at least I did. I don't know what I want now."

I surprised myself at how open I was being with this guy I barely knew. But he had that effect. We sat like that for a long time looking at the stars in silence.

***

I was awoken from the deep woolly layers of a passively stoned sleep (I prided myself on never having smoked either weed or cigarettes but I couldn't have failed to have inhaled the clouds of smoke going around the fire that night) and found myself under the deep woolly layers of the twelve blankets piled on top of me. My nose was icy cold, as were Rich's fingers when they found me beneath the layers. He pressed against my warm sleepy body and as he stroked me into consciousness, all thoughts of his insensitivity and my embarrassment, melted away; we made love in a sleepy fumbly dream under the mound of blankets in a creaking hut in Pai.

Chapter Sixteen

The next morning, I awoke feeling toasty beneath all the blankets. My breath came out in puffs of cloud as I stuck my head out. I thought for a moment that Rich had become lost beneath all the blankets but after searching for a while, I realised he wasn't there. I braced myself to climb out of bed and after throwing on a horrible sensible khaki fleece, I peeked out through the bamboo shutters that covered the glass-less window in the thatched roof of the hut. I looked out onto a dewy green field, dotted with palms and other pointy, stilted huts like ours. The grass was bathed in a blanket of mist and the sun was just peering over the top of the distant mountains. The scene looked like something from a fantasy film, an Ewok village or something. I knew that once the sun came up, it would warm everything up very quickly, and so I waited for a few more minutes before heading out for the open-air shower. When I got back to the hut, humming, I found Rich curled up in a ball. He opened one eye and groaned when he saw me.

"I shouldn't have had that curry," he gasped.

"Oh no," I sat down next to him and stroked his head.

"It's back," he said nodding, "Not as bad as last time, but pretty bad. I spent most of the early hours on the sodding freezing outdoor loo."

I tried to hide my smile at the thought but he saw me. Surprisingly, he smiled too.

"Still, at least I got to look up at the stars."

I leaned down and kissed his forehead.

"What about the trek today?" I asked. We had booked a trek into the mountains the day before with Dazzer and Tuna.

He shook his head.

"I can't go. I need to be near a toilet at all times. Besides I don't feel too hot either," he sighed, "But you go, sweetheart. I don't want you to miss out."

I shook my head.

"No, I'll stay and look after you."

"Don't be silly. I just need to rest. And you have been dying to do an elephant ride. You might not get another chance."

I sat there, feeling undecided. I had really been excited about the trip because it involved a forest trek to an ethnic minority village (which I would have happily missed if I could), bamboo rafting down a river (which sounded like a bit too much effort to me) and a trek on an elephant's back (which sounded like the most amazing thing in the world, and which I knew would make this whole trip worthwhile).

"Go on, Rubes. I'll be fine here, honestly."

I felt bad leaving Rich there in bed but I went to the dining hut of the guesthouse to meet Tuna and Dazzer as arranged, changing my mind every minute and nearly turning back. However, the thought of that elephant kept me going, and I found myself sitting on cushions eating breakfast, listening to Bob Marley on the ancient stereo as we chatted excitedly about the trek. Dazzer was a no-show, undoubtedly too hung over to make it, and so we headed off to the trekking agent's office to meet our guide. There were three other people on the trip and I was really pleased to see that two of them were Rob and Kim, the Canadian couple, from the night before. The other one was Patrice who had seemed like a moody sod but at least we knew him. He surprised me by giving me a huge beam when he saw me.

"'ello Ruby and Tuna," he said happily, "I am glad to know some people on this trip!"

We were introduced to our guide, Lap, and after he outlined the trek for us, we all clambered into a mini-bus and headed out of Pai. After about forty minutes of driving along impossibly winding roads and climbing higher and higher into the hazy hills, we finally stopped at a small clearing on the roadside. From there we set off at a brisk pace into the forest and Lap kept up an interesting commentary about the forest, Thailand in general and the village people we were going to visit. I usually detest any form of outdoor exercise and was a bit worried I wouldn't be able to keep up. But after half an hour, I realised I was really enjoying myself and chatted openly with Kim and Rob about their honeymoon and our respective lives at home. Patrice was also very chatty but seemed reluctant to talk about his trip so far. He changed the subject every time it was broached.

The scenery was breath-taking; dense, green forest blanketing soft hills. There was a lot of clambering over fallen logs and sloshing through muddy rivers but despite earlier misgivings I really enjoyed it. Eventually, after about three hours, we rounded a corner and the path led us to a rather rickety, muddy-looking village. As we walked along the road, children in dirty clothes ran out to stare at us. We passed a man weaving baskets who waved at Lap and women and children washing clothes crouched by a small river that ran through the village. Finally, Lap stopped at a large wooden hut and gathered us around him.

"We are going to meet the oldest man in the village. He is ninety-seven years old. He cannot speak English so if you want to ask him a question I will translate."

He beckoned us to follow and headed up the steps and into the hut, stopping on the top step to remove his shoes. We all copied and as we went in, Lap stooped to hold the hand of a very small and wizened old man sitting on the floor and greeted him loudly. We all bowed our heads slightly, placed our palms together in front of our chest and said 'sa wai dii' as was the custom. An elderly lady gestured for us to sit down. We sat on bamboo mats on the floor, and the lady gave us all tea. The old man asked us questions through Lap about where we all came from. Then he told us that the old lady was his wife and that she was seventy-two – very young he said with a laugh. She smiled and patted his arm. Rob and Kim asked if they could take a photo of him and his wife and he nodded eagerly, grinning a toothless smile. They then showed him the photo on the screen of their digital camera. He was amazed when he saw it, and astounded when Lap explained that the camera could hold hundreds of photos. He turned it over in his hands looking puzzled.

"But it's too small," he told Lap. He then beckoned me to sit by him and said something to Lap who grinned.

"He says he wants a picture taken with the beautiful one."

I felt taken aback and embarrassed. I wasn't sure if he was joking because I was hardly a beauty at the best of times and especially not when I was all sweaty, red and dirty after our trek. I realised briefly in surprise that it was the first time I had thought about what I looked like all day. I beamed at Rob and Kim as they took our photo and then at Tuna who had also produced his camera. He had to put the camera down quickly though as a pretty young woman had entered the hut and was carrying a tiny, beautiful baby which she thrust into his arms, smiling at him encouragingly. It was my turn to click away with my camera, as Tuna sat holding the baby girl awkwardly, smiling down at her. A dimpled smile broke across her face and she balled her hands into fists and giggled. She cuddled into his chest and he held her for twenty minutes contentedly until she decided to wee on him – disposable nappies had apparently not reached this village yet. Tuna held her out at arm's length to her mother who took her laughing heartily. I expected Tuna to be pissed off – I knew Rich would have been – but he just grinned at me.

"It's not like real wee is it, baby wee?" he said looking down at his sodden t-shirt.

Eventually, two more elderly ladies appeared carrying bowls of rice and vegetables doused in chillies for us to eat. We ate heartily – well as heartily as you can with chopsticks. I had been trying my hardest to learn to use them but still found myself being clumsy and dropping the rice all over my lap. After watching me for a few moments, embarrassing myself, Tuna leaned over and taught me how to hold them properly. I managed to get a mouthful of rice to my mouth without dropping a grain after my second go and I smiled at him gratefully.

"Like a pro," he said and Patrice laughed.

"I think this mean prostitute," he said quietly to Tuna and me.

I hit Patrice on the shoulder and he guffawed heartily.

After lunch, we were led outside where the elephants were waiting. Lap explained that an elephant cost as much as six thousand pounds but a village man would try as hard as he could to save up for one, as the payback from tourist elephant treks was more than worth it.

"It would make a man very rich," Lap said.

We were led up wooden steps to a platform from where we had to climb into a basket on the back of the waiting elephant. I gazed at the elephants; I had never seen one that wasn't in the zoo before. They looked so huge, and slow and...and wild. My heart was pounding. I wasn't quite as sure now that I wanted to do this. The platform was so high off the ground; it was a long way to fall off the back of one of these animals. I clutched Tuna's arm.

"Can I go on with you?" I whispered worriedly.

He looked down at me in surprise.

"Of course," he smiled and took my hand, "I'll look after you."

His hand felt big and warm and dry as it closed around mine, and I suddenly felt a bit weird. I hadn't held a man's hand other than Rich's for years. Tuna seemed to sense my sudden tension and casually dropped my hand. I felt immediately stupid. He was only being friendly after all.

He climbed onto the basket and then patted the seat next to him. He held out his hand for me to hold and I sort of fell gracelessly into the seat. The basket lurched and swayed violently as the elephant moved away from the platform and I fell sideways, my hands clasping Tuna's knee.

"Steady on, Rube," he said, "You'll be on my lap next."

I blushed and pulled myself away. And while I should have been completely consumed by the amazing feeling of the steady plodding of this majestic animal beneath me, all I could concentrate on was the proximity of Tuna's leg to my own as we swayed along the road.

After a while of the jerky, steady rocking, I relaxed in the basket and took in the scenery around me. Eventually, the huts of the village petered out and the path led deep into the forest again. The elephant herder stopped and spoke to Lap who was walking along beside us.

"The guide says you can ride bareback on the elephant if you wish," Lap explained.

I couldn't hide the delight on my face and Tuna looked at me and nodded.

"Go on, Ruby, you can't get much better than that."

I slowly slid myself down onto the elephant's back as I saw Kim doing on her elephant, and then edged myself forward until my knees were tucked behind the elephant's ears. Let me just say that elephant hide is not soft, and with the constant motion of his awkward lurching, my shins and inner thighs were rubbed raw. But I didn't care at all. All I could do was marvel at the feeling of this enormous creature's head beneath the palms of my hands, the steady thud of his feet travelling up through my body as they hit the ground far below, and the feel of his huge ears flapping against my legs.

"Is amazing, yes?" Patrice called over his shoulder to me, from where he was also perched behind his elephant's ears. He had the luxury of being on an elephant all on his own. I nodded happily, too ecstatic to reply.

Eventually, we reached a river and the elephants had ideas of their own. They had decided they had had enough of plodding along; they wanted a drink and a bath. Before I knew it, a jet of water had been shot over me from a huge trunk. I heard Kim squeal as her elephant had obviously given himself, and her, a bath as well. Then mine decided to have a drink and kneeled down on his front legs. I gripped on for dear life.

"Bloody hell!" I cried. I glanced over my shoulder at Tuna who was laughing hysterically and hanging onto the basket so he didn't fall out.

All too soon, the ride came to an end. We were helped down from the elephants onto a fallen tree, and with a trumpet, the elephants were led away by their keeper. We were all exhilarated and couldn't stop babbling about what a great experience it had been. Lap raised his voice to get our attention.

"Now, it is time for the rafting," he said before leading us through the trees to the banks of the river, which had widened considerably. There was a man lying on the pebbles of the bank and a long raft was tethered up beside him. The raft was made simply of long bamboo poles strapped together with twisted reeds. It looked far from sturdy and the river looked like it was flowing pretty fast to me. Lap introduced us to our driver and told us to take our shoes off. We clambered aboard, he told us to find a good handhold – which is pretty impossible on bamboo – and before we knew it, Lap had untied the raft and we were off down the river. The driver stood at the front of the raft and guided us along the river expertly and effortlessly, using another long bamboo pole, which he pushed from side to side on the riverbed. He edged us around floating logs and took us perilously close to slippery boulders and rocks.

Eventually, we gained enough courage to stand on the raft and sway with its movements. And this was how I fell in. One minute, I had been laughing at something Tuna had said, the next the raft had jerked to one side and I had fallen off the other in spectacular fashion. I plunged into the cool water which was surprisingly deep, splashed around frantically for a bit and finally managed to get my head above water, gasping for air, my heart racing. I was floating along at a terrific rate, and I kept scraping my knees against rocks and pebbles.

"Ruby!" I heard Tuna's voice across the water. The raft was on the bank and he was wading towards me as I floated along with the current. He was holding out his hand.

"Grab it! Grab my hand!"

I reached up and grasped onto his outstretched arm. He held me tightly and pulled me towards him, my bum dragging along the pebbles. He yanked me gracelessly to my feet, and I coughed and spluttered a bit, beginning to feel, now that the shock had passed, like a prize idiot.

"You OK?" he asked me, looking into my face.

I grinned and nodded. He shook his head and smiled in relief.

"I thought you were a goner then."

"You must know me by now – if there's something I can fall off or over, then I will."

I noticed the driver further down the bank, perched on the river's edge, ready to hold out his arm if Tuna had missed me, and Lap a few feet further on than him.

I padded damply towards the others, Kim and Rob were looking concerned and Patrice was hooting with laughter.

"Ha! You fell like a sack of potatoes!" He chortled. "Plop! You were just gone!"

"Yeah, thanks for the concern, Patrice," I said wryly, wringing out my t-shirt.

"No problem," he chuckled. "Hey, I knew you would be OK. You are a tough girl."

I felt strangely pleased with this compliment. I had always thought I was rather pathetic.

It became apparent from the annoyed shouting of the raft driver, that in the haste to moor the boat after my exit, it had become badly damaged on the rocks. The twine that held the poles together had been ripped and two of the bamboo poles had floated off down the river. Lap was placating the driver.

"There is a village near here," he said to us, once the driver had calmed down, "we can go there to get the raft fixed."

It took a twenty-minute walk through the forest to reach the village. We were greeted with even more interested stares than in the previous village, this one obviously not being as accessible to tour groups.

We sat outside a hut as Lap and the driver went inside and played with a tiny monkey chained to a tree.

"It's so cruel," Kim said, stroking its little head, as it gazed up at her with big eyes.

"Why? It gets food," Patrice pointed at a pile of vegetables in front of the monkey, "And it gets to run up and down the tree." He shrugged.

"Why is it cruel?"

"Because…because it should be free!" Kim spluttered.

Patrice shrugged again and lay down on a big pile of hay with his hands behind his head.

"Americans," I heard him mutter.

Lap, the raft driver and a couple of men from the village worked hard at fixing the raft as we perched on rocks watching them, but very soon the sun was low in the sky, and the raft was still not finished. Eventually, after some hushed conferring, Lap approached us and explained that it was getting too late to raft back.

"The sun will be gone soon and it will be too dangerous to raft all the way back. The villagers have very kindly offered to let us stay with them this evening and we can head back in the morning."

He spread his hands apologetically.

"I am very sorry, it will be basic, and we have to sleep on the floor."

Kim was about to open her mouth to protest but Tuna spoke over her.

"That is fine, Lap. Please tell them we are very grateful."

Kim shut her mouth and looked a bit sheepish. We trooped back to the village. I was silent, feeling really guilty. This was all my fault.

We were led into a large hut and two ladies motioned for us to sit on the floor before bustling out. About twelve children huddled outside the window and gawped at us silently.

"I'm so sorry guys," I blurted.

"Why?" Tuna looked puzzled.

"Well, if I hadn't gone and bloody fallen off the bloody raft, we wouldn't be in this mess."

"Ruby, we have an opportunity here to experience something most other people never will. Yeah you can do a tour and see lots of nice things and meet lots of nice people. But we are getting the chance to be guests in the homes of these people, some of whom will probably never have met a foreigner."

"Here, here," said Rob, giving a disgruntled-looking Kim a warning look.

"So let's enjoy it," Tuna patted my knee.

The two Thai women eventually reappeared and brought us glasses of some very strong rice wine. Lap, the driver and the other village man also joined us and very soon we were chatting and eating bowls of rice and stir-fried vegetables.

We talked to our hosts through Lap because they didn't speak English and had more and more rice wine poured down our throats. After our meal, we were beckoned into the hut next door. Inside was a rotund and very proud-looking man. He motioned towards an ancient-looking TV perched on a rickety table. The aerial was huge and wires seemed to be poking out everywhere.

"W.W.F.," the large man said happily and turned on the television. We settled down on the floor along with what seemed like the rest of the village; all the children were still peering in at the window and about twenty adults sat alongside us. We were treated to about three hours of W.W.F. Apparently, this is what the villagers thought we watched at home, and heads kept turning to look at us to see if we were enjoying it. Tuna smiled and nodded and put his thumbs up whenever something exciting happened. Gasps of disbelief from the villagers would accompany these bouts of violence. A small movement next to me caught my eye; Tuna was sitting with his legs crossed and a small elderly man was stroking his leg, fascinated by the downy fair hair growing on them compared with his own smooth nut-brown skin. Tuna was smiling at him.

"Hairy," he said laughing. The older man was amazed by the hair and continued to stroke him.

He muttered something to the man sitting next to him and motioned towards Tuna's leg. This man then leaned over and started to stroke Tuna's leg. Tuna looked at me and raised his eyebrows.

"This is strange," he said out of the corner of his mouth.

I snorted into my hand and then had to pretend I was coughing. I thought of how Rich would have reacted if it had been him – he would have been horrified. I grinned at the thought.

After a while, I could hardly keep my eyes open, but my need to use the toilet was even stronger. The food that had given Rich his repeat stomach problems was obviously making its way through my system now as well. I kept peering around to look for a toilet or bathroom, but this hut just seemed to consist of the one room.

Lap had disappeared so eventually I asked a young girl who was sitting near to me. I motioned pulling an imaginary flush. She stared at me blankly. Eventually, I squatted on the floor. She continued to stare at me blankly. I made a face as if I was straining. Finally, she cottoned on and burst out laughing. She quickly told the people she was sitting with, and pointed at me, and they all joined her in laughing. I blushed, even though I knew she wasn't being malicious as she was smiling at me and nodding happily. She took my hand and led me outside and around the back of the shack. She pointed at a pile of leaves and nodded, still smiling. She stood and waited for me to walk over to it. I gazed at the pile of damp, dark leaves from where a smell of rotting vegetation and other 'organic material' was being emitted. So this was it, I was just supposed to whip my knickers off and squat over this mound. Hmm. I turned to see the girl heading back around the corner to the hut, still giggling to herself, so at least I wouldn't have an audience. I headed away from the huts into a clearing and found a piece of metal roofing on the floor. I picked it up and lugged it behind a bush. With one hand holding the metal sheet in front of me, I managed to pull my shorts and pants down and I squatted down. And once it started, it didn't stop. Not even when a local village man wandered past and decided to peer over the metal sheet. He watched me; his face expressionless. I resigned myself to a loss of all dignity and stared at the ground. In the end, he wandered away towards the huts, as if he had seen nothing out of the ordinary. I had a balled-up piece of toilet roll in my pocket, which I was most grateful for, and prayed that all the food had exited my system in one go.

By the time I made it back to the hut, the W.W.F. had thankfully finished, most of the villagers had gone, and a small woman was bustling around Tuna, Rob, Kim and Patrice, giving them threadbare blankets.

"Well, that was one of my most memorable toilet experiences," I murmured to Tuna, as he handed me a blanket. He grinned at me, his eyes twinkling.

"This is what memories are made of, Ruby. Toilet visits. At least you didn't have your leg stroked by five different men."

"No, I just had one watch me while I did my business."

Tuna chuckled as we all settled down in a circle on the floor.

"Rich would have died if those guys had started to stroke him."

Tuna shrugged as he lay his blankets out.

"It's not unusual for men to be affectionate here," he said sitting down and pulling the blankets around him.

"Can you imagine if it had happened to Dazzer?"

Tuna laughed at the image: the look of horror that would no doubt have crossed Dazzer's face, the loud shouts of protest that would have followed.

The generator that the TV ran off had been turned off. I imagined it was only used on special occasions. There were a couple of candles in the middle of us on the floor. The only noise other than crickets was the giggle of the clutch of children still huddled around the window watching us. We were all exhausted but somehow the exhilaration of being there in that situation meant that none of us could sleep. We chatted well into the night. Kim and Rob told us all about their travels in South America. I told everyone my rather boring story of how Rich had bought me this trip for my birthday. I suddenly felt rather embarrassed admitting that I hadn't wanted to come away at all; I found myself telling everyone that it had been a dream of mine for a long time and it was amazing to finally fulfil it. Tuna looked at me from the corner of his eye and I felt my cheeks colour. Finally, it came around to Patrice. When Rob asked where he had been on his trip until now and whether he had travelled alone, Patrice hesitated, before sighing.

"Well, I guess you will probably find out soon anyway," he sniffed. He went onto to explain that he had come travelling a year ago with his girlfriend. They had been together for three years and had seemingly lived a charmed life in Paris. They had been so excited about travelling together and had started their trip in Vietnam before moving on to Cambodia, Laos and finally Thailand. Then his girlfriend had left him for someone else.

"No!" I said, horrified for him. He nodded.

"My girlfriend is Nicole. You know, she works in the Riverside bar."

"No!" I said again. Kim looked as shocked as me.

He nodded.

"We met Tam and Jonny one night. I went to bed early, she stay up drinking and smoking with them. The next day, she is with Tam. Just like that," he shrugged, "She tell me, very cool and calm, that she is in love with him, that she is going to run the bar with him and stay in Pai."

I realised I had my hand to my mouth.

"That's awful," I murmured, putting my hand on his shoulder. He shrugged.

"How long ago was this?"

"A month. I hang around to wait for it to go wrong. For her to come back to me," he shrugged again, "But she is still with him. She is happy. So I think now I should leave. I should move on."

Tuna nodded.

"It would be for the best, mate," he said.

The mood was suddenly sombre. I sat there thinking about poor Patrice and what a shock it must have been for him. How could he have stayed? Just waiting and watching her with someone else. I just couldn't fathom it.

The big round man who owned the TV interrupted us. He entered the room carrying what looked like a grubby plastic petrol can. He also had some cups and placed them in the middle of the floor with great ceremony. He poured us a cup each and handed them round. It was the incredibly strong rice liqueur that we had drunk earlier. He grinned and said something to us in Thai as he held up his cup. We raised ours.

"Cheers!" said Tuna, and we all downed our drinks.

***

I awoke to a pounding headache and felt like I had been beaten up. The wooden floor was like concrete. Tuna was lying next to me, his eyes open and watching me as my vision came into focus. His blue eyes looked amazingly clear and he smiled.

"Feeling good?" he asked me quietly.

I groaned. A furry animal appeared to be inhabiting my mouth.

"What happened?"

"We got rip roaring drunk on that rice wine. It didn't take much, it was very strong."

"Was I bad?" I asked thinking of my performance in Ko Pha Ngan.

He shook his head.

"You were very funny. And then you fell asleep very suddenly with your head on my lap."

"God, sorry."

"Not at all. You mumbled a lot in your sleep though."

"About what?"

"I am sure I heard you say sheep. And you definitely murmured I love you."

"Oh dear."

I forced myself to sit up. Sun was blazing in through the window. Miraculously, there were no children peering in.

And then something hit me. Richard. I hadn't even thought about him. He must be worried sick. I felt terrible. Poor Rich, he must be going out of his mind. I got to my feet hurriedly. There were blurry mumbles coming from the other figures that were emerging from their tangled blankets on the floor.

"I think I'm dead," Kim murmured.

"God, my head," added Rob.

The petrol can lay empty on the floor. Tuna stood up, looking relatively bright-eyed.

"How on earth do you look so good?" I grumbled, gathering my sheets together.

Tuna grinned.

"It's a beautiful day and I'm waking up next to a beautiful woman. What better hangover could there be?"

I felt my cheeks redden maddeningly and looked away from his smiling eyes. I mumbled something about getting back and tripped over my trailing blanket as I headed outside into the unforgiving sun.

***

We arrived back in Pai a couple of hours later. We had tried to give the TV man money for all the food and drink we had had but he had declined gruffly. The final part of the raft trip down the river had cured much of my hangover, with the cool water splashing onto my skin. The children had run along the bank with us as far as they could, waving and calling goodbye.

We clambered out of the bus at Lap's booking office and after thanking him heartily for the trip, we strolled back to the river where we were all staying in various guesthouses, chatting and laughing about our eventful couple of days. We said goodbye to Kim, Rob and Patrice at the riverbank and arranged to meet for a drink and food later, and Tuna and I headed on towards our guesthouse. As we passed the riverside bar, my eye was caught by two people lazing back on cushions, with their legs dangling off the platform into the river. I noticed them because the girl was Nicole, but the guy, who had his arm around her shoulders, was clearly not Tam. As we got closer, my heart lurched into my mouth. It couldn't be. Tuna was in the middle of a sentence and he trailed off when I abruptly walked away from him and up the steps to the wooden platform of the bar. The couple looked up at me languorously as if sitting there so closely together was the most natural thing in the world. Nicole's head was resting on Rich's shoulder, and her fingers were entwined with his. I couldn't quite compute what I was seeing. Rich seemed to not recognise me as he gazed up at me. They were clearly stoned.

"Rich, I… I'm back. It's OK. We're all OK."

He finally registered that it was me standing there, and his smile faltered.

"Ruby?"

I nodded looking at his arm draped over her shoulder and the way her long fingers clutched his wrist. They were just stoned, I said in my head, and being friendly. That was all.

"The raft broke. So we had to stay overnight…" I carried on weakly.

Nicole looked at me lazily. She turned her head and whispered something in Rich's ear, and he nodded, sitting up straight.

"Ruby, we have to talk."

Nicole got to her feet.

"I will just go and get us some drinks, darling," she murmured in her silky voice. My mouth dropped open. I felt as if she had just swung back her leg and kicked me in the stomach.

"Rich," I said in a low, wavering voice, "What is going on?"

He had the grace to finally look uncomfortable.

"I'm, uh, I'm with Nicole now."

I shook my head as if trying to clear it or to wake myself up.

"We, uh…well, that night that you passed out by the fire, we uh…just talked and talked all night. And we really hit it off."

"The night we made love when you came back to the hut?" I said, my voice low and shaking.

He nodded, screwing up his face ruefully and squirming slightly.

"And then yesterday," he continued, "We spent the day together. And well…we're just meant to be, Rube. We're soul mates."

The sky felt like it was rushing in on me.

"You weren't ill…"

"Well, I was a bit."

"It was a set up. So you two could be together."

He looked at me his eyes pleading.

"We needed time to talk, to get to know one another. And we both realised that we felt the same about each other. Please understand, Rube. This is nothing to do with you. I've never felt this way before…"

His words were fading because I was running, running away, past the blur that was Tuna, and along the river.

***

There was a soft knock at the door.

"Ruby, it's me, Tuna."

Another knock.

"I'm coming in."

I heard the door squeak as it opened behind me. My face was buried in the pile of thick blankets.

"Ruby."

I lay still. If I didn't move, maybe I would fall asleep and then wake up and it would all have been a nightmare.

I felt the mattress move as Tuna sat down beside me. He didn't speak, but I felt his hand on the back of my head. He stroked my hair gently. After a few minutes I lifted my head and looked at him.

"Rich..." I said, my voice croaky. He nodded.

"He said he hadn't felt this way before... He wasn't ill... They just wanted to be together..."

Tuna nodded.

"I know, I heard."

"I don't...I don't know..." I said, my voice breaking, as a huge wave of desolation overwhelmed me. He pulled me gently into his arms as the first of my tears started to fall.

It felt like I cried for hours. Tuna just sat holding me. Eventually when my crying subsided, he went and got me some tea. I took a sip and then lay and stared at the ceiling.

"I can't believe it. I just don't see how this has happened."

"What are you going to do?" Tuna asked, "Will you go home?"

I looked at him blankly.

"Home? I can't go without Rich. He *is* my home."

Tuna nodded.

"No. I've got to talk to him. He's just confused. She probably threw herself at him. And he couldn't say no..." my voice broke and a fresh wave of tears overwhelmed me as I imagined them together, their bodies entwined. I groaned and I curled up into a ball. I was in agony. It was physical pain. My insides felt raw. The whole world had turned upside down.

***

I got to my feet purposefully. I had been lying in a ball for almost half an hour. Tuna had fallen asleep beside me. I had made a decision. I was going to have a shower, get dressed, go over to the bar and talk to Rich. Bring him to his senses. He was just stoned before and was bound to be sober now. Tears threatened again so I grabbed my toiletry bag and towel and marched over to the showers. The welcome jet of water ran over me, through my hair and down my body. It tingled; it was almost painful. My nerves were so acute, everything was so visceral.

When I got back to the hut, Tuna had gone. I was glad; I needed to be on my own, to be hard and sensible. I pulled on my floaty skirt, trying not to think of that day in Chiang Mai that I had bought it, when we had been so happy. I needed to look nice. I combed my hair, put on a slick of mascara and blusher. I took a deep breath and headed outside. It was early evening; there was that soft, lazy glow over the hills.

Music floated from the main hut, people lazed on their verandas, two children splashed in the water at the edge of the river and giggled.

I walked along the riverbank, my heart thudding in my chest. I kept seeing them together, lying there on the cushions, their fingers entwined, smiling, whispering. As I approached the bar, I saw Patrice, Rob and Kim sitting on cushions together holding bottles of beer. They were chatting and laughing. I also saw Tam behind the bar, and Jonny sitting on a stool in front of the bar. There was no sign of Nicole or Rich. Kim spotted me and waved. I took a deep breath and headed over to them.

"Hey, Ruby," Rob said cheerily, "Feeling refreshed?"

"It was good to have a shower, wasn't it?" Kim chirped.

But Patrice was staring at me, frowning.

"You OK, Ruby?" he asked, "You look…sick."

"Nicole. She's done it again," I said mechanically.

Patrice looked at me blankly. I saw Rob and Kim exchange glances.

"Nicole?" he asked.

"She and Rich…"

They all stared at me.

"I must speak to him," I walked over to the bar.

Tam didn't smile when he saw me. He looked strained and had dark circles under his eyes.

"Tam, where's Nicole?"

He looked me in the eye, as if wondering whether I knew or not.

"She's with Rich."

"So you know then?"

He nodded.

"But…but, don't you care?"

He shrugged.

"I love her," he said simply.

I looked at him speechless. Surely, he would want to fight for her.

"She wants to be with him. I want her to be happy."

He shrugged again.

"Where are they?" I asked, exasperated.

"I don't know; she left our hut. They stay somewhere else."

"If you see them, tell Rich…tell him I need to talk to him."

He nodded, polishing a glass with immense concentration. I glanced at Jonny, who offered a small sympathetic smile. Tam put the glass down on the bar and poured me a huge gin and tonic.

"On me," he said, turning his back to me.

I wandered back over to the fire, clutching my gin. Rob, Kim and Patrice were whispering furiously and stopped when I was within earshot.

I told them in a monotone what had happened when we returned from the trip. Kim sat in horrified silence. Rob kept shaking his head.

"I don't believe it," he muttered.

Patrice's face was like thunder.

"Bastard," he spat when I had finished. I swallowed my drink in two gulps and winced. Rob slunk off to the bar and returned with drinks for everyone and another particularly strong gin and tonic for me, which I finished equally quickly.

"What are you going to do, Ruby?" Kim asked softly. "Will you go home?"

I looked at her in surprise as I had done with Tuna.

"Of course not; I'm not going anywhere without Rich."

She and Rob glanced at each other but I caught Patrice's eye and we looked at each other for a long moment. I hadn't been able to see twenty-four hours before, how he could have stood it, how he could have waited around for so long. Now I understood. It was as clear as water.

Rob and Kim chatted quietly between themselves, and Patrice glowered into the fire. Eventually, Tuna and Dazzer appeared. They nodded greetings at the others and Tuna sat down quickly beside me.

"You alright?" he asked quietly. I shook my head. I looked at Dazzer. He caught my eye and then looked shiftily down at his feet.

"Were you with them?" I asked him loudly and spitefully, "When it happened?"

He shook his head unconvincingly and fiddled with a beer bottle cap.

"What happened?"

"Ruby," Tuna put his hand on my arm, "It's not going to help…"

"I need to know," I hissed and leaned closer to Dazzer.

"Tell me," I said in a steely voice, "What happened?"

Dazzer sort of shrugged and then spoke haltingly.

"They just…uh…hung out by the river all day…and then…then…"

"Then they went off to her hut, did they?"

He fidgeted uncomfortably.

"Did they?" I prompted. He nodded.

"When they came back, they were like, together. That's all I know, Ruby, honestly," he looked up at me, and for once Dazzer actually looked like he meant it, "I'm really sorry. Honest."

Then I saw them. They were strolling along the riverside path hand in hand. Nicole was wearing a long floaty white skirt and a miniscule white crochet top. She was tiny, so skinny. I could picture Rich's hands around her waist. His hand was holding hers now as she threw back her long dark curls over her shoulder laughing at something Rich had said. I sat rigidly, waiting for them to notice me. My mouth was dry. They stopped at the steps leading up to the bar and Tam walked over to them. They stood talking for a while. I saw a muscle clenching in Tam's cheek. Then he held out his hand and Rich shook it. I couldn't believe it. Nicole was smiling gratefully at Tam, who was trying to smile back. But when he turned to walk back up to the bar, his face was drawn and pale. Patrice meanwhile was glaring at them. As they neared, he snarled something in French. Nicole looked up, startled, her happy expression instantly gone. Rich's smile dropped as well when he saw us all sitting there.

Nicole whispered something to Rich and they hurried past. I got to my feet quickly and ran after them, down the steps.

"Rich!" I called breathlessly. They both turned to look at me as I stood there on the dusty path. Rich's eyes met mine for a moment, before he turned and walked away.

I sat up with Tuna that night on his veranda. I couldn't face going back to my hut (no longer ours, but mine alone – all Rich's belongings were gone). I couldn't face going to sleep. Tuna eventually fell asleep on the hammock on his veranda. I put some blankets over him and then huddled under some myself on the floor under the hammock and sat wide-awake all night wondering how on earth this could have happened. At dawn I walked over to Dazzer's hut. I hammered on his door. He appeared bleary-eyed.

"Where is he Dazzer?"

"Wh…uh?"

"Where is Rich?"

He saw the look on my face and woke up immediately.

"The Sunny Side guesthouse, further down the river, past the tented accommodation."

I marched off purposefully. I passed huts with snores emitting from them, chickens crossed my path clucking indignantly. An old lady doing washing in the river looked startled as I stomped past. When I reached the Sunnyside Guesthouse, I wandered around amongst the huts and spotted theirs almost immediately. I recognised Rich's swimming shorts hanging up to dry next to an impossibly small red bikini. I took a deep breath and knocked hard on the door. After a few moments, a tousle-haired Nicole opened it. She had wrapped a black transparent sarong around her and I could see her pert nipples poking through the thin fabric. My heart gave a jolt.

"Ruby," she murmured wearily as if I was some annoying pest, like a mosquito or something.

"I want to speak with my boyfriend," I said, avoiding eye contact with her, and peering over her shoulder. I could see a tangle of sheets, and a familiar looking leg poking out from beneath them.

"He is asleep."

"I don't care…"

"Ruby. I am very sorry. It's true," she said when I snorted, "We did not mean to hurt you. It just happened."

She shrugged. Her mannerisms reminded me so much of Patrice. I couldn't think of anything witty, or cutting, or withering to say to her.

"I…I hate you," I said, my lip beginning to quiver. She sighed and padded over to the bed. She leaned down over Rich's head – over *my* Rich's head – and murmured to him. He mumbled and then when the words sunk in, he sat up abruptly in bed and looked at me, blinking.

"Ruby. What are you doing here?"

I just stared at him. He was so familiar. I wanted to hug him.

"I've just got to get some clothes on," he indicated the door, "Do you mind…?"

"Rich, I've seen you naked before. You're my boyfriend."

Nicole walked towards me and gently shut the door avoiding my eye contact.

I slumped down on the wooden bench on the veranda. When Rich appeared, he was unshaven and rather ashen looking. No longer stoned, the reality of the situation was clearly hitting home. My hopes were raised ever so slightly. He took my arm, pulled me gently to my feet and led me away from the hut. We walked along the river.

"Rich, what are you doing?" I asked him desperately.

He shook his head.

"I'm in love, Rube."

"You're not in love! It's lust!" I choked over the word and the images it conjured, "This is just a silly fling, because we're on holiday, away from the real world."

Once I started, I couldn't stop.

"This isn't reality, Rich. It's not love. What *we* have is love. *Real* love. Going shopping together, doing up the flat together, paying the bills together, looking after each other when we're sick. You can't give all that up over a…a…shag!"

A sob tore out of my throat, but I kept going.

"Think of our life at home, Rich, our life together. We can go back now. I'll forgive you; I'll forget this ever happened; we can go back to the way it used to be."

I was smiling at him maniacally and nodding. He shook his head slowly and looked down at his feet.

"Ruby, I don't want to go back."

"Yes, you do! You just don't know it, that's all!"

"No, Ruby," he looked me in the eye, "I wasn't happy. I know that now. And neither were you if you are honest with yourself. You didn't even want to come on this trip. We want different things."

I looked at him desperately and put my hands up to his face. I couldn't imagine not kissing those lips again, not breathing his smell again, not touching his hair again. He pulled his face away.

"Ruby," he said firmly, locking eyes with me, "Go home."

Chapter Seventeen

"Ruby, you look amazing."

Tuna gawped at me as I walked up to his hut. He was having a sundowner on his veranda before we went out with Patrice, Rob, Kim, Dazzer and Tom who had finally turned up a few days earlier. It had been a week since Rich had left me. After our chat, I had holed up in my hut for five days, not eating, not moving and staring at the walls. Tuna had come by and kept me company and brought me food, but I was inconsolable.

And then on the sixth day I had awoken from a deep sleep, and for some reason the black despair in my stomach didn't feel quite so black. I decided that I needed to do something. I had got washed and dressed, and wandered out into the streets, browsed the market stalls, and tiny boutiques looking for something. And I finally found it, a beautiful silk, ethnic-patterned halter-neck dress that floated around my knees. I bought some beautiful sandals decorated with shells to go with it and headed over to Tuna's hut.

"I want to go out," I told him, "tonight. To the Half Moon Party at Riley's Bar."

He nodded in surprise.

"OK. I'll get everyone together."

I turned up at his hut feeling better than I had in days. The dress was something I would never have worn at home, very bohemian, but I loved it. I had made myself up fully and my hair was tousled and damp. And judging by the look on Tuna's face, I didn't look bad. I was determined I was going to show Rich what he was missing.

We all met at the riverside bar. Tam was there looking glum but there was no sign of Rich. Tom gave me a tight hug when he saw me and asked me quietly if I was OK. It was the first time I had seen him since Chiang Mai. I nodded and smiled brightly.

"Of course! Why wouldn't I be?"

Tom shot Tuna a quick glance and then smiled at me but I was already looking away.

I was on edge watching every single person that walked past. No sign of them.

Eventually, we headed into town, got some food at a busy restaurant. I barely picked at my noodles. Tuna told me I should eat something.

"You've lost so much weight, Taff," Tom pointed out through a mouthful of food.

"I know," I grinned and knocked back my gin, "At least there's one good thing about being dumped!"

I carried on glancing around. Eventually, we saw them, in a small bar. My stomach lurched. Nicole was wearing tight jeans and a tiny backless top. Rich's hand was on the small of her back as they stood at the bar. I felt a pang of sadness when I realised he was wearing a top I hadn't seen before. It was a vest. He would never have worn a vest before. He was a bit too chubby for it. But he still looked gorgeous, so familiar, so Rich.

They were with a group of people I didn't know. They looked completely relaxed with them, like they were old friends. Rich had a whole new world now. A world I wasn't a part of. I pushed these destructive thoughts from my mind and marched purposefully up to the bar. From the corner of my eye, I could see Nicole turning her head to stare at me. I smiled brightly at the barman and tossed my hair over my shoulder. I could see her whispering something to Rich and he looked in my direction. I held my head high and grinned at the barman as he gave me my drink before sauntering back over to the others. Tuna was watching me carefully. I smiled at him brightly. I glanced over my shoulder and my heart sank when I saw Nicole and Rich leaving. I finished my drink at breakneck speed.

"Next bar," I told everyone.

***

By the time we reached Riley's Bar, I was pretty drunk. I spotted them straight away. They were dancing; Nicole's arms were around Rich's neck and his were wrapped around her tiny waist. He'd never danced with me like that; he didn't like dancing. He was nuzzling her neck. I grabbed Tuna's hand and edged between the crowds to where they were dancing. I pressed myself against him.

"Ruby," he tried to extricate himself. I was watching them over his shoulder.

"Just dance with me, Tuna," I demanded. He relaxed and held me lightly.

"Ruby, I think we should go."

"No."

I saw Rich look up from amongst Nicole's hair and spot me. I laughed loudly and threw my head back as if I was having a ball.

"Uh, what's so funny?" Tuna asked in a confused voice.

"Nothing. Just…I'm just laughing because I am happy!"

"Uh, OK."

I watched Rich take Nicole's hand and lead her over to the bar. She glanced over her shoulder at me; he'd obviously just told her I was there.

I took a deep breath and walked over to them.

"Rich, Nicole," I said before I had time to think, "I just wanted to say that I am totally over it. I'm totally fine. And I wanted to wish you all the best."

A small, pitying smile played around Nicole's mouth. Rich grinned, looking relieved.

"Oh, Ruby, that's great. I knew you'd come around. Let me get you a drink."

As he turned to the bar, Nicole met my eyes, and my smile dropped. She shook her head ever so slightly.

"It won't work," she said in a low voice.

When Rich turned back to me with my drink, I grinned again. I raised my glass.

"Cheers," I said, "To us!"

"To us!" Rich said knocking back his drink. Nicole sipped hers.

He grasped her hand.

"Come on, Nic. I can introduce you to my mates now."

He dragged her over towards the others who were watching the whole thing worriedly from a few feet away.

"Hey everyone!" Rich was cheerful. They all mumbled greetings back at him, looking awkwardly around at each other or the floor.

"Tom mate!" Rich said clapping him on the back, "When did you get here?"

Tom mumbled hello, avoiding eye contact with him. He met my eyes and looked away nervously until he ended up staring at the ceiling.

"Alright, Tuna?" Rich held out his hand. Tuna shook his hand without smiling.

"Alright, Rich."

But Rich seemed blind to all the tension and he turned, smiling, to Nicole. He put his arm around her waist and pulled her forward.

"Everyone, Ruby has finally told us that she's feeling much better, and has given us her blessing," he smiled at me gratefully. I felt if I smiled anymore my face would crack.

"So I brought this lovely, wonderful girl over to meet you all. Nicole this is everyone. Oh wait, I forgot. You all met the other night, didn't you?"

There were slight nods and murmurs of assent.

"Anyway, just to remind you, this is Rob and Kim and uh…Patrice, isn't it?" Rich seemed completely oblivious to Patrice's glare. He obviously didn't have a clue that his beloved Nicole made a habit of flitting from relationship to relationship.

"You know, you're both French. You'd have loads in common…" Rich said nodding his head at Nicole like an enthusiastic puppy.

"Fuck you," Patrice spat at Rich's bewildered face before storming off.

That little exchange managed to sober me up. Rich and Nicole continued to kiss and canoodle next to us, Rich so wrapped up in her that he just didn't realise…well, anything. Tuna kept trying to lead me away from them, but I couldn't go. I just wanted to stare at them. Kim and Rob kept looking at me pityingly, and Tom kept trying to engage me in conversation to take my mind off it.

Eventually, Kim sidled over to me.

"Ruby. How can you stand it?" she asked me as we both watched Rich and Nicole with their tongues down each other's throats, "Why are you staying here? He's a bastard, Ruby. Look at what he's done to you, at what he's *doing* to you. I don't want to be cruel honey, but if I were you, I would just leave. I wouldn't be able to stand it anymore."

I looked at her, and she put her arm gently around my shoulder.

"Why don't you go home sweetie, to your family? They can help you put your life back together. You're better off without him."

I looked into her kind blue eyes. She was right. I couldn't stay here anymore. I told her I was going to the toilet but I left the bar and went home.

***

I stood at the bus stop as the sun rose. Kim was right. I couldn't stay. But I couldn't go home. There was no way. I had no home anymore. I couldn't face anyone I knew, I felt too ashamed. And the thought of trying to carry on in my old life without Rich was too awful to contemplate. I was leaving. But I didn't know where I was going to. It was only when I got on the bus heading to the Laos border that my decision was made.

Part Three
Laos and Cambodia

Chapter Eighteen

From: hottuna@yahoo.com
To: Rube99@hotmail.com
Subject: Where are you?

Hi Ruby

Are you OK? We were all worried when you took off like that. Please let us know you're OK.

Tuna

From: welshhottie@yahoo.co.uk
To: Rube99@hotmail.com
Subject: Bollywood here I come!

Well, it's booked Rube! Leaving on the 3rd January. Can't bloody wait! Bit hard to buy floaty sari type things to wear cos middle of bloody winter here. Mam doesn't know yet so don't tell her. Will tell her at Xmas or something when she's a bit mellower. Really moody cow at the moment.

Oh yeah. Got a tat. Thought I would need one when in a bikini. On my lower back. Mam went ballistic. Went through the roof. Even Dad told her to calm down.

Think know why she's so touchy lately. Think she's having affair. Always in work and running off to help that Simon bloke. Dad's in own world anyway and wouldn't notice if came home and saw her shagging Simon bloke on coffee table.

Have started stocking up on Tampax.

Jess

From: babygirlsteph@hotmail.com
To: Rube99@hotmail.com

Hi Rubes

Don't hate me, but I'm still seeing Mark. I can't help it; I love him so much and am so happy when we are together. I met his wife the other day though. She came into work and she was really nice, and dead pretty. I felt really bad, and sort of gurgled at my desk when she spoke to me. But Mark isn't happy with her so it can't be right can it?

He has said he will leave her after Christmas. He's got two sons see so he wants one last Christmas with them as a family. I hate myself for doing it to them but I can't help it. I can't live without him Rube. Do you hate me? I wish you were here to help me! Bet you're having such a wonderful time, in the sun and being all loved up with Rich whenever you want to be.

Miss you – hope you're OK. Haven't heard from you in a while.

Love and hugs

Steph xxxxxxxxxxxxxxxx

From: hottuna@yahoo.com
To: Rube99@hotmail.com

Ruby

It's me again. Just want to check you're OK. Let me know.

Tuna

Chapter Nineteen

Tammy and Trish and I had been in Luang Prabang in the North of Laos for three days. I had read in Tammy's *Lonely Planet* that the small town is a World Heritage Site and it used to be a holiday destination for the wealthy French during the days of French Colonisation. I was completely won over by the charming mix of Asia and Europe. Situated on the banks of the Mekong, with swaying palm trees, and bushes of brilliant pink bougainvillea, the streets were filled with ageing French architecture: tall terraced houses with peeling paint, wooden shutters and wrought iron railings. There were French influences everywhere, especially in the food, with cafés and patisseries selling beautiful croissants, éclairs, quiches and cakes. We wandered the streets stopping for food at least every hour on Tammy's insistence; we sat by the river enjoying the sweeping views; we strolled through the night-markets that lined the streets; we lazed in one of the many bookshops with cushions lining the floors, and mobiles tinkling in the breeze; we wandered around the various temples, watching monks banging enormous tin drums, their sinewy arms glistening in the sun as they drew back their hammers, and we climbed the steep steps to the temple overlooking the town and the hazy countryside. We had coffee and bagels every morning in a small French-style café called Jo Ma's that soon became our favourite. It was the perfect place to lose myself, to be anonymous, and to try to forget what had just happened. I refused to allow myself to think about it. I had told Tammy and Trish that I was travelling alone, and when they once asked about my life at home, and I clammed up, they got the message and dropped the subject. They were the perfect travelling companions; they didn't pry into my past or my life away from here, they just greeted me every day in their cheery sunny way, including me in everything they did.

We went out for drinks a couple of nights, to low-key, laid-back bars dotted around the small back streets. I got chatted up once by a guy called Charlie from Canada. He had long, dark, thick, heavy dreads and a bit of a beard but even under all the hair he was gorgeous. I was polite and friendly as we chatted but strangely detached from the whole thing. Tammy and Trish tried to egg me on, but they stopped nagging after I told them for a third time that I wasn't interested.

The days slipped by. I wasn't sure where I was headed, or what I was going to do. I didn't have a plan. I seemed to be detached from everything, unable to see from one day to the next. I found myself just floating along, seeing where the tide took me.

One day, we took a trip to a nearby waterfall. It was buried in a forest; the main falls thundered down into a milky green pool that then tumbled off into further falls and pools winding through the trees. There were lots of tourists there, but we found a quiet pool in a clearing and we eagerly jumped in, Trish swinging from a vine into the water. It was a twenty-foot drop once the vine swung out from the ledge and I watched her admiringly. She was afraid of nothing. She surfaced, gasping for air, in the ice-cold, milky-blue water, that I was trying to edge my way into.

"It's amazing guys!" she shouted, her voice echoing through the trees, "You gotta try it!"

"Nah, Trish," Tammy said alongside me, "You know I can't swim that well."

"Ah go on, you nancy boy!" Trish jeered.

"Fuck off!" Tammy said, before clambering out of the water, climbing up to the ledge and taking a running jump onto the vine. She plummeted into the water and surfaced, making lots of whooping noises.

"Come on pommy," Trish turned to me, "Your turn. Show us what you're made of!"

I started to shake my head as usual and then stopped. What the hell did I have to lose? Why was I always so bloody careful? I suddenly felt angry with myself and marched up to the vine. I took a deep breath, grabbed hold of it and swung. I felt myself flying through the air, let go of the vine when it was high above the pool, seemed to hang there for a millisecond and then dropped with a huge splash into the water. As it enveloped me, I felt a huge rush. A moment of silence, a roaring noise came rushing back in and I kicked for the surface. I broke through into the air, laughter bursting from my lungs. I had done it.

"Bloody hell!" I cried and looked around to see Tammy and Trish laughing.

"Your face was a picture mate!" Trish cried.

I couldn't stop smiling all day.

We left Luang Prabang reluctantly and headed South to Vang Vieng.

The scenery here was breath-taking; towering limestone cliffs and emerald-green rice paddies surrounded the riverside town. But it was a party place, and I was disappointed when I saw the ubiquitous cafés and bars lining the streets, selling 'happy' shakes, banana pancakes and showing episodes of Friends on loop on their mandatory TVs. Travellers lounged on cushions, stuffing themselves full of cheap pizzas, and engrossed in the telly. Not that I didn't partake of some of this myself, it was pretty relaxing, but wandering away from the main streets, seeing the locals working in the rice paddies, leading their ox through the fields, I realised how quickly their way of life had been invaded. We had met a couple the previous evening in a café who had been to Laos a mere five years before, and they said that Vang Vieng then was paradise; it was a quiet, laidback river town and untouched by tourism in a way that the rest of South East Asia wasn't. But tourism had inevitably sneaked its way in, weaved its fingers through the winding streets and taken a stranglehold. I ruminated to myself as I sat on my hammock outside my chalet that once a place is considered paradise, we descend upon it, squeezing every last drop out of it that we can, until we renew the search for the holy grail – that untouched, undiscovered place that we are all trying to find. I sat there brooding on this while watching the oxen bathing in the river, and an elephant being led on a chain by some children through the water. There were still flashes of the old paradise evident in the gold glinting off the water; in the palms framed against the craggy cliffs that soared into the sky; in the laugh of the children as the elephant sprayed them with water. I heard a familiar screech from behind me.

"Taff! Get off that hammock. We're going tubing!"

Tubing had become the main draw for backpackers in Vang Vieng after an enterprising farmer had taken some inner tubes from tyres and hired them out for people to float down the mighty Mekong as it snaked amongst majestic cliffs. In the past, I imagined there may have only been one or two people doing it, but now there were dozens. We trooped to one of the many cafés that were offering the excursion, collected our huge tubes and then were driven in the back of a *jumbo* – a small truck with benches in the back for passengers – for about twenty minutes up river. We clambered out onto a riverbank, from where we settled ourselves inside our tubes, lay back and let the current wash us down the river. There was laughter echoing from around the corner, bouncing off the cliffs from people that had set off before us. I put my head back to gaze up at the towering cliffs as we floated between them, carried on the river's gentle current.

Eventually, we heard the loud echoing call of 'Beer Laos'! Some locals had set up makeshift bars along the river – little more than wooden platforms and some iceboxes containing beer. They would throw a rope or a long stick out to you as you passed, and if you wanted a drink you grabbed on and they drew you in to the bank. Trish and Tammy stopped at the first one we saw and we clambered onto the wooden platform. We sat there in our bikinis, drinking ice-cold beer in the sun admiring the scenery and watching other people float past sporadically. A small elderly lady sat close by as her husband called out, "Beer Laos!" to the next group of people floating past. She watched us closely, smiling and nodding as we drank our beer. We grinned at her and finally climbed back into our tubes and set off again. I managed with some effort to convince Trish and Tammy to by-pass the next two bars – it was still only 11:30am. Eventually, the river became shallow and I felt my bum brushing against the pebbly riverbed. I could see someone sitting still on a ring, beached on the pebbles, clutching his beer. He had long dreads and sunglasses on and didn't seem to be in any hurry to shift himself. He turned to look at us as we drew closer and waved. It was Charlie from Luang Prabang.

"Hey, Ruby!" he called.

I pushed my feet against the pebbles so I came to a halt alongside him.

"Fancy seeing you here," he said, smiling at me lazily. He was clearly pretty drunk already, and probably stoned too. I smiled at him; he looked so funny just sitting there, wedged on this pebble bank, in his tube, clutching his beer.

"I got stuck."

"Yeah I can see that," I said laughing as Tammy and Trish pulled up alongside me.

"Can we give you a push mate?" Trish asked.

He thought about it for a moment.

"Well, I was just gonna sit here until the water got a bit higher. But I guess that could take a long time."

"Ya think?" Tammy said, clambering out of her tube, which was a funny sight in itself as she flailed around until she got to her feet. She heaved against the side of Charlie's tube until he was free of the pebbles. We floated along in a group for the next few hours, laughing, chatting, stopping for Beer Laos now and again, and just simply enjoying ourselves.

We ended up drinking into the evening with Charlie in bars around the town. He took us to a bar he said only a few people knew of. It was across a rickety wooden bridge that led over the river to a small sand island in the middle. There was a thick cluster of bamboo reaching into the sky above us. Charlie led us through the middle of them. We could hear music up ahead and there were lights twinkling through the bamboo cane as it swayed in the breeze. We came to a clearing with a small wooden bar, wooden stools, and hammocks strung between trees. A handful of people stood around drinking, chatting and smoking. There was a circle of people around a small bonfire. The night seemed charmed; the air smoky. Someone handed me a reefer and I stared at it for a moment. I didn't do this; I didn't smoke. I took a deep drag and, after a loud coughing fit, I had another and finally felt myself melting into the atmosphere. The dull ache that had existed somewhere in my chest since Pai, seemed to disappear into thin air. I felt at peace, at ease with the world. I smiled at Tammy and Trish. I felt Charlie's arm around my shoulder and I leaned back and looked up at the stars.

"I really like you, Ruby," Charlie murmured.

I smiled.

"You seem so…so hard to pin down. You never talk about yourself."

"Not a lot to say," I was enjoying the breeze on my face.

"Why are you on your own?"

"I'm not; I'm with Tammy and Trish."

"But before them. They said you met in Laos. What about before?"

"Before, I was nothing. There was nothing before."

I sat forward and reached for the reefer again. I really meant that. I really did. I felt numb; my past was nothing. Now was all that mattered.

***

Charlie came with us as we travelled South to Vientiane. The bus journeyed along impossibly winding mountainous roads and my childhood travel-sickness came back with a vengeance. I sat next to Charlie on the bus and he kept handing me a plastic bag every time I threatened to be sick. I was lucky enough to be able to hold off until we stopped, and I raced off the bus and stood by the roadside heaving. Charlie rubbed my back, until I stood up, and I saw Trish and Tammy smirking at me. I shot them a withering look before clambering miserably back onto the bus.

Vientiane is the quietest capital city I have ever been to. Orderly and neatly laid out, with wide clean streets, little traffic, and lots of glittering gold temples. We hired bicycles to ride around and explore for a day. We cycled to the replica of the Arc de Triomphe in the centre of town – the Patuxai – and climbed up the steps to the top. The city was laid out calmly and prettily below us, its roads spreading out from the Patuxai like the spokes of a wheel.

We visited the Pha That Luang temple – the emblem on the Laos flag – glistening gold in the sweltering mid-day sun. I was surprised at how much I was enjoying myself. I briefly let my thoughts wander and began to imagine how it would have been if Rich and I had come here together. I stopped myself quickly and wiped my mind clean. To keep it blank and to allow no thoughts to enter it was the only way I could get through each day.

We managed to find a chemist selling toiletries so we could stock up. As we wandered around the clinically white shop and giggled at the various products such as boob-increasing soap, we gradually realised we were the centre of attention. The shop assistants were following us, always a few paces behind, and whispering to each other. Every time we looked at them over our shoulders, they would beam at us. Tammy stopped to point out some obesity-reducing cream.

"Hey, Rubo, look," she said holding it up and chuckling. The shop assistant who had been hovering over her shoulder leaned forward and patted Tammy's belly with an innocent smile on her face.

"Yes, good for you this is," she said in a soft voice, "will make you not fat."

She patted her own flat stomach and nodded enthusiastically at Tammy who glared at her.

"Jeez Louise," she muttered putting the cream back on the shelf with a thump as the shop assistant continued to nod happily at her, "That's almost as bad as when a woman in Thailand told me that I would have to leave her shop because they didn't make clothes in my size!"

Trish nodded.

"It's true," she said, "Tammy's such a heifer."

"Aw c'mon," Tammy said sucking in her stomach, "I'm not *that* bad."

"Hey girls, what about this?" I said holding up a box of nipple pink. So obsessed with having fair skin are the South East Asian girls it seems, that they bleach their underarms and nipples.

"Yes, yes," the ever-present shop assistant said into my hair, "Nice pink nipples. Just like you."

We bought a bar of boob-increasing soap and left the shop almost bursting with the effort from not laughing. Charlie who was waiting outside wanted to go in and see if they had willy-increasing soap.

"Don't bother, Charlie, they'll just tell yeh you're obese," Tammy muttered darkly.

We stopped at a Mexican bar and restaurant for early dinner, and found that it only served noodles, just like all the other bars and restaurants. It did sell packets of Nachos though – hence the 'Mexican' tag. I allowed myself to be persuaded to play pool. I used to hate pool, I would refuse steadfastly to play it, because I simply didn't know how, and I didn't want to look a fool. Here and now, I didn't care. Nobody really knew me. And who cared if I looked stupid?

We worked our way through jugs of beer and played pool with some local Laos people. At one point, Tammy and I sat at a table on our own, while Trish played a Laos guy in pool, and Charlie went off to the bar to get me a drink.

"He really likes you, you know Ruby," Tammy said as we watched Charlie ordering.

I didn't say anything.

"And, my God, look at him. He's such a spunk!"

He was smiling at the barman: a perfect row of white teeth; warm, cinnamon-brown eyes.

"Yeah he is," I agreed.

"So why are you not…you know? Interested?"

I played with a beer mat on the table.

"I was badly hurt."

"Yeah," she nodded sympathetically, "We thought so."

"Am I that easy to read?"

"Nah mate," she shook her head, "You're the most evasive person I have ever met!"

She chuckled and I smiled.

"But it's the most obvious conclusion, isn't it?"

She patted my arm.

"Listen, we're not going to pry. And you know, if you ever need to talk…well, we're both here."

I smiled at her gratefully.

"Thanks," I whispered.

We were all sharing a four-bed dorm, and Charlie had to wait outside for us to get changed.

"OK, you perv!" Trish shouted when we were in our bedclothes, "You can come in now!"

We clambered into our bunk beds, shattered from our day cycling. I lay there in the dark, trying to stop the thoughts whirling round in my head. Trying to think of the day's events rather than let my mind wander and remember.

Trish was snoring gently and Tammy mumbled in her sleep. I sighed. Insomnia was becoming a regular occurrence.

"Ruby," I heard Charlie's soft whisper from the bed below me.

"Yes?"

"You awake?"

"Uh, yes!" I whispered back.

"Wanna go for a smoke?"

I dropped off the side of the bunk without replying.

Charlie and I headed up to the veranda on the roof of the building. The lights of the town twinkled before us. We perched on the wall and Charlie rolled a spliff. We didn't speak until we both took a drag.

"Can't believe I'm smoking," I said eventually, "Rich would kill me…"

As soon as I said it, I felt a sick thud in my stomach.

"Rich?"

I looked down at my feet.

"So this must be the guy that hurt you big time?"

I looked up at Charlie, and he smiled.

"It's not difficult to tell."

I nodded.

"Yeah, he was the guy that hurt me. Big time."

And before I knew what I was doing, I found myself blurting out my whole story to this guy I barely knew, on a roof, at night, overlooking a city that, a few months ago, I had never even heard of. Charlie listened in silence and, when I finished, he draped an arm around my shoulders and we sat for hours watching the city sleep.

***

From: hottuna@yahoo.com
To: Rube99@hotmail.com
Subject: Are you OK??

Ruby

Please let me know if you are OK? Have you gone home? I am really worried about you.

Tuna

From: babygirlsteph@hotmail.com
To: Rube99@hotmail.com

Hi Rubes

Only a month and a half until Christmas, and then Mark and I will be together properly. It feels like forever, but I know it will be worth the wait. We went away for a weekend recently, to Cornwall. Mark told his wife it was business – such a cliché. But it was wonderful. We stayed in a cottage, with a fire and it was right by the beach.

I hope you're not too angry with me. I haven't heard from you in ages. Please try and understand.

Email me soon!

Love and kisses

Steph xxxxx

From: lataandTom69@yahoo.com
To: Rube99@hotmail.com
Subject: Hello?

Hello sweetie

Hope you are OK? Steph said she hasn't heard from you in a while. I said she was probably worrying needlessly and that you are just having a fabulous, debauched time and are far too busy on the beach to bother with email!

Let us know you're safe though darling if you can.

Not much news here. Tim is still on a diet, and although I won't tell him, he looks HOT. Don't want to make him too big headed, now do I?

Tamsin caught her fiancé – the one with the smooth cock – in bed with her sister. So that's well and truly off. He was a dick anyway – a smooth one!

Kisses

Lata

Chapter Twenty

After the surprisingly decent buses in the North of Laos – big coaches with reclining seats – the public transport became steadily worse the further south we travelled. We caught the night bus to Pakse. This was my first night bus and I was to grow to detest them – blaring Laos pop music from the TV all night, potholed roads, no room to sleep, lights flicking on and off whenever the bus driver felt like it, toilet breaks by the roadside for the men but with nowhere for the women to go. From there we made our way to Tadlo Falls on the Bolaven Plateau. We balked when we saw this bus – little more than a rusty box crammed full of people, boxes and sacks of food that were packed in tightly around our legs, and various animals tied to chair backs. I ended up next to a guy with about twelve kids who insisted on trying to talk English to me all the way there but who could only say, "Where you going?" One of his babies kept pulling my bra straps down so I had to hold them up forcefully for four hours.

The destination was worth the journey though. Tadlo was a cluster of wooden huts settled around a small lake and waterfall and surrounded by forest. The huts had wagon wheels perched outside them, and cracked, wooden verandas with rocking chairs that gave the place a Wild West feel. However, instead of horses, tame elephants lumbered around in the trees.

The huts we were staying in only slept two per hut, so I shared with Charlie, making it clear to him that we would be sleeping in separate beds. He grinned and kept silent as he unpacked a couple of things from his small rucksack. He continually ribbed me about the size of mine, whenever I struggled to pick it up off the floor or lift it onto buses.

"If you hate your clothes so much," he pointed out as he sat on the rocking chair on our veranda with a spliff in his mouth, "why don't you just throw them away?"

"I would like to try and retain some semblance of cleanliness," I retorted, pointedly staring at the t-shirt he had been wearing for the last five days. He apparently didn't pick up on my sarcasm. But I thought about what he said and finally threw away the hideous khaki fleece that took up three quarters of my rucksack, and which Rich had made me buy when we were in a camping shop. I also decided to get rid of some horrible trousers that you could transfer into hideous shorts by unzipping the bottoms. They had an elasticised waist that reached almost up to my armpits. I shook my head as I held them up to Charlie's laughing inspection.

"What was I thinking of?" I muttered.

A little local child that hung around our fence went home happy that night wearing his new oversized clothes. A couple of pairs of shoes I never wore also made the chop – some sensible trainers and my hated shandy sandals – I only ever wore flip-flops anyway.

I flopped down on the bench next to Charlie as he rocked back and fore in the rocking chair watching the hazy sun as it lowered between the trees.

"I feel lighter, not only in my luggage, but in myself!" I announced.

He smiled and took a deep drag on his spliff.

"I was just trying to be someone I clearly am not anyway, with all that outdoorsy, hikery stuff. I would never normally have worn stuff like that," I said. I looked down at my baggy fisherman's trousers. I had sworn not to buy any – because they were so 'backpackery' – but they were just so damn comfy! And they came in lots of nice colours and were so cheap… I thought of my smart trousers I wore to work, and my crisp shirts. I looked down at my nails. I couldn't remember the last time before this trip that I had seen my nails without nail colour – my toenails were usually a deep vixen red; my finger nails a perfect French manicure. Now they were un-filed, long and strong after weeks of no damaging chemicals; they looked so healthy and so unlike me. I put my hands up to my hair falling all around my shoulders in a messy tangle of waves and thought of the neat ponytail I usually wore to work, my hair straightened to within an inch of its life. I thought of all the clothes I had just got rid of. I may have been trying to be someone I clearly wasn't, but who was I? Who was I now? I wasn't the same girl that had left London pining for my Whistles dress, and my high heels, or the one who had gone to Pai, in love and counting down the days until I went home.

I decided to go for a walk. I wandered across the rickety bridge to the wide falls that fell into a clear, deep pool. I wandered past an empty upmarket resort, and up a track that led into the woods. I found myself feeling almost light-hearted for the first time in weeks as I listened to the birds around me, and the wind in the trees. I followed a smaller track that branched off the main one and led to a huge wide reservoir. I sat by the water and allowed myself to think about the last few weeks. I couldn't believe I had got through three weeks without Rich. I wondered what he was doing now. A dull ache started in my chest. I wondered if he was missing me yet, if he had realised what a mistake he had made. Maybe he would go home once he realised I was gone and would spend his time regretting what he had done. There was no way Rich could stay in Thailand forever. He would have to go home sometime. And when I returned home, he would beg me for forgiveness…*when* I returned home. The thought of it now was too huge to comprehend. Facing everyone I knew, admitting what had happened, trying to pick up the pieces if my life without Rich. I tried to picture London without him. London equalled Rich to me; I couldn't walk around the streets without seeing him there. I couldn't go to all our old haunts, our local bar, our favourite restaurant. I shook my head. I couldn't go back, not yet, not now. I just had to keep going for a while, just keep going…

A noise in the trees startled me. It sounded rather like a growl. My mind flew to the warnings in the Lonely Planet about tigers in remote parts of Laos. We had heard on the traveller grapevine that there had been a tiger attack on a backpacker recently but it had been about 150 km away. I hadn't even considered that they might be in this area. I glanced around and got slowly to my feet. I tried to think of the advice I had once read about coming face to face with a lion when you're on safari. Try not to have an adrenalin rush and back away slowly. Yeah right. I walked tentatively back along the path, my eyes darting left and right. Don't turn your back or act like prey. And whatever you do, don't run. I heard a twig crack behind me and I ran like…well, like a tiger was after me. My heart felt as if it was going to burst from my chest. I sped through the trees and lost the rough path I had been following, and then another thought hit me – landmines! I had come off the beaten track! And how many times did people warn you not to? Laos was littered with unexploded mines from the American/Vietnam war. I started to run on tiptoes – as if that would help.

I finally hit the main road and kept running, over the bridge, through the huts and right up to our veranda. Charlie was still in the rocking chair and looked at me in mild surprise as I ran up, arms flapping like a windmill and gasping for breath. Trish and Tammy were sitting on the bench next to him and started laughing when they saw me.

"Bloody 'ell mate!" Tammy exclaimed, "Where's the fire?"

I made lots of gasping noises as I tried to catch my breath and leaned over with my hands on my knees.

"What the hell are you doin', Rube?" Trish asked.

"Just…uh…you know…fancied a run," I managed to splutter, feeling the sweat trickle down my forehead. I knew my face must be beetroot.

Charlie laughed out loud.

"Just fancied a run. Just like that?"

"Mmhm," I said nodding, trying to regain my composure and heading inside, "going to have a shower."

"Nuts," I heard Tammy say as I closed the door.

***

From: hottuna@yahoo.com
To: Rube99@hotmail.com
Subject: ?

Ruby

Just checking in again. Seriously just let me know you're OK, and I'll leave you alone.

Tuna

From: welshhottie@yahoo.co.uk
To: Rube99@hotmail.com
Subject: What the f is a Visa?

Rube

Where the fuck are you? Haven't heard from you in like forever. Just let me know you haven't been eaten by sharks or kidnapped or whatever.

Can't wait for India now. Going to Goa to lie on beach. Also to ashram, one of them spiritual places. Counting down days until leave mam – still being a bitch. Keeps making comments about me being like Jordan with my tat. Speaking of which, maybe should get boob job before I go. Won't need to take bras then. Will investigate cost.

Btw, what's a visa? Taylor said we need one for trip. Said I thought it was credit card but she laughed a lot. When asked her what it was then, she got all embarrassed and pretended had to go to the loo. Don't think she knows either.

Say hi soon.

Jess

Chapter Twenty-One

We took the ancient bus back to the small town of Pakse where we stocked up on toiletries and essentials, before heading south again. A number of uncomfortable *jumbo* (Laotian *tuk-tuks)* rides ensued where we had to wrap scarves around our mouths to block out the dust and endure the company of unusual travelling companions such as live ducks that flapped around on the floor. We reached the drop-off point where we were to catch a boat to Si Phan Dhon, or the Four Thousand Islands. The flat area of this archipelago was completely different from the ethereal, mountainous north of Laos. In the south, Charlie had explained to me, the Mekong widens and many islands have been formed, cut off from the mainland and are consequently even more remote and untouched by tourism than the rest of Laos.

We clambered aboard a tiny, rickety, wooden boat clutching onto our rucksacks so they wouldn't topple overboard. The driver started the meagre-sounding engine after a great deal of tugging and pulling that made the boat rock violently. Charlie continued to try to convince us that we were heading into paradise as I gazed at the muddy bank, lined with other precarious boats and dirty oxen wading into the water.

"No electricity, no roads, no way to get to the mainland except on boats that come past now and again," Charlie said wistfully, "heaven."

I wasn't so sure. But I went along with it as I had nowhere else to go. We chugged along slowly, the brown water lapping against the boat and lulling me to sleep, palms swaying in the breeze and children waving at us from the riverbanks.

Finally, we were dropped off on the island of Don Dhet, and we lugged our rucksacks up the muddy slope, cursing and sweating in the sweltering heat.

"This had better be good," I glowered at Charlie.

There was a dusty path running along the edge of the island and not much else as far as we could see, so we hoisted our packs on our backs and set off. After five minutes we came across a small bamboo hut that advertised itself as a bar. We dumped our bags and drew straws – two people would sit with the bags and have a drink, and two would go off and hunt for accommodation. Tammy and Trish were the lucky ones, and they flopped down onto some bamboo chairs, ordering two large Beer Laos. Charlie and I set off, Charlie smiling happily at everything and everyone and me grumbling. I was so hot, sweaty, dirty and dusty, and all I wanted was to climb into a cool shower.

"Come on, Ruby," Charlie said after I moaned for the twelfth time about my aching feet, "look around you; have you ever been anywhere like this?"

I looked around grudgingly. The river ran idly along beside us; palm fronds drooped low to the water as if sipping the water. The path we were following snaked lazily ahead of us and was swallowed by more palms. A chicken with her tiny chicks crossed our path, clucking busily whilst a wild pig snuffled in the grass and ran off into the trees when we disturbed it. A dilapidated hut stood amongst the trees; a man was chopping wood in the grass beside it, his little girl staring at us open-mouthed from where she was playing on the floor. Two women chatted as they squatted on the river bank, washing clothes and draping them over rocks to dry.

"It's like going back fifty years," Charlie murmured.

I nodded.

"I didn't expect to ever see anything like this," I replied.

"What did you expect to see then Ruby?" Charlie picked his way over a bundle of dried palm leaves lying across the path.

"I didn't expect to see anything I guess," I frowned, "I had no preconceptions because I didn't really care. And now..."

Charlie looked at me.

"Well, now I can't believe how lucky I am," I surprised myself as I admitted it.

"I know," Charlie said shaking his head, and smiling, "It must be overwhelming to be in the company of someone as devastatingly good-looking as me..."

I hit him playfully and we were laughing as we rounded a corner and saw a cluster of bamboo huts facing the river. I was still laughing as I looked towards the veranda of the first hut, and noticed a figure lying in a hammock. He turned his head towards us and my heart lurched in my chest. A mixture of emotions passed over his face; recognition, shock, relief and confusion.

"Tuna."

I had stopped dead in my tracks, and he hadn't moved from his hammock. We were barely ten feet away from each other.

"So," he said not taking his eyes from my face, "This is where you've been hiding."

Tuna swung his legs down from the hammock and got to his feet. I swallowed; my throat was suddenly dry. I felt a bit sick to my stomach. Here was a reminder right in front of me, of what I had run away from. He came down the steps towards me. I could feel Charlie's eyes on me.

"You didn't go home then," Tuna stopped in front of me. I couldn't tell what he was thinking. I shook my head feeling like a naughty little girl.

"You look so different," he said, his eyes roving over my hair and clothes.

He looked at Charlie and gave him a small smile.

"This girl was always immaculate," he said politely.

Charlie gave him an unconvincing smile. I looked down at my dishevelled self.

"Well, I've had other things on my mind lately," I said quietly.

"So have I," Tuna replied dryly, "I was really worried after you took off. I wish you'd emailed."

"I just didn't get onto the internet for ages," I said lamely.

"Yeah you did," Charlie started, "In Vientiane..."

I shot him a sharp glance.

"Sorry," I tried to regain my composure, "Charlie, this is Tuna."

Charlie's face broke into a grin and he held out his hand. Strangely, he almost looked relieved.

"Sorry mate, I thought you were someone else," he said shaking Tuna's hand, before glancing at me, "I thought this was the famous Richard."

My stomach tightened at the casual mention of his name. Before now, nobody had known him so I had been able to be detached whenever I talked about him. But here before me was someone who knew him, someone who knew what he had done, someone who had been there for me. With a flash of clarity, I realised the carelessness with which I had treated Tuna. I remembered those nights he had sat with me in the hut, the way he had brought me food, and held me when I cried. I looked at him now, standing awkwardly before me, acting like a stranger, and I stepped forward and put my arms around him. He hugged me back tightly.

"I'm glad to see you again," he said into my ear.

Tuna's hair had grown since I had seen him last. It was light brown, spiky and messy and he was very tanned – a far cry from the pale, skinhead I had met a few months before.

"You look more Australian now," I told him. He rubbed his hair.

"Yeah, I've got over that whole Irish yob look," he smiled sheepishly. He rubbed his chin which was lined with stubble.

"I still hate shaving though."

We sat on his veranda and talked and talked while Charlie booked us into a few of the huts alongside Tuna's, and then went off to get Tammy and Trish. I told Tuna all about what had happened since I had run away from Pai: how Trish and Tammy had been my saviours even though they hadn't realised it; how I hadn't been able to face emailing people at home yet; how I had been concentrating on just getting through each day.

"I never thought I would have been able to carry on travelling without Rich. If someone had told me six months ago that I would be trundling my way through Laos with a couple of people I had only just met, I would have laughed in their face."

Tuna was leaning back in the hammock, giving me an odd look. I was sitting on a cushion on the floor beside him.

"What?" I asked him, feeling uncomfortable under his scrutiny.

He shrugged.

"I don't know. You're…different."

"I know; I'm a mess."

"No. You're not. You're lovely. And I wasn't talking about the way you look," he said. I felt my cheeks colour at his compliment.

"So," he said casually, pushing gently against the railing of the veranda so that his hammock rocked from side to side, "what about this Charlie?"

"What about him?"

"How long have you…?"

I looked at him blankly for a moment before cottoning on and laughing darkly.

"Oh no, you've got the wrong idea there," I shook my head vehemently, "I'm right off men for a long while."

We sat silently for a moment. There was a slight awkwardness between us that hadn't existed before. I took a deep breath.

"Well," I said, "I have to ask…"

"Rich was still in Pai when I left," Tuna answered quickly, "He was still with Nicole. I'm sorry."

It felt like someone had kicked me in the stomach even though I knew what Tuna had been going to say.

"I told Rich you had left," he continued, "he seemed to think you had gone home. I hung around for a week or so after you went just in case you came back."

I looked at him apologetically.

"You're a good friend, Tuna," I reached up and placed my hand on his arm that was hanging out of the hammock, "thank you. And I'm sorry I treated you the way I did. I was really selfish."

He shook his head.

"I know what it's like. It completely consumes you."

He looked out over the river.

"Where are Tom and Dazzer?"

"Tom went back to Chiang Mai to meet Mali again," he grinned, "He's pretty smitten. He said he'd catch up with me later on. I didn't feel like hanging around like a gooseberry. Dazzer went with him. Poor Mali."

"Oh God, I bet Tom was pleased with that – having Dazzer around to insult Mali for a while!"

We sat in companionable silence for a few moments before Tuna looked at me with a nervous smile on his face.

"So are you up for having another travelling companion for a while?" he asked.

I smiled at him and nodded, feeling something akin to happiness for the first time in a long time.

***

Days passed into each other easily on Don Dhet. We spent hours swinging on our hammocks, swimming in the river or going for walks around the island. At night we would eat by candlelight at one of the small riverside cafés, and wander back to our huts, the moonlight and the stars our only source of light. We would talk into the small hours, about anything and everything. Our huts were basic: a bed with a mosquito net; a couple of nails to hang things on and a hammock on the balcony. The bathrooms were small wooden cubicles in the field behind the huts, with buckets of cold water to wash in. I loved it. I couldn't believe that I could live with so little and yet be so happy. I even grew used to the wildlife: spiders the size of my hand; scorpions that dropped on my head when I squatted over the toilet; cockerels that sat under my hut and crowed in the middle of the night, making me shoot up in bed so I became entangled in the mosquito net.

I would lie on the small beach by the river, watching the others playing *tak-tak,* a game played by the local kids, where you had to kick a small sack filled with beans into the air and not let it touch the ground. We would then slink into the cool water of the river, letting it wash off the sweat and sand, feeling the mud squelch between our toes. It felt like I was so far away from everything; it felt like I was in a safe cocoon, and I didn't want it to end.

One evening, Charlie and I were wandering back from Tammy and Trish's hut. It was about one o'clock in the morning. Tuna had gone on ahead of us to bed. I was looking up at the moon and marvelling at its brightness, when its light was suddenly blocked. Charlie had stepped up to me and was leaning down to my upturned face. Before I knew what was happening, I felt his dry, warm lips on mine. It felt strange kissing someone else other than Rich; it felt awkward. I pulled away.

"Sorry," I whispered.

"No, I'm sorry. I did it without thinking."

I looked down at my feet even though I couldn't see them in the darkness.

"I'm not ready. It's Rich…I guess I'm just waiting, until…until he and Nicole break up, and he…wants me back," I was embarrassed to admit it.

At that moment, there were a few cracking twigs, and the light of a torch came swinging towards us.

"Guys," came Tuna's voice, "I'm locked out."

Charlie laughed and walked towards him, offering to help. I lagged behind, feeling like a complete idiot.

The next day, we dragged ourselves off Don Dhet and back to the mainland for a daytrip to see the rare Irrawaddy dolphins that live in the Mekong. It took a series of rickety bus and boat rides to get to the wide expanse of river where the dolphins live. The water was flat, calm and dark and there was no sign of them. Trish and Tammy waded straight in to the water to swim. I lay on the bank, my old familiar nervousness holding me back.

"If there are dolphins in there, what else is there?" I asked Charlie, when he tried to drag me in. I sat on the bank and watched as he and Tuna walked in after Trish and Tammy. They had become good friends, the awkwardness that had been there between Charlie and Tuna when they first met had disappeared. Watching them all in the water laughing, I realised what I was missing because I was always so scared to try anything, always so scared of looking like a fool. I stood up, dropped my sarong on the sand and ran into the water to the sound of loud cheers from Charlie and Tammy. The water was beautifully cool and I swam quickly trying not to think about what was below me. Tuna swam over to me and I held onto his shoulder.

"Welcome," he said, and I laughed happily.

After a few hours, our boat driver indicated that we should go back. We clambered into the boat, disappointed at the no-show from the dolphins. As we were driving away, however, something glistening broke the smooth surface of the silver water. The dolphins crested just ahead of the boat. In the setting sun, they were a beautiful lilac colour. I had read this in the guidebook and I hadn't believed it. We watched in silence, open-mouthed, as they arched out of the water, gleaming in the sun. I grinned at Tuna and he winked back.

Chapter Twenty-Two

A few days later, with great reluctance, we finally set off for the boat that was going to take us away from Dhon Dhet and back to the mainland. I walked away from my little hut, feeling like I was being wrenched away.

"Why are we going?" I asked Tuna, puffing under the weight of my rucksack. He was looking down at his feet as he walked alongside me. He shrugged.

"Because we feel like we should."

"I'm a bit bored of this place now," Tammy called over her shoulder, from behind her huge backpack.

"Things to see, places to go," Trish added, her voice muffled by her equally large bag.

We trudged along in silence. The beach loomed ahead of us; I could see our boat waiting.

"I don't want to go yet," I said quietly to Tuna.

He shook his head and his eyes flickered to my face.

"Nor me."

The others swung their rucksacks off their backs and loaded them onto the boat. I stood there watching. I always went along with other people. I didn't want to go. And therefore I didn't have to go.

"I'm not going," I said firmly. Charlie, Trish and Tammy looked at me in surprise.

"Let's stay."

"My visa runs out in two days," Charlie said shame-facedly. "Sorry to be so boringly law-abiding but I've already been fined massively twice for running over; can't afford it again."

Trish and Tammy smiled at me understandingly.

"It's OK, Rubo," Tammy said reassuringly, "you can stay if you like. It's your call. We can meet up again."

"Yeah, I fancy a good pizza and a bit of luxury in Siem Reap," Trish said, "we can meet you there if you like, in a few days."

I nodded. I looked at Tuna.

"Do you want to stay with me?"

His face broke into a relieved grin.

"I thought you would want to stay on your own."

I shook my head.

"I hate being alone," I murmured so only he could hear, "too much time to think."

He nodded.

"I would definitely love to stay," he said.

We waved to the others as the boat pulled away from the bank. Charlie winked at me. I felt a slight lump in my throat.

"See you in a few days," Trish called, waving frantically and beaming her big-hearted smile.

"I'm gonna miss your whingeing, Pommy," called Tammy. I grinned as the boat chugged away. A poor ox was tied to the front of the boat and he was paddling frantically alongside them.

"I hope this animal doesn't drown," we heard Tammy shouting loudly over the put-put of the engine, "It'll bloody sink the boat!"

With that they disappeared from view around a sand island, and it was suddenly very quiet.

We managed to get our old huts back and we fell quickly into our hammocks dropping our bags onto the floor. I had two on my balcony so Tuna sat next to me and we swung in unison. We looked down at some children playing in the river.

"This is a good place to disappear from the world isn't it?" Tuna asked, his eyes drooping.

I nodded and watched him as he dropped off to sleep. The air was so moist there was a sheen on his skin. His long eyelashes rested on his cheeks. My eyes moved down over his tanned shoulders and over his chest where a light smattering of hair travelled down in a darker line along his lean stomach and disappeared into his low-slung shorts. I hadn't really paid attention before to how toned his body was, I had always just thought he was thin. But studying his cheekbones, and the sinewy muscles in his tanned arms, and the long muscles of his legs, I felt a warm feeling uncoiling in my stomach and with a sudden jolt I realised that I fancied the pants off Tuna.

We wandered down to the river later and floated on the current in the crisp water. At one point, my leg brushed against Tuna's underwater and I felt a rush of warmth flood through me. Tuna didn't notice anything unusual; he was busy waving at the children on the riverbank. I was so confused. I wasn't ready for this. I wasn't anywhere near over Rich, I was still missing him with all my being; his presence, or lack of it, had left a huge hole in my life, like I was my arm. I had to learn how to function without him. I had even told Charlie that I wasn't ready for anything more than friendship, and Charlie was gorgeous. I was obviously just confused, I told myself, just looking for affection. I most definitely did not fancy Tuna.

We went for dinner at our usual place. It was a small hut with an adjoining raised outdoor platform with low tables and cushions on the floor and candles dotted around the place that bathed everything in a warm, orange glow. Music was supplied by the crickets and delicious smells of frying noodles and chillies danced on the warm air. Tuna chatted away telling me all about a place called the Gili Islands in Indonesia, just off the coast of Lombok.

"They are like little droplets of paradise in the ocean," he said dreamily, pushing some very hot and spicy potatoes around his plate, "pure white sand stretching for miles, and you have the beaches all to yourself because there's hardly anyone else there."

The candlelight was flickering on the tawny skin on his shoulder. I couldn't take my eyes off it, or the tattoo that curled from underneath his vest.

"I have a secret place that I stay, away from the main town on Gili Trewangan," he smiled conspiratorially. "When you get off the boat that brings you to the island, on the main beach, you walk left through the town until the hotels and guesthouses peter out. The path becomes a sand track and it looks like it's just leading you into the trees, but you follow it along the coastline, and eventually you'll see a little wooden sign saying, 'Sunshine Guesthouse'. That's the place to stay. It's in a little glen amongst palm trees and flowers, and the beach is directly opposite. I used to lie on my bed there and look out at the sea from my little window."

He pointed a piece of potato at me, pierced on his fork.

"*That's* where I'm heading, before I go home. That's definitely where I'm going to end my trip," he nodded, popping the potato into his mouth. "Anyway, I don't know why I'm telling you how to get there, because I'll just show you. You can come with me."

My stomach flipped, and my mouth opened and closed like a fish. I could think of nothing I would like more than to be on a paradise island with Tuna at this moment in time. I smiled to myself as I realised I already was.

Tuna suddenly looked a bit shy and embarrassed.

"I mean, you know, if you'd like to come," he said poking his potatoes again, "I don't know your plans. You may not even be heading in that direction."

I shook my head quickly.

"I'd love to go there Tuna," I said in a rush, "I didn't have any plans or ideas of where I was going on this trip. Rich organised the whole thing. I just went along with him. Like a sheep."

Shut up! My head was telling my mouth to stop, but it wouldn't. Tuna was gazing into his bowl.

"But you know, that was before he went swanning off with *Neecurl*," I said in a terrible French accent.

He raised his eyes.

"I know you can't blame him," I spat, poking my potatoes angrily, "I mean she was gorgeous and tiny and all …French."

God, now I sound like I'm trying to get a compliment out of him.

"…but well she wasn't *that* gorgeous, was she?"

Now I sound like a bitch! Stop talking!

"…but well she had lovely hair…and…and… a lovely accent."

Tuna grinned.

"I like *your* accent."

My stomach did another little flip.

"It's funny," he said, "With that Welsh twang. You sound like that woman from that show, what was it? Hi-de-hi or something?"

Great. Ruth Madoc. Not Catherine Zeta Jones.

"She was pretty."

Bloody hell he fancies Ruth Madoc! Maybe I'm in with a chance.

"Well, if you like older women," I said in a wary voice, not sure where this was going.

"Nicole wasn't older?" Tuna looked confused. My stomach dropped when I realised he'd been talking about her and not Ruth Madoc.

"Anyway, what I was going to say was that Nicole was pretty, but I thought she was just really boring," he shrugged. "There was nothing special about her and she never had anything interesting to say. Not when I spoke to her anyway."

My heart soared, and I couldn't help beaming.

"Thanks, Tuna," I said shovelling some potato into my mouth, "I know you're just saying that to be nice, but thanks."

OH GOD! I spat some potato on him. It's on his arm! He hasn't noticed.

I stared at the little blob of moist potato on his arm, but he was looking into the air above my head thoughtfully.

"I'm not just being nice, it's the truth," he looked uncomfortable all of a sudden. "You know, she came on to me as well."

I opened my eyes wide, startled, all the while trying to figure out how I could brush against him to wipe the potato off. I squirmed a little and flung my arm across the table so it lay next to his. He glanced down at it and frowned.

"Dead arm," I said by way of explanation, and jiggled it about. Unfortunately, I whacked his arm with it, and he edged it away nervously. I got the potato off though.

"So when did she? You know, come on to you?" I asked casually. I felt inexplicably jealous.

"The night they did that thing to you," he tried not to smile, "you know, put the spliff up your nose."

I rolled my eyes and laughed.

"God how embarrassing, I was a stupid blubbering wreck that night, wasn't I?"

He shook his head.

"No, you were upset and you had a right to be," he grinned at me. "It's pretty funny now you think of it though."

I glared at him, but a small smile tugged at the corners of my mouth.

"Anyway, when I got up to leave, before you woke up, she followed me down the steps, pretending she was going to go to the toilet. But when we got around the corner, so we were hidden by a hut, she grabbed me, kissed me and tried to drag me towards her hut."

"No?" I asked him wide-eyed.

He nodded.

"But like I said, I just didn't find her that attractive, and I liked Tam."

I shook my head.

"God she's a cow."

Uh-oh, sounding like a bitch again.

"I mean, uh I'm sure she's lovely when she wants to be," I added quickly.

Tuna was looking at me with a strange expression on his face.

"Are you OK?" he asked, "You're acting oddly tonight. Sort of…skittish."

I laughed a high, shrill laugh that drew a worried look from the owner of the small café we were sitting in.

"I just think it's the food," I said indicating my potatoes, "It's all so hot and spicy here, isn't it? And everything just goes straight through me."

Great – nice image to put into his head, Ruby.

"And I mean it's hard enough going to the toilet here anyway, squatting over a hole and trying to avoid scorpions dropping on your head," I added for good measure.

Shut up! Stop talking!

"I think squat toilets are better than western ones anyway," Tuna said conversationally, "They're cleaner because you don't actually touch the toilet."

"But I always pee on my foot," the words were out of my mouth before I could stop them. I could kill myself sometimes. Tuna laughed loudly and I gave him a wonky smile, half mortified by what I had said and half pleased that I had made him laugh.

After that I was quiet, partly to stop ridiculous comments coming out of my mouth but also trying to hide what I was feeling, because I knew I didn't really mean it. It was just that I felt lonely that was all. It wasn't Tuna I wanted, it was Rich, I repeated inside my head. I made myself remember when Rich and I had met. I made myself think of the morning we woke up in our flat together for the first time; our first kiss; the first time he told me he loved me…I looked up into Tuna's twinkling eyes in the candlelight, and thoughts of Rich were washed away like the river cleansing the riverbank.

We wandered back to our huts in silence. When we reached mine, I stopped by the little wooden steps that led up to my balcony. Tuna stood facing me. I couldn't see his face because the moon was behind a cloud, and there was no other light. I saw the flash of his eyes looking down at me, when the moon finally emerged. I held my breath. I felt my body flood with heat. I was sure he would notice. He was so close I could smell his warm skin.

"Goodnight," he said finally, his voice barely a whisper.

"Goodnight," I gasped, almost relieved as he stepped back and wandered away along the path, his hands in his pockets.

Chapter Twenty-Three

We finally left Don Dhet a few days later. I still didn't want to go, but I knew that things had to end. We were beginning to get itchy feet; the temples of Angkor Wat lay ahead of us, and we had spent the last couple of days reading about them in our guidebooks. I watched the island grow smaller as the boat pulled away from shore. The palms waved at us, the huts sat sleepily in the afternoon sun, the river moved sluggishly in the heat. I felt like I was leaving my heart on Don Dhet. We were silent on the journey to the Cambodian border which consisted of a series of dusty truck rides. The Laos border post was a wooden hut on the riverbank. Inside, a man in uniform was asleep on his chair with his feet on his desk. He woke up grumpily when Tuna cleared his throat loudly and he barely glanced at our passports. While Tuna was getting his passport stamped, I studied a poster that depicted a cartoon woman being swallowed by an enormous snake. I hoped this wasn't a regular occurrence in these parts.

We crossed the river to the other side for the Cambodian border post, which consisted of another hut with another sleeping man inside, and then we were bundled into a tiny boat with about seven other people, who were waiting on the bank – all backpackers, so we had huge rucksacks to squash in as well. I was utterly terrified, the canoe-type boat was so flimsy, and we were precariously low in the water. Tuna laughed at my panic-stricken face as the boat took off at break-neck speed. This was no gently motoring boat like we had ridden on in Si Phan Dhon. It was even worse when we hit some rapids, and jumped over the top of them, tilting from side to side. I gripped onto Tuna's arm and felt my stomach fly into my throat. After an hour, my nerves were in pieces, and I was so relieved when the boat pulled to a sudden stop on a riverbank at the tiny town of Stung Treng, that I almost laughed when my feet touched solid ground. Hotel touts met us at the quay, young Khmer boys who all tried to catch our attention first. One of them had a perfect London accent. I stared at him in surprise.

"My name is James Bond," he explained, as if it was the most normal thing in the world.

"Are you English?" I asked.

He grinned.

"No, I learned my English from a guy from London. He stayed here for six months and taught me."

He was a bit of a wheeler dealer, which was rather bizarre with his South London accent – it was a bit like meeting a Cambodian Delboy – and before we knew it we found ourselves at his father's hotel, a rather pretty, low, white building, with pink bougainvillea and every room leading out onto a long veranda. We even had proper showers, and I stood underneath the hot water gratefully. Si Phan Dhon seemed like a world away already, and my sudden fancying of Tuna seemed to have been left behind with it. When I opened the door to his cleanly shaven, smiling face later on, he was just Tuna again, my travelling companion.

From Stung Treng it was another boat journey down the Mekong. This was a different kettle of fish however – a thirty-seat speedboat with a large upper deck. Although we had seats inside, the cabin was dark and cramped, and full of passengers, so Tuna and I chose to sit on the deck and watch the river and the countryside slip by. The trip was winding as the boat had to avoid sandbanks and small islands, so we clung onto the railing and let the splashes of water cool us. We waved to small children playing on the banks, or others leading their ox down to the water to drink. Sometimes a small bamboo house would appear surrounded by a well-tended plot, and a lean farmer would be digging or hoeing, pausing only to wave as the boat passed. The journey took eight hours so Tuna and I spent a lot of time talking, mostly about the recent history of Cambodia and the Khmer Rouge rule which hadn't ended all that long before. As we watched children waving to us from the bank, Tuna pointed out that forty percent of the population was under fourteen years of age because so many generations of people had been wiped out during the Khmer Rouge rule. I was horrified to hear about the gruesome campaign that wiped out people indiscriminately – men, women, children – and at the same time amazed at, and ashamed of, my own ignorance. I had always been so wrapped up in my little world at home, I rarely worried about anything outside that sphere; things that happened on the other side of the world seemed so far away, they didn't matter.

When we reached the small town of Kompong Cham, we quickly settled ourselves into a hotel that was reminiscent of a mental institution with long white corridors, nearly empty rooms with ceiling fans and bare light bulbs that couldn't be turned off, and iron beds. I didn't fancy staying inside for very long so we went for a wander around the town which was dusty and rundown with faded, crumbling, colonial buildings. We soon discovered that our hotel looked like the best of the lot. We ended up back by the river near our hotel sitting on plastic chairs at a makeshift bar where we chatted to the owner and local tour guide, Mr Vannat, and an ageing hippy called Mike who was also staying at our hotel. He would stroke his greying beard and nod slowly at everything anyone said. Everyone we had encountered in Cambodia so far had been immensely friendly and welcoming, and Mr Vannat was no different, chatting happily to us once he had established that we didn't need any tickets for anything, or a tour guide to take us anywhere. The sky grew darker, and our tongues grew looser with the beer and inevitably talk turned to the elephant in the room – the Khmer Rouge. Mr Vannat instantly clammed up and, after making a few vague references to his life during the Khmer Rouge rule, he wouldn't be drawn on the subject again. Instead he quickly got up to tidy up his little bar, even though nobody but us had visited it that evening. Whether he had been a supporter or had lost loved ones during the rule it was difficult to tell but we learned a quick lesson that it seemed to be a subject best left alone.

After a while I sat back in my seat and looked around at this motley crew. I tried to picture myself on a Friday night at home in a bar in Clapham, and it seemed like a lifetime away. If someone had told that girl back then, where I would be this night, three months into the future, she would have laughed heartily before going to buy another cocktail. This situation would have terrified me; the thought of being with these people from completely different walks of life in a remote and mysterious country that I knew little about, would have seemed terribly lonely and scary. Yet sitting here, watching Tuna talking animatedly, I felt completely content and it was the thought of being in that bar in Clapham that now seemed lonely and empty.

***

From: welshhottie@yahoo.co.uk
To: Rube99@hotmail.com
Subject: What the f is going on?

Hia

Rubes, something's going on. Can tell. This is not like you. Mam keeps asking if have heard from you, and keep having to lie and say you're OK.

Where are you?

Dad being weird lately. On phone a lot in study and when walk in, puts it down quickly. Maybe has realised Mam is having affair and is trying to catch her out.

Jess

From: donnamjones@infosystems.com
To: Rube99@hotmail.com
Subject: Hello

Ruby

Your sister is a terrible liar. She keeps saying she has heard from you and everything is fine but I can tell she is not telling the truth. I know you're busy, but please let us know you are OK.

Mother

From: misskitten@yahoo.com
To: Rube99@hotmail.com
Subject: Conundrum

Hello darling

Didn't know who else to talk to about this. You see Ruby, I have fallen in love. And not with Tim. With someone else. It's a guy I work with. He is fabulous. Don't want to say too much yet because I just don't know what to do about it. It began as an email flirtation, and the messages ended up becoming filthy. Went out for a work do the other day and we ended up kissing, even though I swore I wasn't going to do anything.

I love Tim, I really do, but we've been together so long. And this guy is just so exciting. I feel weak every time he walks into the office and I become a gibbering idiot. And you know me. I am *not* a gibbering idiot. I managed not to sleep with him after the do but I'm worried it's only a matter of time.

What should I do?! Reply on this address I set up, so that Tim can't read my emails.

Hope all is well. Hi to Rich.

Lata

From: Rube99@hotmail.com
To: misskitten@yahoo.com
Subject: Sort it out

Lata

I'm shocked at you. You and Tim have got such a sure thing. Don't throw it away on a silly work infatuation that will fizzle out in a few weeks. I would have expected better from you.

Ruby

From: Rube99@hotmail.com
To: welshhottie@yahoo.co.uk
Subject: I'm fine

Jess

There's nothing to worry about, I'm fine, all is well, just been really busy travelling. And I've been in the middle of nowhere most of the time anyway so I just haven't been able to get on the internet.

Mum is not having an affair – she may be a workaholic, but she wouldn't do that to Dad. Give them both my love.

Ruby

From: Rube99@hotmail.com
To: babygirlsteph@hotmail.com
Subject: Honestly…

Hi Steph

I know you think you're in love, but I just can't condone what you're doing. I'm sorry, before I may have been more understanding but, now I just think you're being unfair to Mark's wife and to yourself. Think about what you're doing.

I'm OK, everything's OK; I've just been really busy lately that's all…

Love Rube x

From: Rube99@hotmail.com
To: donnamjones@infosystems.com
Subject: Hello

Mother

I'm absolutely fine, I've just been travelling in some remote places and so it's been hard to get on email. Hope you're all OK.

Ruby

From: hottuna@yahoo.com
To: Rube99@hotmail.com
Subject: Ready to go?
☺

I looked up from my computer screen to see Tuna's smiling eyes peering over the top of his. I smiled back and nodded. I was quiet as we left. I was thinking of the emails I had just sent. I couldn't help but be harsh with Lata and Steph after what had happened to me. I knew that a few months ago I probably would have told them both it was her choice, and had a giggle with them about the dirty emails and the thrill of elicit meetings. But now I thought of Tim and the anonymous figure of Mark's wife being hurt and the horrible sick feeling in my stomach when I had seen Nicole and Rich together that first time, and there was no way I could condone it.

"So did you email everyone?" Tuna asked as we went through the door of the tiny internet café. Tuna knew that I had been dreading emailing everyone at home and telling them about Rich and Nicole. I nodded and avoided his eyes.

"Yeah," I said breezily, "I told them everything that happened."

Tuna put his arm around me shoulder and gave me a quick squeeze. I don't know why I lied. I supposed I just wasn't ready to face it yet.

Chapter Twenty-Four

The jungle lay before us bathed in mist. It was coming to life sleepily, shaking and stretching its limbs; trees seemed to unfurl and stretch as the sun warmed them. We gazed at the sight before us as we huddled under our chequered *khramas* – cotton scarves – in the cool dawn. The pointed spires of Angkor Wat in the far distance gleamed in the rising sun. We were perched on the hilltop temple of Phnom Bakeng, amongst tumbledown pillars and statues. Even Tammy and Trish were impressed into silence, and we sat for a while not speaking. This was the start of two dream-like days filled with visits to temple after temple, each one different and impressive in its own way. We spent the days weaving along the newly tarred roads that wound through the jungle, perched on the backs of motorbikes. Each of us had our own driver; Tammy and Trish were on the back of one, Tuna and I on another and Charlie on his own. I felt inordinately happy with the wind in my hair as we passed leaning huts on stilts hiding behind stooping palm trees, and children waving and running after the bikes as fast as their tiny legs would carry them. We flitted past green fields, beautifully ploughed in rows; steadily plodding oxen were led by farmers whose skin was darkened by the sun, their loose shirts sticking to their bodies with sweat. The jungle was surprisingly light, with tall trees dappling the sunlight on the road. Sometimes a temple would emerge from the trees, its tumbledown towers spilling towards the road. At other times, we would have to park the bikes and walk into the trees, across ornate wide bridges, their banisters decorated with *nagas,* mythical Hindu serpents. At the temple of Ta Prohm, the jungle had begun to reclaim its own, as magnificent ivory coloured tree roots snaked their way around the walls and pillars of the temple and slowly dragged them to the ground, strangling them over the years. It was a wonder to wander through the corridors, stepping over fallen blocks, admiring the fading carvings on the stones, marvelling at the size and power of the roots and trees that had staked a claim over the temple, and had grown in it, on it and around it. Trees towered over old walkways and perched precariously or proudly on top of doorways. It was at this temple that Tomb Raider was filmed, and we found the famous doorway that was framed by a huge tree root and which was used in the film. Surrounded by a group of people Tuna took my picture as I posed against the doorframe, in my baggy linen trousers, grimy vest, and hair tied back in my *khrama*.

"Lara Croft eat your heart out," he said loudly. I cringed by the door as dozens of eyes turned to stare at me. I glared at him and his face broke into that infectious, wide smile, banishing my annoyance immediately.

The Bayon probably captured my imagination more than any other temple. Its disquieting grandeur was intimidating as it rose up through the jungle. Uneasiness arose in me as we parked the bikes and walked slowly towards its towers, and I realised the reason behind my wariness. The temple is covered in faces twice the height of an adult, staring down from all angles. As you wind your way around its corridors, staircases and towers, you feel eyes on you constantly, some faces scowling, some smiling enigmatically. Nobody yet knows the history behind the faces, who they were, and why the Bayon, unlike all the others, is filled with them. Some inspire in you a feeling of peace, some a feeling of malevolence. I was gazing at a face above me, its eyes looking through me and beyond, when I turned to find the Tuna, Charlie, Tammy and Trish had disappeared from view. I could hear their voices inside a doorway that lead into a narrow tower. I followed, always one step behind the voices. I heard them echo along a dark corridor. I walked towards them, feeling along the walls with my hands. The voices got further away. I couldn't see ahead of me. A small wave of panic grew inside me, but I quelled it and pressed on.

"Tuna," I called out quietly, and then more loudly, "guys?"

No answer. I pressed on into the darkness. My heart started to beat more quickly. I could feel the eyes of the faces looking down at me, even though I couldn't see them.

"Tuna, where are you?" I called anxiously as I started to trot. My heart was pounding now, my fingers felt along the damp wall. I decided to turn back and I came to a crossroads I hadn't noticed before. Each corridor was at an angle so I couldn't tell which way was straight on. How hadn't I noticed before? I picked one and plunged on into the darkness. My breathing was ragged when I suddenly stumbled into a chamber and fell over a bundle on the floor. Some gentle words were mumbled in Thai, as my eyes adjusted to the light and I got to my feet, brushing down my knees that were stinging. The light came from a single candle, and the bundle was an elderly female monk; her orange robes glowed warmly in the candlelight and her head was shaved. Her eyes peered out from the folds and wrinkles of her serene face and she grinned toothlessly up at me. She beckoned me towards her. My breathing had slowed, along with my heart. She held out an incense stick, and then motioned to the statue of a Buddha that was nestled in an alcove of the wall. Garlands of flowers hung around its neck, and incense sticks burned at its feet, stuck into an urn of sand. I placed the incense stick into the sand. She smiled and nodded.

"Where…?" My voice was muffled in the darkness. She pointed a knobbly finger over my shoulder. I turned to see a dark passage that had a dim light at the end of it. I nodded and smiled my thanks. I backed away from her, holding her shining eyes until the flickering of the candle no longer lit her face. I turned and ran, and found myself very quickly blinking in the brilliant sunlight; I was standing on a parapet just around the corner from where I had followed the others into the corridor. I could hear their voices around the corner, and I walked around a huge stone face to find them.

"You led me on a goose-chase!" I said, surprising them from behind, they looked at me with puzzled expressions.

"What do you mean?" Trish asked.

"Well, you disappeared into that doorway over there," I pointed to the door that I had their voices disappear into, "And you didn't tell me, so I followed and got lost and…"

Tuna was shaking his head.

"No, we didn't. We've been here all along."

Tammy nodded.

"Yeah mate. We were looking at this face here and when we turned around you were gone."

I shook my head in confusion.

"No, I followed you down there," I protested, "And there was this female monk…"

Tuna placed his hand on my shoulder.

"We were right here, Ruby, the whole time. We haven't moved."

I looked into his light eyes, as glassy and bright as the sky above us, and I knew he was telling me the truth.

"Come on," Charlie said, forcing us to break eye contact, "we've got one more left. The big one: Angkor Wat."

We trooped down the steps and along the rubble-strewn walkways to our bikes. As we drove away, I glanced over my shoulder at the Bayon. Its faces smiled down at me. I smiled back and watched the jungle swallow up those eyes once more.

We clambered up impossibly steep steps using our hands as well as our feet to pull us up. Charlie's flip flops were in front of my face; Tuna was below me. Trish was way ahead being skinny and fit and Tammy was far behind us looking red in the face and puffing and panting.

I glanced behind me once and caught a glimpse of her face, before feeling dizzy and turning back to face the stone steps. The reason for the steepness of the steps leading up to towers in the central courtyard was to ensure worshippers stooped low as they approached the Gods. It was not something someone with vertigo would enjoy.

As I reached the last few steps, I saw Charlie hold out his hand to help me up. His eyes were lit up and I knew that the view from the top was going to be worth it. I turned to look out at the red globe of the sun as it lowered itself sleepily towards the earth. The courtyard below was patterned with multi-coloured groups of milling tourists and fleeting figures of orange-clad monks as they scurried along the walkways. Beyond the walls of the Wat were beautiful gardens stretched out and dotted with trees, like manicured European gardens rather than the gardens of ancient Khmer ruins. I looked down at the dizzying drop of the steps below my feet. Tuna had gone back down the steps and was helping Tammy to climb the last and steepest section, with a hand on her back. He glanced up and caught my eye and winked. I couldn't wipe the silly grin off my face. I sat on a block of stone next to Charlie and Trish to enjoy the view. Tammy finally joined us, panting, and sat down between Charlie and me. Tuna sat down on my other side. I turned to look at the profiles of my friends, lit up by the setting sun. Trish turned lilac-blue eyes upon me; her tawny skin was glowing in the setting sun, and she smiled her goofy smile. I studied Charlie's face; sunglasses hid his eyes from me. He was exhaling a long plume of smoke from his perfectly formed lips and gazing out at the horizon. Next to me, Tammy's wispy blonde hair was dancing about her face, which was still pink from the climb. Dimples marked her cheeks and she broke into a smile when she caught my eye.

"What's up?" she asked.

I shrugged and moved my gaze to Tuna. His short messy hair had become fairer in the sun; his dark eyebrows were knitted together as he watched the scene before him. His eyes were the colour of shallow waters over white sand, flecked with silver and framed by dark, thick lashes. He felt my eyes on him and turned to meet my stare. He returned my smile.

"It's good to see," he said quietly.

I nodded.

"It's quite a sight," I agreed turning to admire the view.

"I meant it's good to see you healing," he continued, turning to look at me again.

I looked into his silvery eyes and smiled.

"It's been down to all of you."

He shook his head.

"No, Ruby, it's been you. You've done the hard work yourself. You should take some credit for it."

I felt a rush of happiness sitting there, on that tower in the middle of the jungle amongst my friends. I turned to watch the sunset with them.

Chapter Twenty-Five

We arrived in Phnom Penh at the obligatory dusty bus station and prepared ourselves for a lengthy hike across the city. We were met by the usual crowd of hotel touts, gesticulating frantically and calling out to us. Feeling tired and irritable, I walked past them, my head held high so as not to meet their eyes. I just couldn't deal with it all right now; I wanted a shower, food and a drink. But Tuna surprised me as always with his patience, answering each person in turn as he walked past them, "No thank you, we know where we are staying, thank you." There was one particularly persistent man who kept trotting after us, a little older than the others, a wide smile on his leathery face and a twinkle in his eye. A tall lanky man walking beside him looked surly and muttered something to him as he skipped after us, but this guy shook his head, and carried on smiling.

"Hello? Hello? Lady, sir, you need a hotel? I know good hotel, wonderful. I can take you there now. Very cheap; very nice." I shook my head, not meeting his eye. Tuna suddenly stopped in his tracks as I marched on ahead after Trish, Tammy and Charlie.

Trish was busy smiling at everyone she passed and saying, "How are ya?"

"OK," Tuna said to the man who was bobbing up and down expectantly, "How far is it?"

I turned and looked back at Tuna. I had become so accustomed to being followed by touts that latched onto you for days, that I just found it easier now to ignore them.

The older man was nodding and grinning at Tuna.

"Not far my friend, not far," he said pointing a shaky finger up the road, "You just come with me, my friend has taxi, and I get you good rate at the hotel."

Tuna smiled and held out his hand. The man's grin widened and he shook Tuna's hand eagerly.

"Sure OK," Tuna said flashing me a smile, "why not?"

Tuna's friendly gratitude made me feel a flash of shame. I had come to think that an experienced traveller was one who was not taken in by touts, who did not fall for their tricks. Even now, I looked at this guy warily. He nodded and smiled at me.

"My name is James Taylor," he said holding his hand out to me. I shook it and smiled.

"Sure it is," I said under my breath to Tuna as James trotted on happily ahead of us, "we've already met James Bond, so why not James Taylor?"

Tuna shrugged and grinned and we trudged after James, with Trish, Tammy and Charlie trailing behind us.

"You know we won't be able to get rid of him now," I murmured to Tuna. He shrugged again and walked along humming happily to himself.

James joined Tuna and I in the taxi which was a *cyclo* – a small carriage drawn by a motorbike. It was a cosy ride what with our rucksacks balanced on our feet and James squeezed in the middle of us in the open-air carriage. The other three were in another *cyclo* behind us. I grinned at Tuna as James talked loudly about Phnom Penh, his voice nearly being drowned out by traffic.

"Very wonderful, good city," he was saying, his eyes gleaming and his mouth smiling, "Lots to do, see. Plenty nice restaurants to eat."

He nodded enthusiastically as the *cyclo* turned down a quiet road and then again into a smaller alleyway.

"Nice hotel by the lake," James said as the *cyclo* drew to a halt, unable to go any further down the rocky, dirt road. The other *cyclo* pulled up behind us.

James leapt down from the *cyclo* after Tuna and then hoisted my bag onto his back.

"No, no," I said hurriedly, climbing down after him, "it's OK, I can carry it."

James smiled into my eyes. His own eyes twinkled.

"'S'OK lady, you can trust me," he patted his skinny legs beneath dusty trousers, "I am old man now, can't run away with your bag."

I felt my cheeks burn.

"That's not what I meant," I said weakly, embarrassed that he had thought that I was worried about him stealing my bag, but he bounced away, with a spring in his step. I just felt guilty about this older man carrying my heavy bag when he looked so frail. I sighed, and followed him and Tuna, who were deep in conversation.

The narrow road was lined with small cafés, little stalls selling baguettes or noodles, and open doors that led into various guesthouses with whimsical names like '*Happiness Guesthouse*' or '*Loveheart Hostel*'. Backpackers mingled with motorbike-taxi drivers and young, beautiful woman that were on the lookout for 'customers' amongst the wealthy, young Western travellers. James led us to the very end of the road to "Number 9" guesthouse and gestured for us to go in through the open door. It led onto a wide long veranda that jutted out over Lake Boeung Kak. The veranda contained a reception desk which doubled as a small bar, a pool table, hammocks and tables and chairs dotted amongst potted plants, upon which people lounged and looked out over the lake. Rickety wooden walkways led off the main veranda to small wooden bungalows perched on stilts over the water.

"Come, come," James said bustling past us and up to the reception desk. He dropped my rucksack with a crash by the desk, and then chatted with the young man who sat behind it and who greeted him warmly. James turned to us with a grin.

"This nice guesthouse yes?" he asked us, nodding. We nodded back enthusiastically.

If it had been a pigsty, I would have nodded not wanting to offend this genial man who seemed so earnest in his desire to help. Of course I knew it was for money – he would get commission from the guesthouse for bringing us – but he seemed to really want us to like it.

"Yeah this is cool mate," Charlie crooned as he looked around dreamily, clearly envisaging himself swinging on a hammock as he got stoned.

James stepped back so we could check-in. We were given keys and when I lifted my rucksack again, and turned around, I saw James sitting in one of the bamboo chairs, chatting to a small child. He grinned and jumped to his feet when he saw me watching him.

"Toona and Boobee," we had told him our names in the cyclo, but he still couldn't quite get the hang of mine. He nodded at Charlie and the girls.

"If you or your good friends want anything arranged, please come to me; I can do for you, organise taxi, get tickets for places to see, even take you on tour of city."

Tuna smiled and shook his hand, and I knew he had money in his palm that he had passed him as a thank you.

"We will come to you James," he said warmly.

"Just ask anyone for me," James said nodding and waving his hand around vaguely, "I am always around. Everyone knows James Taylor."

He gave us a small bow and with that, bounced away, a spring in his step.

"You've got a friend," Trish sang loudly as she strode along the wooden walkway towards the rooms.

"Ain't it good to know you got a friend," Tammy sang after her.

***

I clung to the *moto* (motorbike-taxi) driver – a friend of James – and Tuna clasped my waist lightly as we weaved through the streets of Phnom Penh. It was a city I loved immediately. Golden pagodas glinted in the sun; the glistening gold and silver tiled spires of the Royal Palace rose up over the high exterior walls tempting people inside; citrus-robed monks scurried along under umbrellas protecting them from the glaring sun; huge golden statues of lions lined the wall of the wide river along which barges and fishing boats glided.

We headed into the bowels of the city to the Russian Market, a dark, musty maze of stalls selling jewellery, CD's, fake designer clothes, Buddha ornaments and intricately carved wooden boxes. We strolled along the narrow alleys between stalls, stopping now and again to muse over something or other. Tuna haggled like a pro. I, on the other hand, didn't have a clue. The stallholders could name any price and I would breathe "Ooh that's good!" Tuna would roll his eyes and drag me away clutching my '*bargain*'.

We blinked as we emerged into the searing sunlight and flagged down another bike-taxi to take us to Tuol Sleng, the famous prison used by the despotic Khmer Rouge leader Pol Pot during his reign of terror. The sights we saw there soon washed our carefree moods away. In an ordinary suburban street, Pol Pot had turned a high school into a prison where he tortured and killed his prisoners, who ranged from babies to his own faithful guards and soldiers. It is now a museum left as it was in order to remind people of what had happened only a short time ago. Fragrant frangipani trees in full bloom dotted the gardens, jarringly incongruous with the barbed wire that topped the exterior walls. We saw scenes of torture within those prison walls that turned our stomachs. We left in sombre moods and flagged down another passing motorbike to take us to the Royal Palace. Wandering around the breath-taking gardens filled with orchards and manicured lawns and gazing at the glittering palace buildings decorated in gold, silver, and mirrored tiles, it was easy to forget the images of the prison, but they hovered at the back of my mind all day.

We headed back to our guesthouse wearily at the end of the day, glad to be able to come back to an oasis in the middle of the city. Sitting on the veranda looking out over the lake was a good way of leaving the bustle and noise of the city behind. Constantly moving islands of water lilies floated around the surface of the lake so that the view was always different. Tuna and I flopped down onto a sofa next to Charlie, who was smoking, as usual, with his feet up on a coffee table.

"How was your day guys?" he asked us lazily.

"Excellent," Tuna sighed, "but exhausting."

"Well, at least you didn't spend it in the bank like me. Fucking banks, fucking society, why do we have to have banks, and rules and societies man? Fuck them. Fuck it."

I smiled, having listened to this rant from Charlie more than once.

"I mean, I don't want to live in any fucking society man, with all its rules. But I really hate the way Western society, *our* society has leeched into these beautiful countries, with our *banks,* and our *laws,* and even our fucking food," he motioned towards the half-eaten hamburger on the table in front of him, "I just want to travel around, free to come and go as I choose. But no I have to go to fucking banks to sort out shit."

"So what were you doing at the bank? Did you have traveller cheques to change? Because I could have lent you the money," Tuna said, leaning forward to rest his elbows on his knees. Charlie took a long drag on his spliff and exhaled just as slowly.

"Nah man. My old man was wiring me some more money, 'cause I spent all of mine."

Tuna and I looked at each other and burst out laughing. Charlie turned his head to look at us although we couldn't see his eyes behind his ever-present sunglasses.

"What?" he asked innocently.

"What's the joke guys?" Tammy asked as she and Trish flopped down on cushioned chairs beside us. I shook my head.

"Charlie is just having his usual rant against society, whilst accepting money from his dad – who's a lawyer," I added for Tuna's benefit, "...so he can keep travelling and smoking and 'experiencing the world'."

Trish clipped Charlie over the head and he scrunched himself lower in his seat, grumbling to himself about society and rules and McDonalds.

"So you guys fancy the Heart of Darkness tonight?"

"Well, I've seen it before..." I started, not relishing the thought of ploughing through the heavy film again.

"Not *that* Heart of Darkness," Trish said enigmatically, "the real Heart of Darkness. A club. t*he* club that everyone has to experience whilst in Phnom Penh."

"Hell yeah," Charlie said, his face lighting up, "that's one thing about society I *do* like. Clubs."

As we walked through the door, I wasn't struck by the throng of people all moving together at the same time to the music as if one, nor the bluish haze created by the fluorescent lights, nor the pleasing mix of nationalities all sharing the space together, laughing together, drinking together, dancing together. I was struck by a poster on the wall, of a very young, handsome boy with dark hair, and smiling eyes. Underneath his picture I read these words:

Missing

Our son Julian Thomas, age 19, has been missing for 3 months. He was last seen in Heart of Darkness nightclub in Phnom Penh. If anyone has seen him, or has heard anything about him, please contact us on the numbers below.

Any help at all would be most appreciated. We have not seen our son in person for 18 months.
Robert and Magda Thomas

"A sad story," Tuna said over my shoulder. I turned my head to look up at him.

"I was chatting to James outside our guesthouse last night about it. The boy turned up in Phnom Penh, just like any other backpacker, and pretty quickly got himself hooked on opium. He started hanging around with a group of working girls and their pimps, before he went missing. His stuff was found in his room two days later, including his wallet and passport."

I looked back at the picture.

"Poor kid," I murmured. It was so easy to just disappear here, to escape, to forget who you were and become someone else. Everyone and everything from home seemed so far away. I thought of my family; I hadn't emailed them for weeks. They were probably worried sick. But it was just too much effort having to keep up the lie, about Rich and me. Thoughts began to clamour into my mind, thoughts I had pushed away for so long: thoughts of going home and facing up to the truth, of telling everyone about what Rich had done; thoughts of going to all of our local bars and not seeing his face there; thoughts of our flat, empty except for me and Moggy.

I felt Tuna's hand on my shoulder as he steered me towards the others standing at the bar. I let their smiles wash away thoughts of the boy, of Rich and of home.

We began to feel at home in Phnom Penh. It was the first city I had been to in ages that I felt like I wanted to stay in for longer than a couple of days. We would either eat breakfast on the veranda overlooking the water – big bowls of fruit and yoghurt – or we would eat from one of the small stalls on the street selling hot baguettes full of butter and marmite, standing on the roadside and watching people go about their business. James would sometimes appear, puffing on a cigarette, his thin frame hunched beneath his clothes and the same sparkle in his eyes. Tuna would often buy him a baguette as well which he would devour ravenously before asking what we were doing that day. If there was anything we wanted him to help us with – directions, taxis, tickets – he would organise it immediately. If we made it clear we were just going to relax that day, maybe take a walk later on, but with no particular goal, he would nod patiently and not push his services on us. Similarly, whenever he organised something for us, he never asked for payment, although we would always give him a tip. When we were with him, it struck us how everybody knew him, everyone waved at him as he passed – stall owners, taxi drivers, guesthouse owners, working girls. If we were with James, we had preferable rates. We became more than just his customers – we were his friends.

Most evenings we ate at restaurants near the lake, geared towards backpackers, with burgers and pizzas on the menu, or a couple of Indian restaurants. A few of them offered "happy" burgers or pizzas, sprinkled with hash. Charlie often opted for these even if the rest of us weren't up for it, and we wouldn't see him for the rest of the evening, until later when we would find him passed out in a hammock.

One evening, Trish decided to have an early night suffering from a particularly bad hangover and Tammy decided to join Charlie for a "happy" burger. Tuna and I were not hungry yet, and had tired of visiting the same old backpacker haunts. We headed off the main restaurant road down a small alleyway, where we had heard there was a bar patronised by local people. We couldn't find any sign of it whatsoever on our way down the winding alley – we just encountered two little boys playing with an old bicycle tyre, and a rat that scurried for cover behind some dustbins when it saw us coming. The alley came to a dead end so we looked at each other, shrugged and headed back. When we reached the corner that met the road, I decided to stop and browse in the small curio shop on the corner that sold wooden carvings of Buddha, shell necklaces and postcards. Inside sat a wizened old woman behind a high desk, snoring quietly. I could hear music coming from somewhere and took it to be coming from one of the nearby bars or guesthouses. But as I wandered to the back of the shop and found it winding around a corner, it opened onto an open-air courtyard and there was our bar.

We were the only foreigners there but nobody batted an eyelid as we walked in. A few Khmer people were sitting at plastic tables and chairs, and a wire mesh separated the courtyard from the water of the lake. A small wiry man stood at another table chopping dead chickens into pieces and dropping the meat into a wok of bubbling hot oil. I smiled at Tuna. This was more like it. No cocktails or fancy pizzas. I sat at a dirty plastic table and he went to the bar which was fronted by more wire mesh. He returned with a large bottle of the rice liqueur that could be found all over Asia, only with a different language on the label depending on which country you happened to be in. It all tasted equally revolting and was guaranteed to put you in a stupor very quickly. He had also bought two cans of Coke and two glasses which he placed on the bare table with a flourish. The next twenty minutes passed in a pleasant haze as we chatted about meaningless stuff. I felt at peace with the world and I smiled at the other people sitting and drinking. Very soon a familiar face appeared by our table. James was smiling down at us.

"My friends," he said delightedly, his eyes dancing "I not see you for all day, and now I find you here. Tourists not come here often."

Tuna nodded.

"We know, that's why we're here," he stood up and grabbed a nearby empty chair, "Please join us James."

James shook his head.

"No, no, I do not want to be in your way," he grinned again, "Nice romantic drink yes?"

I glanced around at the chicken-chopping man, who was now plucking a freshly expired chicken. Really romantic.

"Please James;" he patted the chair, "We're not romantically involved. We are just friends. We would like you to join us."

James winked at me.

"Just friends yes?"

I thought of that brief few days on Don Dhet when I had found myself thinking I fancied Tuna and felt my cheeks colour. James nodded, his eyes twinkling as they met mine.

Tuna meanwhile trotted to the bar, grabbed another glass, returned and filled it half full with some liqueur. At the sight of the drink James quickly sat down.

"So," I said quickly, before he could bring up the subject of romance again, "What is your real name?"

"James Taylor," he said sincerely.

I smiled.

"No, really."

"Really, really Ruby," he said seriously, "my father, he knows English man. His name James Taylor. He was good man. My father call me after him."

I started to laugh but could see that James was deadly serious and so turned it into a cough.

The drink loosened James' tongue and he was soon telling us about how, before the Khmer Rouge, he had worked as a lecturer in university. He stood up and enacted different techniques he used to teach, pretending we were his class and he was our teacher. He was witty and sharp and had us in stitches more than once. Then, he explained, once the Khmer Rouge took over, he had to play down his intellect in case they tortured and killed him along with all of the thousands of others they deemed a threat. He went back to work on his father's farm. He had spent so long playing dumb, that he had learned to hide his true self so well that he could blend into the crowd, as a farmer or a hotel tout or whatever his role was at the time. I gazed at this man in wonder; what kind of a world would make him have to pretend to be less than he was. His eyes glistened a little and his smile faltered before he changed the subject to us and our travels.

"You know," he said eventually, looking at Tuna with narrowed eyes, "when I see this man here, I think he is good man."

He met my eyes and smiled.

"You, I think when I see you at the bus station, are afraid, and so you not want to look people in the eye," he nodded his head as I raised my eyebrows. "My friend, he say – forgive me Ruby – but he say 'leave her alone, she is racist'. But I say no, I can see you are just afraid."

I spluttered over my drink.

"I'm not racist," I said indignantly.

"I know; I know that. I can see. This man," he waved at Tuna, "is good man. And you are lady with him so you must be good lady."

I wondered to myself if he was right. Did my fear show through that easily? And all this time, I thought it came across as confidence, not talking to people who are trying to sell me something. I thought I was saying, 'don't mess with me, I'm an experienced traveller, I'm not falling for your routine'. But I was merely showing my fear. I met James' eyes and they were soft and warm.

"I suppose I am afraid James," I found myself saying, "afraid to be alone."

"But you have nice man here; you no need to be alone."

I felt my cheeks begin to burn again, and studiously avoided Tuna's eye.

James' eyes became misty and he settled back in his chair.

"I am not alone, with my beautiful wife in my home. She work so hard all day, sewing, making clothes. I work so hard too, meeting new people, meeting tourists. This is where the money is, I tell her."

He finished his drink.

"She want me to go back to teaching, or work in the bank," he shook his head, "but I like meeting good people, like you. And I need to earn as much money as I can…"

His eyes suddenly filled with tears and he shook his head to try to make them stop. He smiled.

"But life is hard for everyone no?"

Tuna nodded but James' smile faltered.

"This country has been through so much. There is so much shame here, so much death," he shook his head. "My brother, they kill him. He was teacher too. His wife, they kill her as well and also his two children. So now I look after my mother and father alone. Then my son, he die last year from illness."

I gazed at this poor man, shrunken in on himself in his chair, all sign of his usual cheeriness disappeared. And then he forced a smile back onto his face.

"I am sorry," he said over our protests, "you not want to hear this."

He waved his hand around in a circle above his head.

"This country, this place, is so beautiful," he drank a large gulp from his glass that Tuna had just refilled. "So much to see. You good people, you must tell others to come. We need help now, the Khmer people. We need more people to come for holiday. And we can rebuild our country for our children."

We nodded and promised we would spread the word, as we raised our glasses in a toast. Very soon James left, staggering away. Tuna jogged after him, telling me he was going to the toilet.

"I offered him money," he said when he returned and flopped into the chair next to me, "But he wouldn't take it."

"Sometimes you meet people that make you see everything differently, don't you?" I said.

Tuna nodded and gazed out at the lake. He drained his glass and got to his feet. He took my hand and heaved me up.

"Come on girl," he dragged me after him, "we need a happy burger."

James organised our *cyclos* for the day we left. As we pulled away down the street waving to him, Tuna suddenly told the driver to stop. He leapt out and trotted over to James. He shook his hand and then ran very quickly back to the *cyclo*.

"Go," he said urgently to the driver. "Go!"

I glanced back at James as the *cyclo* trundled away, to see him gazing down at the bundle of notes in his hand. He raised his head and as his eyes met mine, he smiled a sad and grateful smile.

Chapter Twenty-Six

The beach stretched on for miles, golden sand fringed by palms; the usual beach scene in South East Asia. I had seen better beaches, more pristine, the sea more blue, the sand whiter. But there was something about this place, about *this* beach, Serendipity beach in Sihanoukville, on the South coast of Cambodia, that made you want to stay. It may have been the relative lack of tourists, the happy friendliness of the locals, the beach kids who, although they hassled you constantly with their baskets of fruit or *khramas* for sale, lit up your morning with their smiles. It was a lovely laid-back beach resort and we agreed as a group to stay there for a while, and spend Christmas there. I couldn't think of a better place, to try and bury the thoughts of Christmas at home; the damp London streets lit by fairy lights; strolling arm in arm with Rich, both of us wrapped up in scarves and hats; the turkey filling the smell of the house on Christmas Day; my father with his apron on, a paper hat on his head, a glass of bubbly in his hand and greeting Jess and I warmly with a grin as we emerged dishevelled and hung over from the night before.

This was going to be a beach Christmas with new friends and new family. We were all trying to ignore thoughts of home, and we would do it together.

Days at Serendipity were spent lying on the beach, accepting massages from the local women, buying bags of fruit from the street kids, eating breakfast on the sand at our favourite local beach-bar Eve. At the end of the day we would stroll back happy and sunburned, take cool showers to wash the sand from our bodies and head back down to the beach. We would sit on blankets and cushions on the sand around small, low tables at Eve and the party would begin. A rather gorgeous Maori guy called Bruno who was quiet and enigmatic ran it and would every night put on a fire show. I usually thought these were really naff – "Wanky backpackers with nothing better to do," I was often heard to mutter. But this guy was good; really good. He lit the ends of two ropes or sticks dipped in kerosene and would spin them into a frenzied dance, throwing them impossibly high in the air, twisting them into all kinds of contortions around his body, until he was one whirling ball of fire.

The party would carry on into the night, the music sometimes chilled out and easy, sometimes uplifting, sometimes hard and intense, depending on the mood Bruno was in. Groups of travellers would come and go, sometimes staying for a day, sometimes for a week like us but there were the regulars; those people that had arrived years ago, and had never left. And it was a temptation that crossed my mind on a regular basis.

On our third night, the party was in full swing as I headed to the bar to get my second beer of the evening. I had managed to find a happy medium where three drinks was my maximum. I had forgotten what it felt like to fall over drunk, to feel that dizzying lack of control, or that irrational anger that came with getting paralytic.

As I stepped up onto the wooden veranda which doubled as a dance floor when the mood took anyone, I felt a strong grip on my waist and I was spun into Bruno's arms. I was pressed against his hard chest and I giggled breathlessly. I knew that not just a few girls' envious eyes were on me.

"Dance with me," he murmured.

"I don't...know how," I gasped, having watched him dancing his hip-swaying dance with girls before.

"You don't need to," he said before guiding me firmly and smoothly with his hands gripping me fast, and his legs and feet pushing mine where he wanted them to go, my white long skirt twirling out around me. The whole time he held my gaze with his unreadable dark eyes. After five minutes that seemed to last forever, he spun me away from him so that I landed against the bar, holding on for dear life as he slipped into the crowd, disappearing to carry on running his bar.

Tammy rushed up to me, her face pink with excitement.

"Bloody 'ell mate," she gushed, "you were bloody lucky! He's a spunk!"

I nodded, grinning from ear to ear, trying to catch my breath.

"And you should have seen Charlie's face," she added, laughing darkly, "He was spewin'! Calling Bruno a smarmy bastard. Ha ha!"

"Really?" I asked, feeling a squirm of pleasure stir in my stomach. I strained my neck to see our table over the crowd of people. I could see Charlie looking thunderous and sucking on a spliff as he looked our way. My eyes roamed further. Tuna was in deep conversation with Trish, and they were facing the sea, not the dance floor.

"You like him, don't you?" Tammy asked, smiling mischievously.

"Who? Charlie?" I asked...

She nodded.

I shrugged but couldn't keep the smile off my face.

"He's nice."

She laughed a dirty laugh.

"Well, y'know if you ever have y'know womanly *needs*, he'd be more than happy to satisfy them."

I groaned and nudged her in the stomach as she guffawed.

"Can I satisfy your womanly needs ladies?" an English voice said from over my shoulder.

"Bugger off you pommy bastard," Tammy said laughing as she turned to face the stocky guy beside us. He grinned back at her, puffing out his rugby player chest.

I left them to it and headed over to the table.

"What did you do that for?" Charlie asked gruffly.

"What?" I asked innocently, glancing at Tuna and Trish.

"Throwing yourself at that arrogant bastard," he muttered.

"I didn't throw myself at him," I said indignantly, trying to hide my smile, "he just sort of grabbed me."

Tuna got to his feet, brushing the sand from his shorts. As he headed past me, he leaned down to my ear.

"You looked great," he grinned, "I didn't know you could dance like that."

"I can't," I said laughing and watching his long legs walk away across the sand. But the laugh was hollow. I sat and contemplated the breaking waves beyond us in the darkness. Why did I feel so flat all of a sudden?

After a few days of lazing on the beach, we decided to get off our backsides and go on a boat trip. There was a group of about twelve of us, and we headed out on a rather rickety wooden boat. It crashed through the dark green waves that seemed to be far more choppy and aggressive than they looked from the shore. I began to have my doubts when we were handed life jackets – safety measures were never adhered to in South East Asia unless the risk was great – and the captain tied the bag of bread rolls for our lunch to the mast. I gripped onto the wooden post by my head and hung on as we rolled over the top of the angry waves. The sun was blazing and the sky was blue, but the wind whipped the sea into an angry turmoil that we were trying to ride through. Eventually the water calmed and we neared a small island. Honey-yellow sand stretched the length of the shore and palms dipped their heads to the azure water of the little lagoon we were pulling into. We clambered off the boat, glad to be alive, and splashed through the water towards the beach. We were dealt snorkelling masks and flippers and we set off exploring the little coves and pools around the bay, as the captain and his crew set up a barbeque. Tammy and Trish kept their life jackets on and rolled about in the water like beached whales, screeching and laughing hysterically. My fingers fumbled with my mask nervously as I pulled it on. I watched Tuna and how he was doing it. I had never snorkelled before and I felt sick with nerves. I wasn't a sea person. The sea in Wales is cold, dark and uninviting so I had never found any reason to go in deeper than my ankles. But I didn't want to admit this to my friends who had all taken to the water with relish and ease. I found myself following Charlie and Tuna as they swam through the water, pointing out small fish and rare patches of coral. I tried not to think about the floor falling away beneath me into the deep dark depths of the ocean and concentrated on the small patch of sand in my vision below me.

"Jeez," Charlie said raising his head and looking at Tuna, "this snorkelling is the pits. There's hardly anything here. It must be really bad for you man, being Australian and all."

Tuna pushed his snorkelling mask up on his head.

"It's what you make of it, Charlie. I saw a barracuda back there."

"What?" Charlie said spluttering as he spat salt water out of his mouth, "Where?"

Tuna nodded his head behind me.

"About five metres over there."

I felt the panic rise in my chest and I moved closer to Tuna. Barracudas were like piranhas, weren't they? I yanked my mask up and my hair got into a big tangle in the strap. I frantically trod water as I grappled with my hair.

"You OK?" he asked me looking concerned. "You look a bit white. Are you cold?"

The water was beautifully luke-warm so I was far from cold. I nodded my head.

"Yeah, just a bit cold."

"Maybe you should go and sit on the beach in the sun," he suggested.

I looked back towards the sand. It seemed so far away, a big expanse of water that I would have to swim through, with barracudas and other fishy things with tentacles and teeth between me and it. I shook my head.

"Nah, I'll keep going," I said nonchalantly. "Don't want to miss the awesome coral."

Tuna smiled but frowned at the same time at my choice of words. I *never* said awesome.

"Uh, if you're sure you're OK?" Charlie's hairy head was already back in the water, looking this way and that, his dreads snaking about in the water. He jerked his head up, water pouring from his hair making him look like a creature from the deep.

"A parrot fish," he said excitedly and off he swam. I paddled along after the two of them, feeling the pounding in my ears of my heartbeat as the water became deeper and the sand fell away below us.

We had rounded the promontory of the bay and were circling back into the next bay where the waves were much choppier. I raised my head, feeling the swishing of my stomach as I bobbed about on the waves. I paddled furiously, trying to keep the rising swell of bile that was creeping up my throat. I couldn't believe it. I felt seasick. And I wasn't even in a boat.

"Guys!" I called pathetically, swallowing a mouthful of water as I did, which only served to heighten the feeling of sickness.

I could see their heads and their air-pipes on top of the water, but they couldn't hear me. They were getting further away. I swam after them pathetically slowly as I fought the nausea. Finally, Tuna raised his head and looked around. He spotted me some twenty metres behind them. I waved my hand at him and he began to swim back to me. Charlie raised his head and after spotting Tuna, followed him.

When Tuna reached me, he raised his mask onto his head.

"You OK?"

I shook my head.

Charlie reached us.

"Whas'up?" I opened my mouth to speak and threw up instead into the water in front of us. It swirled around us, and I was sick again.

"Jesus," Charlie said, and Tuna caught my arm.

"Let's get her back to the beach," he said.

Taking an arm each they turned me onto my back and dragged me through the water. I gazed up at the sea. I couldn't believe it. I had thrown up in front of two of the best-looking guys I had ever met. I wasn't made to be single.

Once it was shallow enough, I put my feet down onto the sand and reached down to take my flippers off. We strode through the clear water carrying our masks and flippers. The next thing I knew, there was a piercing pain in my right foot.

"Ahh," I half-screamed and half-gasped as I dropped to my knees.

The two of them stared down at me as I raised my foot to them.

"Damn," Tuna muttered, "you stood on an urchin."

He pulled a small black spike from my foot and threw it into the water. My foot throbbed.

"Jesus Ruby!" Charlie chuckled. "You're in the wars."

They caught me under each arm and they helped me hobbling up onto the sand.

Tuna studied my foot.

"It's only a small one," he said frowning, "I got all of the spike out; it didn't go very far in. But it'll hurt for a few hours." Charlie lay down on the sand beside me and stretched out his arms in the sun.

"We'll just have to lie here until the pain passes," he murmured closing his eyes.

"You guys don't have to stay here," I said feeling embarrassed. Why *why, why* did I have to make such a dick of myself?

Tuna smiled.

"We're not going to leave you here."

"Sorry I was sick on you guys," I said unhappily.

Charlie burst out laughing.

"Well, I've had some girls doing weird sexual things to me before, but I have never had one throw up on me," he said, his eyes glinting in the sun. I felt a warm flush in my stomach as I met his eye. I glanced up at Tuna and met his smiling eyes. He winked at me. I felt another flush of warmth in my stomach that spread down between my legs. What on earth was going on? I couldn't fancy both of them. Could I?

I lay in the sun and thought about how much Rich would have complained about me spoiling his day if I had been with him when this had happened. He probably would have left me on the sand and gone back to snorkelling. I smiled to myself. He really had been a selfish bastard.

"What are you smiling about?" I heard Tuna's voice filter through my thoughts.

"Nothing," I said quietly, smiling even wider, "Just thinking about Rich."

He raised his eyebrows in surprise.

"Really?"

I nodded and lifted myself onto my elbows.

"I was thinking what a dick he was."

He grinned and I laughed. He then suddenly jumped to his feet.

"I can smell the barbeque," he said, wiping the sand down off his shorts that had dried in the sun. "You two stay here; I'll go and get some food."

He trotted away over the sand. I watched him clamber over the rocks, his skin a golden brown in the sun. Charlie turned onto one side and leaned on his elbow. His eyes, the colour of dark sand, watched me.

"So you still think about him?"

I nodded, sighing a deep sigh.

"Yeah, I do."

I couldn't really explain my thoughts to him though. I couldn't explain that my thoughts had changed from missing him, from thinking about his kiss, and his warm skin and his smell, and his dark, chocolate brown eyes, to his selfishness, his childishness, his neediness, his expectations of me and how he wanted me to act. I couldn't tell him that I thought often of how I must not have known him very well at all, because I never thought he could have hurt me as badly as he did; how he must have been so cold hearted, so thoughtless that he would have just left me like that, in a remote country with no-one and nothing. I couldn't explain because I felt embarrassed that I had loved someone like that and that I hadn't known him at all even though I had dedicated three years of my life to loving him.

He nodded.

"I had a girlfriend once," he mused. "We dated for like three months."

I laughed.

"Shit man, she was gorgeous," he said dreamily, "long dark hair, big round hazel eyes, amazing body with big…"

"Uh yeah, I get the picture," I said dryly. It briefly occurred to me that I didn't feel remotely jealous, but the thought was swept away as Charlie continued.

"In fact, she looked just like you…"

I met his dark eyes. There was a smile twitching at the corners of his mouth. I hit him playfully and threw sand over his torso. He flicked sand back over me and before I knew it we were having a writhing sand fight, throwing sand over each other, rolling, kicking and laughing. Finally, Charlie wrestled me onto my back and held my arms over my head.

"Give up?" He panted.

"No!" I wriggled about underneath him.

"Come on," he held my legs still with one of his. I finally gave up struggling and lay still, laughing and spluttering, sand in my face and hair and mouth.

"Say Charlie is the king," he demanded.

"Charlie is the king," I laughed.

"He's the most gorgeous, sexiest man I have ever met."

"He's the most gorgeous, sexiest man I've ever met," I met his eye and held it, feeling uncharacteristically bold. He lowered his head slowly, looking into my eyes the whole time. As his lips neared mine, his grip on my arms loosened and I took my chance. I shoved against his chest as hard as I could and as he toppled to one side, I wriggled out from under him and scrambled to my feet. My right foot was still sore so I sort of hopped on the spot, laughing as he moaned and lay flat on the floor.

"You tease," he said laughing. I looked up to see the figure of Tuna coming over the rocks towards us. I wondered how much he had seen. He was clutching bundles of tin foil on paper plates, with bread.

He walked towards us and smiled brightly at me, showing no evidence of having seen Charlie and me rolling about on the sand.

"Barbecued barracuda!" He said grinning. "Told you I saw one!"

Later that night, after I had showered, I slipped on my white sundress, the one I had bought in Bangkok all those months ago and looked at my reflection in the mirror. I looked tanned and healthy, my arms and shoulders looked more slender in the straps of the dress; it skimmed my hips rather than clung to them. My hair fell, damp and wavy almost to my waist, the layers framing my face were soft. I was wearing an ankle bracelet of shells and my slender leather thong sandals were simple. I put on some mascara and some lip-gloss. It felt wonderful to be ready so quickly, to be comfortable with the way I looked without having to spend an hour getting ready. Tammy lay on her bed watching me, still in her beach gear, while Trish showered.

"Jeez, you look good, mate," she said, brazenly open in her admiration.

I grinned and met her eyes in the reflection of the mirror.

"I'll never forget that pale, tired-looking girl we met, her eyes all red from crying, and looking all wild and lost."

This was an epic sentence for Tammy and I stared at her. She'd never spoken of the time we'd first met before.

"Jeez, we felt really sorry for ya," she smiled, "not in a bad way, like you were a loser. Just y'know, you looked lost and lonely."

I nodded and sat down on the end of her bed.

"I was. I was really scared."

I wanted to tell her that she and Trish had been my saviours, my guardian angels. But that old British reserve kicked in and I couldn't. I felt embarrassed and played with the leather bracelet around my wrist.

"And now look at you. All tanned and thin and gorgeous," she patted her belly. "Jeez look at me. Pity the travelling hasn't made me lose a few kilos. But seriously you really have got over him haven't ya?"

I smiled and thought about it. I thought about Rich and his boyish grin, and I felt fondness, and a sort of regret. But there was no longer the gut-wrenching twist in my heart when his face filled my mind. I nodded.

"Yeah. Yeah, I think I have. A bit anyway."

"So what about when you go home?"

I laughed a little nervously.

"One step at a time. I'll think about that when the time comes. I'm just getting used to life on my own at the moment. Being at home with all the familiar things, and our mutual friends, well that will be the hard bit. And who knows Rich may still be in Thailand. I don't know where he is."

And I realised that I didn't really care all that much. She nodded, her china-blue eyes watching me.

"But I'm not home, am I?" I asked happily. "I'm here and I'm with great mates."

I patted her foot affectionately.

"Ah get off you lezza," she cackled.

There was a knock at the front door as Trish emerged from the bathroom with a tiny travel towel around her. I opened the door and found Charlie standing there with his habitual spliff hanging from the corner of his mouth.

"So who's ready?" he drawled. His eyes flickered over Trish's long tanned legs, "nice legs Trish."

"Fuck off perv," she fired back but I could tell she was pleased.

"Only me, Prince Charming," I said holding the door wide.

"Well, there's a party down at the beach, at some other beach bar. Fancy checkin' it out? We can have a drink; these guys can follow on later."

"Where's Tuna?" I asked.

"Still in the shower, the girl. But he knows where we're going. He said he'll follow us."

I nodded.

"Sure," I agreed.

"It's just further on down the beach from Eve," Charlie called out to the girls. "You can't miss it. There'll be a gorgeous guy with dreads sitting on the beach outside."

Tammy threw a cushion at the door as he hurriedly pulled it shut behind us.

We walked down to the beach, talking amiably as we reached the sand. The last light of the day faded to an inky blue as we passed Eve and carried on along the shore. All of the other beach bars had closed down for the night. With Cambodia and Sihanoukville still being relatively new to tourism, Eve had the monopoly on most of the visitors, being so conveniently located, and more importantly, being the first bar mentioned in the Lonely Planet.

We reached a small beach bar that still had its lights on and chill out music playing. But there was no sign of a party. A lone barman stood behind the wooden bar, a couple of guys rocked in hammocks, and a young Khmer girl breast-fed her baby on the sand.

"Wow," I murmured, "some party."

"It'll kick off later," Charlie assured me, taking my hand and leading me to the bar. It felt strange feeling his fingers wrapped in mine. His hand was big and warm and dry.

He ordered us two beers, and we went and sat on the sand watching a bonfire that had been lit in the hope of attracting customers.

There was a strange awkwardness between us that hadn't existed before. I tried to remember the last time we had been alone apart from the beach that day. I stole glances at his side profile. He was ridiculously handsome. If he shaved his dreads off, he would look like a Calvin Klein model. But one that hadn't shaved for a few weeks, and who had smoked and drunk himself to oblivion every night for the last five years.

"So where are you planning to go next, Ruby? After Cambodia I mean."

I was caught off guard. I hadn't thought much beyond Christmas. I knew that Tammy and Trish were heading to Vietnam for a month before heading back to Australia, and I had a vague idea of going with them. After Vietnam I had no idea. The plan had been to fly to Australia with Rich and travel for a few months there. But could I go without him? Australia was so far away. And Tammy and Trish wouldn't want to travel around with me. They would have jobs and lives to go back to. Maybe it would be time for me to go home then. I shuddered at the thought and pushed it to the back of my mind. I shrugged.

"There it goes again," he murmured looking at my face intently.

"What?" I asked.

"That shutter that falls down over your eyes."

I looked at Charlie in surprise. He wasn't normally so eloquent or shrewd in his observations.

"Sorry," I shrugged and gave a small wry smile, "I just haven't decided yet. My trip plans have changed considerably since leaving home. What about you?"

He shrugged.

"You know me, no plan. I just go with the flow. I might go to Vietnam with Tammy and Trish. Those girls are a good laugh. But I also fancy heading on down to Malaysia and Indonesia. The world is our oyster Ruby, as they say."

I looked up at the stars and knew he was right. I had no ties, no commitments. Why not just enjoy this for as long as I could? I would have to go back one day and pick up where I left off. Why not delay it for as long as possible?

We sat on the sand chatting for a while, Charlie supplying us with new drinks while we waited for other customers and partygoers that didn't come.

Suddenly, Charlie jumped to his feet and dragged me with him. He had spotted something on the beach down by the water and he ran towards it pulling me by the hand.

"Brilliant," he said as excited as a puppy, "Fire ropes."

There were two ropes lying on the sand waiting for a fire dancer to do their display later on in the evening. There was a bucket of kerosene sitting next to them. Charlie dipped the ends of the ropes into it and lit them with is lighter. Two balls of flame swirled around the ends of the rope. He began to swing them around his head, a cigarette clamped between his lips.

"It's harder than it looks," he muttered through clenched teeth.

I laughed as I watched him bang himself on his back more than once with the rope. Each time he was quick enough to swing it away hurriedly so his clothes didn't catch fire.

"Let me have a go," I said kicking off my sandals.

I started to swing the ropes in a wide circle, and Charlie was right, they were really hard to control. I giggled uncontrollably as I swung a bit too hard and had to keep them going round and round and round, terrified I was going to hit myself in the face with them. Charlie lay on the sand laughing out loud as I managed to get the ropes completely wrapped around my middle.

"Shit," he shouted, jumping to his feet. "Your skirt Ruby! Your damn skirt!"

He yanked the ropes from my hand, and they unwrapped themselves from my waist as I rolled away from him. I glanced at the straggly gipsy ends of my dress to check I wasn't on fire, while Charlie stamped the ropes out on the sand.

"Jesus Christ, Ruby, what the hell were you trying to do?" he muttered chuckling and shaking his head as he stamped out the last flames.

I felt like an idiot, nearly setting myself on fire, and I turned to look at the sea. The wind whipped my hair out behind me and I felt a hand on my arm swinging me round. I was face to face with Charlie.

"There was no party," his voice was low.

"Well, I can see that," I said looking over his shoulder at the sleepy bar, "but it might pick up…"

"Will you just stop talking?"

"Um, well, um OK." I nodded.

"I brought you here because I wanted to get you alone," he said softly, "so I could do this."

He lowered his head towards mine until his breath was on my lips. And then he kissed me, pressing his warm lips on mine, and holding the back of my head in his hand. His tongue slid between my lips and before I knew it, I was kissing him back, slowly and warmly and comfortably. He smelled of soap so I knew he had showered just for this moment. The kiss was lovely and I melted into it for a moment. But that was it. It felt nice, and comfortable, and warm. But it felt just like kissing a friend. And there was another feeling bobbing around and trying to surface. And finally I put my finger on it. It was guilt. I assumed it was a left-over guilt from having been going out with Rich for so long. But then I realised it wasn't Rich's face that filled my mind. In my mind's eye I saw a pair of crystal blue eyes and a pursed, amused smile on a face that I wanted to look at all the time; a face that made my stomach lurch when its eyes turned upon me; the face of the man that I had fallen in love with.

I pushed Charlie away firmly but gently and, smiling softly at him, I shook my head.

"I'm sorry, Charlie," I said, "I can't do this. I'm in love with someone else."

He nodded.

"You're still not over Rich, are you?"

I shook my head and almost laughed with the wonderful absurdity of the notion.

"No, it's not that. It's not him."

He looked deep into my eyes and nodded slowly again. His eyes were dark and warm in the night, and he smiled.

"It's Tuna."

I nodded, my face breaking out into a big grin.

"I knew it when we first met him," he said, his hands still on my waist, "I knew when I saw him in the hammock that time in Laos. I could tell by the look on your face. I thought to myself, 'This is the guy; this guy is going to be my rival'. That's why I assumed he was Rich."

I shook my head.

"I didn't feel that way about him then," I protested but Charlie interrupted me, nodding his head.

"Oh yes you did, Ruby. Anyone with half a brain could see it, even me," he smiled wryly. "But despite myself, I grew to really like him. So it was a friendly rivalry."

He lifted his hand to brush back a tendril of my hair that was tickling my cheek in the breeze.

"I backed off because I was happy to step aside, when it was obvious how you felt about him. But since nothing has happened for so long, I began to think I had misread the signals. I began to think there was a chance for me."

I smiled back at him, my heart filling with love for him; but a good friend's love.

"You did have a chance you know. If I hadn't have already met Tuna, if he hadn't have been there for me the way he was, when Rich hurt me so badly...well, you would definitely have swept me off my feet," I narrowed my eyes mischievously, "with your rare showers, and your moaning about the establishment, and your chronic smoking and drinking habit. You really know how to win a woman over."

He pretended to look hurt and taken aback.

"I showered tonight!" he said indignantly.

"I am only teasing Charlie," I grinned, "you're hilariously funny, you're kind, you're free-spirited, you don't give a damn what people think about you and you're drop-dead gorgeous."

I kissed his cheek.

"But most of all, you're a real friend. Thank you, for making me feel so good about myself," I shook my head, "My friends would not believe I managed to get someone like you to fall for me. And hey, did you know I have a twin sister?"

Charlie's eyes lit up.

"Really?" His eyes lit up, and I knew he was half-serious, "What's her number?"

I laughed.

He pushed me away gently.

"Do me a favour," he said lighting a cigarette and taking a deep drag. "Go and put everyone out of their misery. Go and tell that lucky bloke how you feel about him, because believe me, he's waiting for it as desperately as the rest of us."

I grinned and felt a surge of excitement fill my body.

"What if he doesn't feel the same?" The dreadful thought was only just emerging through my elation.

Charlie looked at me and held my stare for a few moments.

"Well, you won't know until you try," he said, and nodded his head down the beach towards Eve. "Go on."

I flashed him a grin, and half ran and half skipped along the sand. I turned to look back at him, and he was at the bar with a drink in his hand, chatting to the bar man. I felt bad for Charlie, but I was under no pretence that he was in love with me, and I knew he would very quickly find himself a nice Khmer girl to keep him company now he had cleared the air with me. I thought about what it would have been like to be with him as I strolled along. We would have been lethal together, my drinking would have doubled again, and I seriously doubted Charlie was the faithful type.

I looked out at the stars, a million of them winking and shining above the dark water. I smiled and breathed in the fresh breeze that had picked up along the shore, and thought of Tuna's eyes, the pupils rimmed with silver flecks. I thought of his gentle smile, that sort of amused smile he gave me whenever I did or said anything stupid or silly. I thought about seeing him playing pool that night when we first arrived in Bangkok and how I had assumed he was just like Dazzer. I thought of him stroking my head as I lay in the hut in Pai, bringing me tea and talking to me soothingly. I thought of his body and felt a flush of heat fill my stomach; his toned arms with the tattoos; the rise of his chest and the dark hair that trailed down to his lean flat stomach and led further down past the line of his hips, disappearing into his low-slung shorts. I felt a surge of excitement. I almost squealed with expectation and nerves. I didn't know what I was going to say, but I was going to do it; I was going to be brave like Charlie and tell him that I had fallen long and hard and deeply head over heels in love with him. I picked up my walk to a jog and trotted along the beach.

The flickering light from the candles dotted on the tables outside Eve, cast weird dancing shadows along the beach. There were little crowds of people huddled around the tables; the music wafted to me on the breeze. *So Bruno felt like a chill-out night tonight*, I thought to myself, as the calming strains of *Café Del Mar* reached my ears. As I grew nearer, I began to strain my eyes to see our group. Thoughts raced through my mind; I had to do it straight away, or I would lose my courage. But how was I going to get Tuna to come away without letting on to everyone else? I studied the different groups of people and finally spotted Trish and Tammy sitting on the sand with a group of girls and a couple with their backs to me. I rushed towards them smiling and Tammy spotted me and raised her hand. She had a worried smile on her face as she waved. As I neared, my jog slowed to a walk, and my gaze fell on the couple. The man looked exactly like Tuna. He was wearing the same khaki green t-shirt as Tuna, he had the same short messy, sun-kissed hair, and the same lean back and shoulders that were highlighted by the t-shirt stretched over them as he clasped his arms around his knees. The girl sitting with him had white-blonde messy hair that curled around her shoulders and was scattered with small plaits. The strap of her loose sundress was falling off her shoulder and her arm was wrapped around the waist of the man.

I looked around the crowd for Tuna. Where was he? I glanced towards the bar. I turned to face the group, glancing down to my left at the couple, and my mouth opened but words didn't come out. It felt like someone had kicked me in the stomach.

The man who was part of the couple, and who looked so much like Tuna, *was* Tuna. He was looking at the girl sitting next to him and smiling. The girl with her arm around him was Karla, the girl he'd met in Ko Pha Nang all those months ago.

"Look who's here!" Tammy said in a too-bright voice.

"Hey, Ruby," Trish said, watching me closely.

Tuna's head swung around to look up at me from where he was sitting. His eyes were shining in the candlelight.

"Hey, Ruby," he said cheerily, "you remember Karla?"

With an almighty effort I dragged a smile onto my face and met her eyes. She looked as pretty as ever, and was smiling happily up at me, her ice-blue eyes sparkling, her tanned little nose scattered with freckles.

"Hi, Ruby," she said warmly, "you have recovered from your hangover, yes?"

I forced a laugh.

"Yes, thanks, Karla. All better now. How are you? Have you had a good trip?"
"Yes, very good, thank you."
"When did you get here?" I asked in a quiet voice.
"Just today, yes?" She glanced at her two friends, identikit pretty blondes with dark tans.
They nodded happily.
"And I was very happy when I see Tuna here," she looked at him grinning. "We have lots of catching up, yes?"
I could see the dimple in his cheek as he looked down at the sand, so I knew he was smiling.
"Where have you been?" Trish asked me as an awkward silence descended on the group.
"Oh, just along the beach with Charlie. That party didn't come to much," I rubbed at my forehead, which was clammy, "and I'm not feeling too good. So I think I'm going to have an early night."
I made a quick exit, not looking at Tuna and waving vaguely at the group as I stumbled away. When I reached the point where the sand met the road, I glanced over my shoulder. Tuna's and Karla's heads were close together in conversation. I turned and ran up the road.
I found myself in front of a computer for the first time in weeks. All I wanted to do was to finally tell Steph, my best friend, everything that had happened; Rich, Tuna, Charlie, Karla, everything. I logged on and found a very full Inbox.

From: welshhottie@yahoo.co.uk
To: Rube99@hotmail.com
Subject: The whole world is falling apart…

Where the fuck are you Ruby?! Because everything is going fucking mental here and I'm the only sensible one it seems in this bloody family – God help us.
Dad has left mam and run off to Spain. You know we thought mam was having affair? Well, turns out she wasn't, just REALLY likes her job, and so spent all time in work. So Dad felt neglected, packed it all in and ran off to Spain. Is apparently running bistro in La Manga.
Weirdest thing is mam went to pieces. She cried for three days solid, and would not let me go out. Ever. Anywhere. Had to call in sick for her. Kept going on about Dad being love of her life and other such crap. Bit sick making, but felt a bit sorry for her to tell the truth.
To top it off, am convinced that you have been seduced by the charms of opium and are wallowing in a drug den somewhere. Or have been eaten by tigers.

Bloody well email me and let me know am not alone in all this madness (and that you are OK).

Jess

From: jeffmjones65@aol.co.uk
To: Rube99@hotmail.com
Subject: Hello

Dear Ruby

You may have heard from your mother by now that i have left home. Ihave movved to Spain to run my own bistro. Your mother and I had not been makin each other happy for a while, Sadly I think she fell out of love with me a long time e agoo and i am sure she willl be happier without me. Youknow that I have long had a dream to cook and so I thought this would be the perfectt opportunity to follow that dream.you were my inspiration going off around the world like that. Evvven if it was not your dream you had the courage to support Richard in his dream.

I hope that this is nottoo much of a shockto you and maybe when you come back you can comeand visit me and we cann talk all this over properly. Its wonderfulhere but lonely withouttt my girls.

Love, as always, Dad.

I sat back in my chair in shock, trying to take it all in. Reliable, loving, ordinary Dad had run off to Spain. I shook my head, refusing to believe it. I thought of Dad's grey jumpers, and his tired, soft eyes, and the fluffy hair on his head. I thought about how distant he and Mum had become over the last few years and realised it wasn't that much of a shock after all. Dragging my eyes away from Dad's email, I flicked back to my inbox. Although I was completely stunned by Dad and Jess's emails, there were more to be read.

From: babygirlsteph@hotmail.com
To: Rube99@hotmail.com
Subject: Help!

Oh God Rube, I think I am going to kill myself. Either that or die from a broken heart. Mark finished with me. You know he said he was going to wait until Christmas and then leave his wife? Well, he chickened out! He came to see me last Saturday and said he couldn't do it to her or the kids. I am such a sucker. I can't believe I fell for it. Since he dumped me, Nerys on the helpdesk told me that he has been sending her dirty emails. I spent an hour in the loo in work crying. He's a bastard I know, and you were right, I shouldn't have got involved. But I love him so much and it hurts so much! What am I going to do? Wish you were here!

Steph ☹

P.S. Where are you?!

From: misskitten@yahoo.com
To: Rube99@hotmail.com
Subject:

Ruby

Frankly I was a bit upset about your reaction to this guy I am falling for, but I guess I can understand it. I never took you for the judgemental type, and thought you would have supported me through this. I know that affairs are wrong, but they do happen Ruby, all the time, all over the world, and quite often it's for the best. People make mistakes and I am far from perfect. As far as Tim is concerned, you were right and it is my feelings for him that have stopped me from taking this 'thing', whatever it is, any further.

Anyway, enough about me. Have you heard from Steph? She is utterly devastated, because that shit of a boss of hers dumped her. She is inconsolable, and I am quite honestly at the end of my tether with my love triangle, and feeling very confused and in need of a break. So I have booked a holiday for Steph and me to Thailand. She doesn't know yet and she will have no say in it, but I know she would love it (and so would I, even though you hate me) if you could try and meet up with us? We are arriving in Bangkok on the 20th December and have booked a hotel in a place called Railey – have you heard of it? It's supposed to be stunningly beautiful.

I must admit I am also a little worried about you, and I get the impression that there is something going on with you that you are not telling us about. So I want to check up on you while we are there as well.

Lata x

From: lataandTim69@yahoo.com
To: Rube99@hotmail.com
Subject: Hi

Hi Ruby

It's Tim here. I'm writing to you because I don't know who else to ask. Lata has been a bit weird lately and really off with me. I am not sure if I have done anything wrong and she won't tell me. She snaps every time I try and ask her. Has she mentioned anything to you?

I had this idea that I have been thinking about for a long time – I was thinking of proposing to her at Christmas time, but I am not sure if it's a good idea. What do you think?

Hope all is well with you and your travels are exciting.

Tim

From: welshhottie@yahoo.co.uk
To: Rube99@hotmail.com
Subject: Am going to kill mam!

Rube

Mam is a nightmare. Preferred her when she was bitch from hell! Now is moping doormat from hell. Lies in bed, smoking and only getting up to eat soup. Bloody Dad.

Mind you, don't blame him after the crap he put up with from mam for so long. Maybe now will realise what she had.

Come home!

Jess

From: babygirlsteph@hotmail.com
To: Rube99@hotmail.com
Subject: OMG

Ruby!!!

Lata booked us a holiday! I don't want to go in case Mark tries to get in touch with me, but I am so excited about seeing you! PLEASE please please please come and meet us! I think it will be the only thing that will stop me from committing suicide.

Steph xxxxxxxxxxxxxxxxxxx

I sat and stared at the screen. I looked out of the window of the small internet café. I could see the candle lights on the beach at the bottom of the hill. I could see tiny flickers of flame flying around like fireflies as Bruno did his fire dancing. I thought of Tuna with Karla's arm around his shoulders, their golden heads close together in the flickering lights.

I quickly opened a cheap flights' website and booked myself onto a flight to Bangkok from Phnom Penh for the following evening. Then I went back to my guesthouse and booked myself on the dawn bus to Phnom Penh for the next morning. Running away had solved my problems once. So why shouldn't it work again?

Part Four
Thailand

Chapter Twenty-Seven

I felt the warmth filter through my skin and into my bones as the sun baked me. Another beach, another azure sea, but this time with weird, turquoise-green limestone rocks towering out of the sparkling water in the sparkling bay – a bit phallic as Lata had commented on our first day here. Railey was one of the most beautiful places I had ever been to. It was a small peninsula stretching away from the mainland with spectacular beaches on all sides. We were staying in the backpacker area on Tonsai beach that consisted of wooden and thatched bungalows dotted amongst towering palm tree groves. Laid-back, rickety, wooden bars lazed along the beach which had bronze sand. Although Tonsai beach was pretty, it wasn't quite as impressive as the main beaches further around the small peninsula, so we strolled most days to one of the other beaches that were favoured by the five star resorts. The jewel in the crown of Railey was Hat Pra Nhang beach, with its sheltered ivory sand, unusual, coral-coloured caves at either end of the beach and an enormous, jade-coloured rock jutting out of the milky blue sea. Lata and Steph gazed at the beach open-mouthed when we first arrived, but I had smiled smugly; I had seen so many of these beautiful beaches by now that I accepted them as the norm.

"Bloody beats the Costa del Sol," Steph muttered as we traipsed along the burning sand looking for the perfect spot to settle ourselves down.

We noticed on the first day a woman lying on the beach, tanned to the colour of an old shoe. She was lying in an odd position in a very tiny bikini, almost like the recovery position but on her back, with one leg hoiked up so her right foot rested on her opposite inner thigh and her knee was flopped down to the sand. The view all in all was rather unappetising. Steph gawped open-mouthed.

"Has she died?" she whispered loudly.

I shrugged and hurried past trying to avert my eyes from the mound of her pink-lycra'd crotch. We lay not far from her, and Steph's eyes kept straying towards the orange woman.

"I think she must be at least in her seventies," she hissed.

"You'd be surprised sweetie, she's probably only about nineteen. You know what sun damage can do to you," Lata drawled from under her floppy sunhat, "especially you and your baby pink complexion."

A curious beeping noise made us all glance towards the woman. She reached into her beach bag, pulled out a small alarm clock, pressed a button to stop it and replaced it again. Then she straightened her left leg and hitched her left leg up in the same position her other one had been in moments before.

"Bloody hell," Steph murmured in awe, "she's timing her tanning."

I pressed my face into my beach towel to try to muffle my laughter.

"If I ever end up like that girls, please put me down," Lata purred, stretching out her golden limbs in the sun.

Every day it became a bit of a ritual to see what body part the woman was tanning that day. It had been wonderful to see Lata and Steph and we hadn't stopped talking since we'd met, screaming and flapping our arms, in Bangkok airport. I had been secretly very pleased and smug when they almost walked past me in the airport. Lata had given me a double look and then stopped in her tracks, her *Louis Vuitton* pull-along case bumping into the backs of her calves.

"Bloody hell," she said and Steph turned to look at me. Her mouth dropped open.

"Ruby?!"

I grinned and nodded as their eyes travelled over my floaty lilac skirt, my skimpy white vest and my hair in loose curls around my shoulders.

Steph threw her arms around me and cried.

"You look utterly gorgeous darling," Lata said silkily, still a little reserved after our email tiff. Steph nodded happily.

"You do. You look so skinny," she breathed, "and brown! And I love your hair like that."

Then she burst into tears and we had to lead her to a taxi as she sobbed her way through the whole story of Mark. The days since then had been filled with mindless, numbing, lovely wonderful gossipy chat about rubbish that didn't demand intellect or digging around into horrible feelings. We just relished being together again.

I let them think at first that I had left Rich in Cambodia and that I was going to meet up with him again after they left. But on the second night while we were sitting at a small beach bar on the sand, I finally admitted to them what had happened with Rich in Pai. They listened in shocked silence to the whole thing. I explained how Trish and Tammy had felt like my saviours in those first few days; I told them about the friends I had made along the way, and how I was finally feeling like I was over Rich.

Finally, I stopped talking and toyed with the umbrella in my drink as Steph stared at me open-mouthed. Then she moved around the table, sat next to me on the sand, put her arms around me and gave me a huge hug.

"You poor thing," she whispered. "Why didn't you tell us?"

"I felt so stupid," I felt tears burn my eyes at her touch, the touch of a friend who has known all of your fears and disappointments. "I was so humiliated. And the enormity of coming home alone was just too much."

"But you must have been so scared going off on your own," she pulled back to look into my eyes.

I shrugged and nodded.

"I was confused and hurt and just wanted to get away. From everything."

Lata was watching me shrewdly.

"So if you're over him, why do you still have that little-girl-lost look?" she asked in a soft voice.

Steph looked from her to me and back to Lata again. And then Lata's eyes opened wide.

"There's someone else!" She hissed. Step's eyes widened as well. I couldn't help the silly grin that spread across my face.

"Who? Who is it?!" Lata leaned forward across the low table, "Tell us!"

I shook my head.

"Come on!"

"Well, I don't know if you remember me emailing you about some of Rich's friends that we met in Bangkok…."

"Tuna!" Steph and Lata both said at the same time. I looked at them in shock.

"I liked the sound of him from the start," Steph nodded.

"And he always seemed to pop up in your emails," Lata added, "The one you thought was a yob and ended up being kind and caring and intelligent. But I don't understand. If he was with you in Pai, and you left there – what – three months ago? Then how…?"

I smiled looking down at the sand.

"We met up again, in Laos. And we've been travelling together ever since."

Lata whooped with joy and clapped her hands.

"Take that Rich, you little shit!"

Steph was beaming.

"So where is he?" she asked breathlessly, "I want to meet him."

My smile faded a little and I shook my head.

"Unfortunately, it was unrequited," I said quietly, "I…well…let's just say I was too late. He met someone else, before I realised what was there right under my nose."

Both girls looked crestfallen and didn't say anything. Lata reached out and touched my arm with perfectly manicured fingers.

"I'm sorry, sweetheart," she said softly, "Maybe it's for the best."

I nodded and forced a smile onto my face, trying to banish the silvery eyes that flashed into my mind, laughing in the sun. I looked at my two friends beside me and grinned. And then the smiling faces of my new friends, of Trish and Tammy and Charlie's, flashed into my mind's eye and I felt a stab of guilt at having run away and left them. I pushed their smiling faces away quickly.

"But you're here," I said, "and I am *so* happy about that. And I have another major drama that I have to worry about anyway. My father ran off to Spain…"

***

The days rolled into each other, waking late, eating pancakes for breakfast, strolling to one of the beaches, lolling in the sun all day, only moving for a cooling dip in the sea, or a furtive glance at Orange Woman to see what part of her anatomy she was tanning today. The evenings would be taken up by lots of pampering, applying of make-up and then the consumption of alcohol – which had dramatically increased again. I felt awful in the mornings and my thoughts would often stray to the clear-headed mornings I had grown used to experiencing; rising at dawn and excited about a new day and its adventures. I was happy to see the girls. I was having fun and I was doing the kind of thing I used to love doing; yet, I felt empty. My days felt pointless. Steph was absorbed in her own misery over Mark but Lata could see that I wasn't myself. I would feel her eyes on me when I was staring out to sea, or when I didn't join in one of their conversations about a gorgeous guy that walked past. If I met her stare, she would smile at me comfortingly, and I would make an almighty effort to smile back.

But my thoughts would be far, far away swaying on a hammock overlooking the river that meandered through the Four Thousand Islands; or on the back of a bike with the wind in my hair, winding through the streets of Phnom Penh, the golden spires of the palace glinting in the sun; or floating down the Mekong on a tube watching the craggy, karst hills rise majestically from the water; or sitting on top of a crumbling temple in a twilit jungle watching the sun set. And all too often my thoughts would return to Tuna's smiling face, to the day he looked after me when I came off the motorbike; or to seeing his face over my shoulder when I sat astride an elephant in the jungle in Pai; or to the grip of his hand on my arm when he heaved me out of the water when I fell off the raft; or to the firm softness of his hug when he held me while my heart was breaking and my world was falling apart around me. And then my thoughts would switch to Karla and her round, cherubic face looking up at him. And I would see them entwined in sheets, giggling and rolling about, his hands in her messy sexy hair. I just knew she was one of those people that wore loads of mascara and was too sluttish to take it off before going to bed but wouldn't wake up with panda eyes in the morning. And she would never have one of those hair days where you've just slept on it funny on one side of your head so it looks flat and a bit like Herman Munster. No, she was the sexy, tousled, bed-hair type…I punished myself with these thoughts daily.

The days were bright and beautiful and clear, but they seemed grey and one-dimensional without Tuna's smile to light them. I didn't have that sense of ragged loss that I had when Rich left me, because Tuna had never been mine to lose. But I mourned him. And I missed him so much that it was almost a physical pain, a dull throb in my chest whenever I realised he wasn't going to turn up at my door to go to dinner, or I wasn't going to be able to slip my arms around his waist as we sailed along palm-lined roads on a motorbike, or I wasn't going to see him laughing silently as I attempted to eat rice with chopsticks and end up giving up and tipping it into my mouth straight from the bowl when I thought nobody was looking…

"He must have been some guy," Lata's voice made me jump as it broke into my thoughts. "You haven't spoken for about an hour and yet I can tell a million thoughts are racing through your mind."

I turned to look at her propped against a palm tree trunk. We had a favourite spot that we came to each day, which was sheltered from the rest of the beach and the other small groups of tourists that preferred the end of the beach nearer to the drink sellers, and hotels. There was a small grove of palm trees but other than that there wasn't much shade, hence the presence of the orange lady who liked this little sun trap too.

Lata was wearing a white tunic that fell open almost to her waist; a bronze coloured string bikini that highlighted her model-toned stomach when she took off her top; oversized Jackie O' glasses and a cream, floppy straw hat over her silky black hair which was pinned up and had tendrils falling down around her slender neck. She looked cool, unruffled and like something out of a Bacardi advert. I, on the other hand, had odd pink patterns where my new bikini that I had treated myself to, revealed patches of skin that hadn't been exposed to the sun before. I had become carried away with my new streamline self and bought a daringly skimpy bikini, but now I just looked pink and ridiculous. I pushed myself more into the shade to protect myself from the sun's glare and sighed.

"Yeah," I nodded, "he really was."

I looked up at beautiful Lata with her book open on her lap and felt a rush of love and shame.

"I'm sorry I was so judgemental, Lata, about what happened with this other guy," I said haltingly, "I was just so hurt by what Rich did to me, that the thought of you doing that same thing to Tim was just intolerable. I know that things are different for everyone, and I didn't know the full story and…well, I'm sorry."

She gave me a small smile.

"I know, I understand it now," she sighed. "It has made me think long and hard about things."

"You haven't mentioned it since we got here."

"Well, you know, Steph and Mark and you and Rich…my infidelity seemed to fade in comparison."

She stared out to sea.

"My God, I want this guy," she muttered, "he's just so…so…delicious."

I nodded, my thoughts straying to Tuna's narrow, lean waist, his shorts hanging dangerously low from his hips, the line of muscle running along the edge of his stomach.

"I think I have to see it through, Ruby," Lata said decisively, "Because otherwise how am I going to know? I will always be wondering what if?"

My heart ached at the thought of Tim and how hurt he would be, but I knew that sometimes you just have to let people make their own mistakes and then be there for them in the fallout; because she would only go ahead and make the mistake anyway but secretly without telling anyone.

"Good God," Lata said laughing suddenly as she stared out to sea, "she never fails to amaze me. What is it do you think? The little-girl-lost thing? The baby-blue eyes?"

I turned onto my back to look down towards the sea to see what Lata was talking about. Steph was walking up from the water, surrounded by three men, who, from where we were lying, looked rather nice.

As they got nearer, we could see that one of them, with wild blonde hair, was clearly the favourite as her smiling face was turned towards him, while the other two walked slightly a step behind checking out her small, pert bottom in its pale-blue bikini.

Her red hair looked dark as it snaked down her neck because it was dripping wet like her body which consequently meant her bikini was slightly see-through and her erect nipples poked through the thin material like beacons. Her chosen guy was clearly struggling to wrench his eyes up to her face. As they neared, the other two guys realised that there was other potential female company when they spotted us, and so politely dragged their eyes away from Steph's posterior. She turned to us beaming.

"Lata, Ruby, you'll never believe this, but these guys are from the UK!"

But I wasn't taking her words in, because as her chosen guy moved in front of the sun so that I was no longer dazzled and I could see his face, I realised that it was one I knew very well. And by the startled expression on his face, I could see that he recognised me as well.

"Fookin 'ell," he spluttered before bounding forward, "Tom mate! It's fookin' Ruby!"

I couldn't stop the grin spread across my face as I got to my feet and he flung his arms around me like an old friend. I never thought I would *ever* have been happy to see Dazzer. Then I felt some more arms around me, and Tom was hugging me too.

"Jesus Ruby," Tom said happily, smiling into my face, "what the hell happened to you? I mean you just buggered off in Pai..."

His words faltered, and the smile on his face lost some of its radiance. I saw Dazzer glance nervously at him. I gave him a big reassuring smile.

"It's OK Tom, I realised what a great big prick Rich is and decided to do it alone."

Tom burst out laughing and slapped me on the back, nearly forcing my shoulder blades out through my chest, clearly relieved to have the awkward moment dispersed.

His mate, who was a tall Indian guy, had jet-black hair, laughing eyes, impossibly white, straight teeth, and a dazzling smile. He hadn't yet taken his eyes off Lata. He coughed politely.

"Sorry girls, this is our mate," Tom indicated the dazzling guy behind him, "His name's..."

"Don't tell me, Tiddler? Toto? Tosser?"

I had meant it as a joke, but the words came out viciously and dazzling-man's smile faltered a little. Tom looked taken aback and confused. Dazzer looked at me frowning disapprovingly.

"No need to be rude, Ruby," he smiled politely. "His name's Razzer."

I snorted through my nose, while everyone looked at me amused and very confused.

We all went out for dinner that night, and Tom and I were very clearly the joint raspberries. Razzer and Lata were wrapped up assuredly in each other's perfection, and Dazzer and Steph didn't stop giggling all night. I couldn't believe the enraptured expression on Dazzer's face as he gazed at Steph in wonder. *Amazement that she's paying him any attention at all*, I thought nastily to myself. Actually, I thought, studying him, he looked pretty good. His hair wasn't quite as wild, and he was looking fit, and had lost the paunch he'd had when I first met him, and with a tan, his eyes looked very blue. And when he smiled, he did look kind of boyishly good-looking. Tom and I glanced at each other and he smiled shyly.

"Looks like it's just you and me," he said, and then looked horrified and spluttered, "I...I mean, you know, not just you and me in that way..."

I laughed.

"Don't be daft, Tom. So what happened to Mali?"

A dreamy expression came over his face.

"Well, she had to carry on working, y'know, so I decided to come down here for a few weeks, and when Spazz goes home after Christmas, I'm going to go back up to Chiang Mai to see her. I'm extending my ticket."

At the mention of Pai, Tom got a wild, nervous look in his eyes and he started to fidget.

"It's OK, Tom; I'm over all that now."

He sighed a sigh of relief.

"Tuna was really chuffed he bumped into you again," he said.

I looked at him quickly and my stomach lurched.

"Really? He told you?"

He nodded in surprise.

"'course. He emails me every week or so. Told me what you've been up to," he fidgeted with his shorts again. "Told me about your new guy. Y'know Charlie or something."

I frowned at him.

"My new guy? Charlie?" I shook my head, "He's just a friend."

He turned the corners of his mouth down.

"Tuna said you were pretty friendly and well…" he hesitated and then shrugged his shoulders, "Well, I may as well tell you, now you're no longer travelling with him. He was pretty gutted to be honest. He's liked you for ages – you should have seen the way he acted when you disappeared. He was really worried about you man, haven't seen him like that before."

My heart was suddenly soaring and hammering in my chest. Tom's words echoed in my head – *he's liked you for ages…*

"You know he hit Rich, don't you?"

My eyes nearly popped out of their sockets.

"What?"

He nodded seriously.

"After you left, he went to tell Rich that you'd gone and Rich just didn't care – sorry," he added quickly but I shook my head impatiently, "and he just got so mad he clocked him one."

I burst out laughing. Lata and Steph shot me a glance, annoyed that I was interrupting their respective tête-à-têtes.

"What did Rich do?"

Tom snorted and then guffawed.

"He actually cried! And that stupid girl he was with, Nicola or whatever her name was, tried to hit Tuna back but he just walked away while she ran after him slapping him on his back!"

He looked at me warily.

"I never liked Rich much you know. Tuna and I both wondered what the hell you were doing with him."

I glowed. Rich not good enough for me? I had always thought that I was lucky to have landed someone like him; I was under the impression that everyone else thought so too. That may have been because Rich would subtly remind me of this now and again – that *he* had noticed me when nobody else had; that *he* could see my beauty; that he no longer wanted to go out with the obviously good looking girls anymore, because they were big-headed/needy/boring. Funny how I had never seen the compliments as backhanded before. I had just felt grateful that I had a boyfriend who could see the real me, who could see past my boring looks. I mean I was OK looking but I wasn't in Rich's league. Was I?

"Really, you thought that?" I asked in surprise.

He nodded and frowned.

"'course. I mean, Rich is quite a good-looking guy – not that I'm gay or nothing," he added hastily, before looking awkwardly down at the ground, "but you're lovely."

I couldn't keep the smile off my face.

"Thank you, Tom."

"Tuna was really into you," he added.

"I don't believe it," I murmured.

Tom nodded.

"He never made a move, because when you were in Pai, you were obviously really cut up over Rich, and then when he met up with you again, you were with Charlie."

"But I wasn't!" I spluttered. "We were just friends. Charlie was into me, but I just wanted to be friends with him. And I told him that."

I suddenly got defensive.

"Anyway, when I left Sihanoukville, Tuna was pretty cosy with Karla."

Tom frowned at me in confusion.

"Karla?"

"That Swedish girl he met in Ko Pha Ngan. You know, pretty, blonde, curvy."

A goofy grin broke out across his face.

"Ah yeah, she was fit," he said gazing into the candle flame, "cute smile, big…"

I raised my eyebrows.

"Uh, yeah sorry," he said seriously, "well, he didn't sleep with her in Ko Pha Ngan, because of you."

"What?" I stared at him in amazement, "But that was before I even broke up with Rich!"

Tom nodded and shrugged his shoulders.

"I know. I told him he was mad. You and Rich seemed so together, and this girl basically lay down on her back and offered it to 'im – sorry," he made a sheepish face, "She made it clear what she wanted. I mean she actually did a striptease for him…"

I raised my hands feeling my gut wrench.

"OK, thanks, I don't need the details, Tom."

"Well, anyway, he turned her down. Said he liked you too much," he shrugged. "He's a one-woman man is Tuna."

I thought of Tuna and Karla giggling by the fire when I last saw them.

"Well, he was with her when I left Cambodia."

He shrugged.

"Maybe he just had enough of waiting for you. I mean, you don't feel the same way as him, so he needs to move on. A good shag will probably get him on the way…"

I stared at him, the horrible truth dawning.

"But I *do* feel the same way as him, Tom! Oh God. I really screwed up."

He was looking at me astonished.

"You like Tuna? I mean *like* like him?"

Oh God, were we five? I nodded irritably.

"Yes. But I think he may have seen Charlie and me together and got the wrong idea," I said groaning. "I was going to go and tell him how I felt; I was all fired up to do it. But when I found him, he was sitting there all cosy with Karla. And…well, I ran away again."

"Again?"

I nodded.

"You seem to be making a habit of that. Did you tell him you were going?"

I shook my head and lay back on the sand.

"No, I just ran off. Got on the bus the next day and came down here. He must hate me. He must think I am a complete cow. First of all snogging Charlie and then running off without a word again."

I twisted my hands in my hair in anguish.

"So you *were* with Charlie? I mean you were snogging him?"

"No! Well, yes, but *he* kissed *me*! But I told him I was in love with Tuna," I groaned and curled into foetal ball. "What a mess!"

I was aware of startled stares coming from people sitting around other tables. Tom awkwardly stroked my hair.

"It's OK," he mouthed to the onlookers before making a little circle in the air by his head and going cross-eyed.

I groaned again and finally managed to gain the attention of my two best friends.

"Rube!" Steph gasped, edging over the sand towards me. "What's the matter?"

I groaned and buried my face in the sand.

Tom relayed the story to her quickly, in boys' language.

"Tuna fancies her; she fancies Tuna. She got off with Charlie; Tuna saw them so he went off with Karla – who is really fit with big jugs – and so Ruby ran away, and now realises her mega mistake and boo hoo!" He even rubbed at his eyes with curled fists as if he was crying.

"Thanks for that detailed and sympathetic rundown of my tragic mess, Tom," I said sarcastically forcing myself to sit up, and spitting sand out of my mouth.

"S'alright," he said amiably.

"Well," Lata said dragging herself away from Razzer's side, "it's OK. Why don't you email Tuna tomorrow and tell him how you feel and try to arrange to meet up?"

I felt a spark of hope that was quickly extinguished.

"Because he's probably tangled up in bed with big-jugged Karla," the thought of it made me dry-heave loudly.

Razzer looked startled. I saw Dazzer lean towards him.

"She's a bit of a basket-case," he whispered loudly.

I shot him an evil look and he shrunk back into the shadows.

"Yeah, probably," Tom said nodding thoughtfully, agreeing with me about Karla. Lata shot him an evil look.

"Actually he's probably not you know," he changed his mind quickly.

I looked at him witheringly and he shrugged, looking a bit terrified.

"Well, you can't blame him if he is," he murmured. I got to my feet, stalked off to the bar, bought a triple gin and tonic and a bottle of tequila, and proceeded to get completely hammered.

Chapter Twenty-Eight

The next few days were miserable. Steph, of course, slept with Dazzer on the first night. Unfortunately, they were sharing the room next to ours, and the bed was placed next to our wall which was paper-thin so we could hear every awful detail.

I then had to endure detail by excruciating detail from her the next day. I didn't want to think of Dazzer humping away like a rabbit. I kept trying not to retch as she told me, and nodded my head happily, trying to look pleased and excited for her. They disappeared off down the beach together to try and shag wherever they could, whenever they could. I even approached them in the sea once, and realised as I got nearer, that Steph, with her arms wrapped around his shoulders, was moving jerkily up and down, and they looked at me like startled rabbits when they saw me. I made a hasty exit. Lata on the other hand, hadn't slept with Razzer, but still spent every spare minute talking about him.

I gazed at orange lady as she got onto all fours on her towel and pointed her skinny saggy bottom up to the sun.

"So she doesn't get those little white wrinkles in the folds of her bum," Steph explained to me in a hoarse whisper – hoarse from all the screaming and moaning she'd been doing.

"Doesn't he have just the most perfect smile?" Lata cooed, watching Razzer laugh as he chatted to Tom down by the sea. "And those eyes; so black, so deep, you could just fall into them."

I watched orange woman push her bum even further into the air.

"And his hands – have you noticed his hands? They are so perfect," Lata purred.

"So I take it your office fling guy is out of the window," I said nastily.

Lata looked stung and disconcertingly confused. Lata was the most sure-of-herself person I knew and I suddenly felt guilty.

"Well..." she said slowly, "meeting Razzer is making me wonder if this is really all about that guy, or whether the problem is actually between Tim and I."

I put my hand over hers as she stared down at the sand.

"I'm sorry," I said, "I don't mean to be a bitch. I'm just a bit...fed up."

I felt the tears sting my eyes.

"Why don't you just email him?" She said softly. "You don't *know* he's with Karla. And you may just be letting him slip through your fingers for nothing. Or get Tom to mention you're here..."

"No! I already made Tom swear under pain of death that he wasn't going to tell him," I said sharply. I had actually told him that I would tell Tuna he had told me about his feelings for me first (and also that I would tell Dazzer he was gay and had fancied Rich) if he mentioned anything to Tuna. He had agreed unhappily to keep his mouth shut.

"I couldn't face another humiliation Lata," I said thinking of how I had felt in Pai, "I couldn't stand getting my hopes up either and being let down again."

Lata nodded and wisely dropped the subject.

***

Finally, Christmas Day arrived. Waking up was sad and lonely even though I was in a room with Lata. We awoke again to the sounds of a banging headboard; Lara was staring at the ceiling and, I could tell, feeling as lonely as I was. I threw back the covers and sat up.

"Come on!" I chirped, forcing myself to be cheerful. "It's Christmas Day! Let's go to the beach!"

"Never thought I'd hear *that* odd sentence," Lata said dryly, struggling out of bed.

We traipsed down to the sand and were soon joined by Dazzer and Steph, looking sleepy-eyed and very loved up, Razzer looking as fresh and handsome as ever, and Tom looking hung over.

After a long day of sunbathing, swimming and discussing the orange woman and her new strange position (on her stomach with the soles of her feet placed together and her knees out to her sides) I insisted that we head over to Krabi on the mainland to have Christmas dinner somewhere. So we all traipsed around from restaurant to restaurant trying to find something resembling a turkey dinner. Eventually, we gave up on that idea and settled for a restaurant called Vietnamese Barbeque. A flash of Trish and Tammy's smiling faces came into my head as I thought of them heading off to Vietnam.

"It sounds exciting," Steph said brightly, in that everything-is-wonderful-because-I'm-in-love voice.

We settled around a table and all agreed to share a Vietnamese hotpot, which was the most British sounding thing on the menu.

When it came it was a pot of boiling water, placed in the middle of the table with a petite bowl of noodles and a handful of prawns to throw into the water along with a few herbs. The boys all looked horrified, and as soon as the prawns had been added, Dazzer did his very best to fish out as many as he could before anyone else and shovel them into his mouth.

"Shtarving," he mumbled, winking and spraying us with watery soup.

I couldn't help my lip curling and Lata glared at him in disgust, but Steph blushed and gazed at him adoringly. Razzer snorted into his soup. We ate in silence.

"God this is crap," Tom eventually voiced what we all were thinking.

"Yeah, water and noodles for Christmas dinner," I added. "Yum."

"Cheer up," Lata said, "at least we'll lose weight over Christmas for once."

Just as we launched into an attack on the food, all the lights in the restaurant went off and one single spotlight was shone upon us. A tiny elderly woman came towards us carrying a tray of melon with sparklers stuck into them and placed it on our table, as all the other diners and staff launched into a clipped and squawky version of "We wish you a Merry Christmas!"

We reddened, suitably chastised that they were celebrating our western tradition with us, even though they weren't Christians. They all clapped at the end and then fell silent. They all stared at us expectantly.

"I think they want a speech," Tom hissed. "Go on Razzer!"

"I'm not doing it!" He hissed back. Lata slid down in her chair, and Steph stared into her bowl of water.

I was always one of those kids in school who hated it when a teacher asked a question and the silence would drag on forever as everyone shifted uncomfortably in their seats and stared at their pencil cases, because nobody wanted to look stupid if they got it wrong. I would end up putting my hand up just to break the excruciating silence, and then would inevitably get the answer wrong and be laughed at.

This was one of those times. I got slowly to my feet. I gazed around at the other restaurant guests and squinted to see them as the lights were still off and our table was lit up like a bonfire with all the sparklers.

"Er…thank you…" I said haltingly, "for erm, a lovely hot pot. It was really delicious and…"

"Is like your nice-nice food you have in home yes? Same-same?" the tiny woman who had brought the sparklers to the table said, beaming and nodding her head.

"Er yes…and thank you for a lovely Christmas and the lovely sparklers. And the melon," I said quickly, "They were lovely."

The other diners gave a rousing round of applause as I sat down. Lata had stuffed her handkerchief into her mouth and Razzer's head was so close to his soup as he laughed into it I thought he was going to fall in.

"Shut up," I hissed, "Someone had to do it."

As the lights came back on, the noise of the restaurant picked up once more. Tom put down his chopsticks and pushed his chair back.

"Sod this for a game of laughs," he declared getting to his feet, "there's a party tonight at the Skunk bar in Railey. Up for it anyone?"

"Hell yes," we all agreed, leaving our watery noodles and a big tip for the sweet little sparkler lady who beamed, placed her palms together and nodded her head slightly as we hurried out. The diners launched into another round of applause as we exited and we found ourselves bobbing and bowing awkwardly as we scuttled through the restaurant.

"That was the most bizarre Christmas dinner I've ever had," Lata muttered as we clambered into the boat heading back to Railay.

"It was lovely," Steph said clinging onto Dazzer's arm and gazing up at him.

I looked at Lata and we rolled our eyes.

***

The Skunk Bar was deep in a forest in a little valley behind all of the resorts. A dirt path wound through trees creaking in the gentle breeze. The only light came from the stars, and we could hear the muffled beat of music. We finally reached a rickety wooden and thatched hut, which was only half covered by a roof. The ground floor had a dirt floor, a wooden bar, a rickety table where a Rastafarian DJ spun his tunes, and beanbags and tables scattered about for people to lounge around on; a couple of split-level platforms made of bamboo held tables and cushions and 'upstairs' was the designated chill-out area, where people could sit and smoke and look up at the stars. The party was already in full swing when we arrived with an eclectic mix of Thai Rastafarians shaking their long dreads around enthusiastically to the music; some skinhead Germans; a Brazilian girl writhing around in the middle of the floor; some tanned, skinny Scandinavian girls in tiny mini-skirts and halter-neck tops who had stumbled their way there by mistake; a group of cool, stylish and disinterested Israelis on one of the platforms, and two Australian guys wearing board shorts and peaked caps, playing enormous bongos and struggling to keep in time with the music.

Drinks flowed freely, and we soon found ourselves in the middle of the throng, dancing away. I grinned at Steph and Lata, riding high on the knowledge that Tuna liked me, even if it was too late now to do anything about it. With him in mind, I limited my drink, and just enjoyed being there, in that moment, with all of these happy people, deep in a woods, dancing under the stars.

Chapter Twenty-Nine

Boxing Day dawned bright, breezy and sunny – and I was the only one who felt any of those things. Lata was buried deep under her sheet and let out a moan when I opened the curtains. I remembered her knocking back some shots of tequila and I hurriedly closed the curtains again. I decided to head down to the beach on my own for a few hours, feeling smug and self-righteous. I knew the others wouldn't emerge until at least lunchtime.

I headed around the coast while the tide was out and found it pretty empty. Apart from, of course, orange-woman. Today she was lying on one side, her head resting on her stretched out arm, and her other arm stretched over her head – I presume this was to bronze the side of her body and that all-important armpit. She smiled at me briefly, not wanting to cause too many creases on her face that wouldn't catch the sun's rays, I surmised. I smiled back cheerfully and settled myself in a nice little corner up near the palm trees. There was a man walking his dog along the shore, and some fishermen pulling up the anchors on their wooden fishing boats. The sea was calmly lapping the shore. A small Thai girl was squatting in the sand a few feet from me, digging for shells. I lay down on my towel and began to mull over the last few days. Maybe I was being stupid about Tuna. Maybe I should just email him. But then this little voice that had been hovering around in the back of my mind chirped up clearly. It said *but what's the point? He lives in Australia. You live in the UK. You'll be heading home soon and then what? More heartache. Best just leave it well alone...*

I sighed and flipped onto my stomach. I was about to untie my bikini strings when I heard this strange noise. A sort of rushing, whooshing noise that grew louder until it became thunderous. I saw orange woman raise her head and look around. I saw a man out to sea on a fishing boat shouting to other men on their boats and waving and pointing frantically off to sea.

And then around the rocky corner of the beach came a wall of water. It was rushing toward me, *along the beach.* My head swam. The whole world was backwards. Why was the water not coming from the sea? Why was it coming over the rocks and *parallel* to the sea? These thoughts passed through my mind, before a slow realisation gripped me. The wall of water was coming towards me. Fast. And it was huge.

I glanced at orange-woman and her eyes met mine. An adrenalin shot of fear pumped through me and I jumped to my feet at the same time as the orange-woman.

"The trees!" she shouted at me. I looked to my right and saw a small Thai girl standing up and looking at the wall of water rushing towards us. I caught orange-woman's eyes. They widened in acknowledgment and we both ran to the girl. I caught her skinny arm in my hand and whipped her off her feet and up onto my hip before racing back up towards the trees, followed closely by orange-woman.

When we reached the palm trees, I copied the way she wrapped her arms tightly around a trunk. I caught hold of the little girl's arms and wrapped them tightly around the trunk underneath mine. She wrapped her legs tightly around my waist. I just had time to glance down towards the shore and see the open-mouthed faces of the fishermen, waist-deep with the ropes tied to their boats in their hands or sitting aboard their flimsy vessels as they watched this rush of water race along the beach. I also saw a man with his dog, running, running, as hard as he could as the water raced towards him. I looked at orange-woman and she held my eyes.

"Hold on!" she shouted, before the water hit us. It hit with such force that my legs were taken out from underneath me. And still the water came, pushing my body up until it was at a right angle to the tree. The little girl clung to my body with her tiny legs with all her might. I felt the soft skin of her arms under mine and gripped them tighter with my hands. I knew I was bruising her, but I didn't care. I couldn't let go. Her face was pressed into my neck. The bombardment seemed to go on for hours. The water was up to my shoulders and I was struggling to hold my head up and kept getting mouthfuls of salt water. I was terrified the little girl would slip under; I could hear her spluttering and gasping as the water hit her face. The bark was cutting into the soft skin of my inner arms, but I held on and held on and held on as the water seemed determined to wrench me from the tree.

And then my grip started to slip. I squeezed my eyes shut against the torrent and tried to hold on tighter but my arms were weak, and I slipped again. And just when I thought I was going to let go, the water subsided and my legs dropped and I felt the sand beneath my feet and I heard the water rushing away towards the end of the beach and then into the sea. I coughed and spluttered. The little girl was sobbing great heaving sobs into my shoulder as she let go of the tree and transferred her arms to my neck. I turned to see the orange-woman, her eyes wide with horror as they met mine.

"You OK sweetie?" she asked me, panting. It struck me that she was a Londoner – one of those inconsequential thoughts that run through your mind when it least matters. I nodded.

"I… think…I am," I looked around me shocked. Orange-woman came to me and gently took the child from my arms. I looked down towards the sea. The fishermen were still on their boats. The water hadn't even affected them. One was rowing his boat back towards shore; another dived off his and swam in. A woman was in the water, shouting and waving her hands, and a man had just reached her and was dragging her towards the beach. The palm trees were bedraggled and wet from the onslaught of the water.

"What the hell was that?" I asked, tears beginning to well in my eyes. Orange-woman put her free skinny arm around my shoulders. She only came up to about my belly button so she had to reach up to do it.

"I dunno love," she shook her head. "I really don't 'ave a bloody clue."

She gazed around and I started to whimper as I looked at my grazed arms, bruises already beginning to show up on my skin.

"Come on love, don't cry now," she soothed, her face still wild from shock. The little girl was wiping her small pale face and gazing at me.

And then I did stop crying because I heard shouts. Local children were running towards the shore because *the sea was disappearing*. Right before our eyes. It was sucking right out towards the horizon. And the children were running after it, screaming in delight.

"Dear God," orange-woman breathed.

There were fish left flipping about on the wet sand where the sea had been only moments before. The children were picking them up and shouting with joy. The fishermen however, were calling to them anxiously, waving for them to go back in.

I looked at orange-woman and she looked at me. Her blue eyes held a fear that put a chill into my heart. My stomach felt like lead.

"Run gel," she said in a husky voice, "run back to your hotel. And get upstairs or get up a hill. I dunno what's goin' on but this ain't right. If the sea's gone out, it's gonna come back in. Go. As fast as you can!"

"What about you?" I asked her, panic-stricken.

"Me 'usband. Gotta go back to me own hotel," she jabbed her thumb over her shoulder, "now go!"

I turned and started to run as fast as I could down the beach, and when I glanced over my shoulder I saw her running in the opposite direction, still clutching the tiny girl in her arms. I clambered over the rocks, slipping and grazing myself and finally I was sprinting across the brown sand of the backpacker beach. Steph, Lata and Dazzer were running down the beach towards me. I was whimpering and each breath was ragged in my chest.

"Ruby!" Steph almost screamed, "Where were you? We were so scared! What the hell *was* that?"

They were all also out of breath more from panic than from running I guessed.

"We've got to get off the beach," I said breathlessly, through my sobs, "Now…Got to get up a hill."

I ran past them and up to the guesthouse and found the staff milling around looking confused about what had happened.

"A wave of water," one was saying to a hippy guy who was looking confused about all the commotion, "came along the beach, the wrong way."

I ran up to the bar and gasped.

"We've got to get out, all of us. Got to go up the hill," I shouted, "the water, it'll come back!"

People looked a bit startled by my outburst, but the owner looked into my eyes and she understood how panicked I was. She barked orders at her son and he started gathering up CD's. She fumbled with keys trying to open the safe, and finally wrenched it open before grabbing bags of money from inside.

Then the next weird thing happened. All of a sudden, there was water again, shallow water that rose steadily up the beach, up the steps to the guesthouse, and up to our ankles. I looked at Lata.

"Go and get Razzer and Tom," I almost screamed, frustrated at their inaction. "Get everyone! We have to get out!"

And with that, we all started running. Dazzer reached Razzer's door and bellowed at him to get up and get out, then it was Tom's turn. They emerged looking terrified, Razzer in a sarong and Tom in his boxer shorts, and they ran with us. We ran right through the guesthouse, yelling for everyone to get out, and then we ran down the steps and out through the trees, shouting at any huts we passed, or bars, or people strolling on the road, to run, run, run. We threaded our ways through the trees until we were eventually going uphill, up through the trees, hearing the faint ominous roar behind us.

Finally, we stopped in a clearing in the trees, exhausted. There were about fifteen of us in a group, and we heard other people following behind us. We looked down below us and we saw the waves. The next one came, looking gentle and harmless until it crashed into the huts and trees and instead of breaking and losing energy, it just forged straight over them and through them, tearing down anything in its path. It is impossible to describe the power in that wave. We saw it crash into people and drag them with it. And then another wave came, and we stared down the slope watching the devastation unfold before us, not knowing what the hell was happening or why and all of us were wondering silently if the world was ending.

Chapter Thirty

We stayed up on that hill for nearly twenty-four hours, right through the rest of the day and the night waiting for the water to subside. At first what struck me was the cacophony of noise; the rushing of water; the creaking and cracking of wood being bent and broken; the loud wrenching of steel-reinforced pillars being torn from the ground; the screaming of children, women, men; the guttural cries of people being dragged under water.

After a while the sounds changed to shouts of panic and screams of mothers trying to find their children. And we sat up on the hill, not knowing what was going on below, being joined by people scrambling up out of the water. We sat huddled together in shock – us, along with the owner of the guesthouse, Mrs Juntasa, and her two sons Som and Praya, Thip the barman, a couple from Slovakia Adela and Dominik, Adam the hippy guy from our guesthouse who was from Poland, and two Canadian girls Naomi and Claire. We were initially shocked into silence. Then came a phase of talking so much we couldn't stop. Then we brooded in silence which was only broken by the occasional sobbing – usually Naomi. But during that night a bond grew between us that was stronger than any I have experienced before. I haven't seen or heard from Adela, Dominik, Adam, Naomi or Claire since we climbed down from that hill. But I know we'll all remember that terrible night up there with the stars above us and the water swirling below. I would meet someone's eye and see deep into their soul – the crazed look of panic in Claire's eye; the bewildered gaze of Thip; the stoic but grim smile on Mrs Juntasa's face as she held Som's arm; the pure terror in Steph's glance. Lata and Steph and I held hands all night, huddling in close as the air cooled. Why was this happening? *What* was happening? Was it just us? Was it the whole world? We just didn't know, and we sat in our ignorance, confused, scared and reaching out for one another.

"Shouldn't we go and help?" Dazzer asked quietly when we heard a woman's crying coming from the trees below.

A couple of times one or two of us would amble our way down through the trees to offer help to people roaming around waist-high in the water, but more often than not, they would ramble inconsolably, and continue their hunt through the fallen trees for their missing son, brother, mother. Sometimes, people would join us, wet, soaking, sobbing, clinging to a friend or relative and sit with us and wait. We didn't know what we were waiting for. When I went down the hill once with Tom, we came across a woman trying to drag an elderly man through the water. We tried to help her, tried to take the man from her, and help them up the hill but she shrieked at us in Thai and slapped our hands away before dragging him on through the trees. We returned to our post on the hill, not speaking, completely at a loss at what we were supposed to do.

At dawn, we edged our way down the hill, exhausted and scared, blinking in the bright sunlight. We met what I thought was devastation although we learned later that Railey got off quite lightly. Walls were knocked down, some of the flimsier guesthouses were in ruins, some trees had fallen or were leaning dangerously, and there was rubbish and debris strewn across the sand. There were shouts and sounds of crying, as people sifted through the rubble and detritus; all that remained of their livelihoods.

Our guesthouse wasn't too badly affected, having been protected by a bar and a grove of trees that stood in front of it. But others were not so lucky. Luckily, we learned from Mrs Juntasa that nobody in the very near vicinity had died that she knew of. We were to learn later that a few people had lost their lives as the waves had crashed over the main peninsula, washing through the five star resorts.

The TV in the guesthouse, which ran off a generator, was perched up high on the wall on a stand and so had escaped the water. Thip turned it on and we were finally delivered answers about what had happened to us. A tsunami had devastated parts of South East Asia as well as far away as Sri Lanka. The death toll grew over the next few days; the extent of the devastation to Thailand as well as other countries affected by it was immense.

We spent the first two days exhaustively clearing up, helping the local people to try and regain some sort of order to their homes and their lives. We worked tirelessly alongside each other inspired by the stoic acceptance of the locals. Food was shared around from the remaining restaurants to all the people, locals and tourists alike.

On the second day after the tsunami, I headed around to the main beach where I had first been hit by the water. I walked around the hotels until I found orange-woman having a cup of tea on a table outside a hotel that was clearly once beautiful but whose façade was now battered and sorry-looking. She looked weary and old but her face lit up when she saw me.

"Thank God lovey," she said putting her wafer-thin arms around me and hugging me like I was a long-lost friend, "you're OK."

I nodded choking back tears.

"How is your husband?" I hastily brushed away the tears.

"OK," she nodded solemnly. "He got washed clean out of our hotel room. Luckily 'e managed to grab onto a stair handrail but he bumped his 'ead and 'e's got a nasty cut. But 'e's OK."

"What about the little girl?"

"When I got back to the hotel, she took off like a bullet," she shrugged, "never saw 'er again. I assume she's OK."

I nodded; I hoped so.

"Listen 'ave you phoned 'ome?" Orange-woman asked.

I shook my head. The phone lines were down, and none of us had a cell phone. She fished in her pocket and produced her phone and handed it to me.

"Oh thank you," I said breathlessly, relieved to be able to put my family's minds to rest.

"Take it to your friends as well," she said nodding, "they can call 'ome too. Their parents'll be worried sick."

"Thank you!" I cried, but before I ran off, I asked her what her name was. I felt too bad to call her orange-woman to the girls anymore.

"Janine, love," she said lighting up a cigarette.

I smiled at her and felt guilty for all those times we had laughed at her and her bizarre sunbathing techniques.

I rang and rang and rang my house but there was no answer. I then tried Mum's cell phone and she answered immediately after one ring.

"Mum…"

"Oh thank God!" She almost screamed down the phone, so that I had to pull it away from my ear. And then she burst into noisy tears. I thought I must have the wrong number, until I heard a fumble while the phone was being wrenched away from her, and Jess's voice came on.

"Rube? Is that you?"

"Yes!" The line was cutting out.

"Are you OK?" she barked.

"Yes! I'm fine…"

"Yes, yes…OK mam…I'll tell her," she said irritably, "Mam says you're to come home. Now."

"Look, I'm fine…"

"Mam says there are no buts about it…*mam*, I'm talking…"

There was more fumbling as they wrestled with the phone and then my mother's voice came on, business-like as usual and I relaxed once I heard the mother I knew.

"Now you listen here young lady! You're coming…ome…ight…ow…"

"Mum!" I shouted, "You're cutting out!"

"…ot taking …o for an answer…"

"I'm fine! I can't come home! I'm needed here!"

"…e'll come and …et you…"

"Look, Mum, I'm on someone else's phone! I have to go! Trust me! I'm OK! I'll call you on a landline as soon as I can…"

The line went dead. I sighed. I could understand their concern. But there was no way I could go home. Not now. I looked around at the people on the beach: fishermen gathering together the wrecked pieces of wood that were once their boats and their livelihoods; woman gathering together scattered belongings from the sand; children sitting on patches of ground where their houses used to sit, looking lost and scared.

I couldn't leave these people; I couldn't go back to my cosy, comfortable life. Not now.

When I handed the phone to Lata, she disappeared down to the beach with it. After about fifteen minutes I went to look for her and found her sitting on a rock, staring out to sea. She looked tired with dark rings under her round ebony black eyes. She looked at me and gave me a small smile, and it was then I saw wet tracks of tears running down her cheeks. I put my arm around her.

"I've been so stupid, Ruby," she said burying her head into my shoulder and sobbing. I had never ever seen Lata cry before, and I found it unnerving. Confident, cool, calm, poised Lata.

"I spoke to Tim," she said finally, when her sobs had passed, "he was so scared, he cried when he heard my voice. He said he thought he had lost me."

I sat down on the rock next to her.

"What a silly cow I have been," she said, wiping her tears away irritably with the sleeve of her black tunic. "Last night up on that hill, I tried to imagine what it would be like if I never saw Tim again. And I couldn't imagine it. He *is* me. I see that now. And I was just flattering myself, thinking that a girl needed the attention to make her feel wanted and beautiful."

She shook her head sadly.

"I told him everything, Ruby."

"What?!"

She nodded.

"I had to. I couldn't keep it from him," she sniffed. "We have never had secrets. Ever. So I told him, about the guy in the office. And about Razzer."

"But nothing's happened with Razzer," I said and then narrowed my eyes, "has it?"

She shook her head.

"No. But I wanted it to. Until last night. Up on that hill. And it all became clear. I don't want anyone but Tim."

"What did he say?"

She took a deep shaky breath.

"He didn't say anything at first. And then he said he needed to think. And he said to call him in a couple of days."

She put her long hands over her face.

"And all I want is to be there now with him," her voice was muffled through her slender fingers.

We sat in silence for a while.

"Well," I said eventually, "if he dumps you, maybe Tamsin can introduce you to that bloke with the smooth cock."

She gave me a half-hearted smile and we walked hand in hand back to the hotel.

***

On the fourth day after the tsunami, I awoke with a jolt from a restless sleep in which I was being chased by an unknown figure. I was running through trees and I could hear him behind me, always just behind, no matter how fast I ran. It was early. Lata was fast asleep. We were all exhausted. I had a shower and headed down to the beach. I didn't know where I was going; I just let my feet keep walking. I finally found myself sitting under the palm tree that I had held onto and that had saved my life. I leaned my head against it and watched the early morning sun glint off the calm, innocent-looking sea. And then the tears came. The first proper tears I had cried since we had run up that hill. And they didn't stop. They came and rolled down my cheeks in a constant stream. I hugged the palm tree.

"Thank you," I whispered, "thank you."

I thought of all of the stupid things I had thought were so important just four days ago. I thought of how scared I had been of leaving home, of how I'd worried about my clothes and straightening my hair. I thought of how ridiculously I had acted over Rich, as if nobody else had ever had something bad happen to them, as if I was the most injured person in the world. And all that had happened was a stupid boyfriend had gone off with another girl. While all around me here, people had lost everything, and still they smiled and they picked themselves up and they carried on. Every morning Mrs Juntasa's sons Som and Praya grinned at me when I appeared sleep-eyed from my room, as they dragged debris from the beach, and tried to help their neighbours rebuild their lives as well as theirs. And I thought of how stupid I had been with Tuna, how I had found someone I truly cared about, someone decent and good, and my stupid pride had got in the way. How I wished he were there now so I could tell him that I loved him, and I had all along.

I watched a lone, tall figure walking along the beach. His stride was long and purposeful as if he was looking for something. I wondered what or who he had lost. The figure stopped at the shore and turned towards me. He stood for a long time staring up at where I sat. I wondered if we both felt the same thing, that man and I. And then he started to walk towards me. And there was something familiar in his walk, something about the swing of the arms. And then he started to trot towards me and something lit up inside me. I got to my feet slowly, and started to move towards him, and as he got closer and his face came into view, I started to run. I ran sobbing towards him and threw my arms around his neck, almost knocking him over as he caught me and held onto me tightly.

"Thank God," Tuna muttered into my hair.

He pulled my head back and pushed the tangled hair away from my eyes and looked long and hard into them. His silver eyes were rimmed with red; he was pale and drawn and I loved him so much it hurt.

"Ruby," he kept whispering over and over again until he took my face into his hands, and I finally felt his lips, his perfect lips, on mine, kissing me with all the pent up passion and fear that I felt.

He pulled back breathlessly and smiled, his eyes disbelieving.

"I'm sorry it took me so long to find you," he gasped. "I knew you were here…Tom emailed me…but there were no buses, everyone was trying to get down here, to find family…I tried…had to hitchhike in the end. Took so long…roads are a mess."

I kissed his warm cheek; the skin was rough with stubble. I kissed his tired eyes, and his forehead.

"I was so scared, Ruby; so many people have died."

"We're all OK," I managed to say finally.

He let go of me and then took my hand and without saying a thing he led me up through the palm trees to the nearest hotel. It was the expensive one that Janine had been staying in. He walked up to the receptionist and asked for a room.

"You want to check in, sir?" she asked in surprise. She, like everyone, looked exhausted. "Everyone else is leaving."

He nodded and pushed a wad of cash towards her.

He led me by the hand in silence upstairs. The room was beautiful, all white flowing curtains and dark wood. Beyond the bed was a small balcony that overlooked the beach. Tuna dropped his rucksack and led me to the bed. I stood in front of him, my breathing slow and calm. It was almost as if time was standing still. He pulled my vest up over my head, and then undid the knot on the sarong around my waist. It floated to the floor around my feet. He undid the knot of my bikini around my neck and then the strap around my back and that too fell to the floor. Then he undid the strings on either side of my bikini bottoms and they joined the pile of clothes. I had never stood like this naked in front of anyone, not even Rich. He pulled his vest over his head, and I reached to undo the button of his shorts. He kicked them off and then he too was naked. I stared at him; he was gorgeous. It was strange; I knew his body so well. He took my hand and led me to the bed. White curtains hung from the posts at either end. I lay back amongst the pillows and Tuna leaned over me and kissed me. I got lost in that kiss, I fell into it and felt like I was falling, falling, falling into the most delicious comfortable dream. We slowly made love. Everything felt so different compared with Rich, so strange, and so right; his hips were narrow and hard as they pushed against me, his hands big and dry as they touched me, his shoulders hard and smooth under my lips as I kissed them. Afterwards, we lay still for ages, our legs and arms entwined. I stroked the back of his head. Finally, he rolled away from me, and lay on his side looking at me, with a big smile on his face.

"Wow," I breathed.

"Yeah," he agreed.

I trailed a hand over his lean stomach, and the rise of his chest.

"God, I'm glad you came," I said.

He started to laugh. I grinned.

"I mean came *here*! To find me!"

He leaned on his elbow and looked down at me, smiling.

"Oh so am I," he grinned, "I've wanted to do that for so long!"

"So Tom told you I was here?" I gave him a sidelong glance.

"Yeah."

I shook my head.

"I made him swear not to tell you."

"Why?" he frowned.

"Because," I fiddled with the edge of the white sheet, "I thought you were with Karla. I thought I had blown it."

"And how did you think you had blown it?" he asked, his tone calm, his eyes giving nothing away.

"I thought that I had waited too long," I shrugged. "Karla turned up just when I had decided to tell you how I felt."

His eyes looked dark and he pursed his lips as he looked away and out through the window.

"You did look pretty *together*, y'know," I said defensively, "that night on the beach by Eve."

"I was trying to make you jealous," he said loudly, saying each word slowly, as he turned back to look at me. "I was hurt and angry. You didn't look much like you had decided to declare your undying love for me when you were kissing Charlie."

"*He* kissed *me*," I said in exasperation, hitting the bed with my open palm.

He looked back at me steadily. I took his face in my hands.

"And I realised then what I had known all along. It was you I wanted. *You.* And even Charlie knew that. When I stopped him, he said he knew it was because of you," I sighed, "and I was so happy, I ran down the beach to tell you, and there you were with Karla…"

"So you ran away. Again," he said shortly.

"Why are you so angry with me?" I asked him, sitting up in bed and holding the sheet over me.

"Because you left without a word of explanation. We were all worried shitless about you," he shook his head and sat up next to me. "You did it once before, and then you did it again. It was pretty thoughtless you know."

"I left a note with Tammy and Trish explaining that I had to go. To meet Steph and Lata…" I trailed off pathetically.

"But not for me," he looked at me. "That hurt you know?"

I nodded feeling ashamed.

"I was just so happy to have crawled out of that shell that I had formed around myself after Rich," I shrugged helplessly. "It felt so good to be happy again, not to just feel sad and hurt. And when I saw you with Karla, the wound felt just as raw. I'd left myself open to hurt again. I dealt with it the only way I knew how. I ran away from it."

I put my hand up to his cheek.

"I won't run away again," I said looking into his eyes, "I promise."

He stroked the bruises and grazes on my arms.

"What happened here?" he asked softly.

I sighed and looked out at the sea that was lapping the shore lazily. I told him in a low voice about what had happened when the waves hit. After I finished speaking, he took me in his arms and held me for a long, long time.

Chapter Thirty-One

The Joneses

I heard them before I saw them. They were bickering as usual. We were sitting at a café having breakfast, and I could hear their voices through the trees, raised and arguing. I could also hear two sets of high heels clopping along the path hidden by the trees.

"Fuckin' sand. It gets everywhere!"

"Watch your language, young lady!"

I suddenly felt cold. It couldn't be. I looked frantically round the table at the others but they were all tucking into their eggs and bacon, apparently unaware of anything else.

"God no," I breathed. Tuna looked up at me in surprise, and then they came around the corner, just behind him, and my worst fears were realised.

"Fookin' 'ell," Dazzer spluttered, eggs spraying from his mouth, "Ruby, it's you! But fitter!"

I shot him a withering look, before glancing back to the three people walking up the steps to the café. I slid down in my seat hoping they wouldn't see me.

"Bloody hell," Tom breathed, "look at that. She *does* look like you Ruby. And she's *gorgeous*!"

I watched him take in the high, wooden-heeled, white clogs, the long tanned legs – suspiciously so for Welsh legs – the tiny cut off denim shorts, the pink shirt tied up in a knot to reveal a toned, tanned stomach and a gleaming cleavage, long tumbling freshly highlighted curls and huge white-rimmed sunglasses. The sunglasses turned towards our table and stopped dead when they saw me looking horror-stricken and scrunched down in my chair.

"Well! Fina – fuckin' – lee!" Jess exclaimed, her hands on her hips. A few heads turned to look at her. Tuna turned round in his chair and did a double take.

"They're right, Ruby, she does look like you," he said in surprise.

"*That's* because it's her twin," Lata muttered darkly. She still remembered Jess making a play for Tim at my leaving party.

A dark head swung towards us, and my mum's *Gucci* sunglasses were pushed hurriedly up onto her head. Her hair was no longer her usual deep-red colour, but jet-black. With her long ebony curls, red lips, expensive white linen trousers and crisp white shirt, she looked like Nancy D'ell Olio. And then she did something completely uncharacteristic of my mum. She burst into tears and ran towards me. She threw her arms around me and sobbed loudly. Over her shoulder I could see my dad hovering awkwardly next to Jess; his white spindly legs, clad in argyle socks that were pulled half way up his calves, were poking out from very short beige shorts. I noticed in surprise that he was, however, wearing a bright lime green Hawaiian style shirt with big cream flowers splattered all over it, instead of his customary checked Marks and Spencer one. I also noticed he had gelled his wispy hair into tufty spikes. And then the thought crossed my mind that he was supposed to be in Spain.

Finally, Mum pulled back and blew her nose noisily into a crisp white handkerchief.

"I'm sorry we took so long to get here darling," she said.

"It was that fuckin' incompetent travel agent friend of Mum," Jess piped up from behind Steph's chair, "Connie, Bonnie or whatever her name is."

"She is *not* incompetent, Jessica. Bronny's been going through a terrible divorce and the menopause all at the same time," Mum snapped at her, and then turned back to me and said in a soothing voice "It's been impossible to get flights out here. Everyone's coming to try and find their children, or families. Some are coming to bring bodies…home…"

With that she burst into a fresh bout of tears. I stood up and patted her back, aware of all the eyes around the table on me (except Dazzer and Tom who were gazing at Jess in awe and Steph who was scowling at Dazzer).

Dad ambled over and gave me a tight hug.

"What are you doing here?" I asked, my voice a bit too shrill. I forced a happy smile on my face.

"Well," Mum smiled at me as if I was simple, or as if she thought I may have hit my head when I got caught in the waves or something, "we've come to take you home, of course, darling."

"Actually, we're taking you home and then we're going to our *new* home," Jess said, grinning like the cat that got the cream, "in *Spain*!"

I frowned in confusion.

"Oh, we'll tell you all about it," Mum said taking my hand and patting it, and trying to lead me away from the table. She nodded a hello to all my speechless friends.

"Oh hello, Steph dear. How are you?" She chirped, "I contacted your parents and told them we were coming out here to get you home safely. You know, to evacuate you."

Steph nodded mutely and I stared at Mum. It looked like my mum, but it had seemingly been overtaken by a Stepford Wife robot. She turned and frowned at Dad.

"Help your daughter, Jeff," she scolded him, "she's been through a terrible ordeal."

He hurried round to the other side of me and started to try and shuffle me along.

"But… Mum…stop it!" I snapped, and immediately felt guilty when I saw the hurt look in her eyes.

"I'm fine," I said in a gentler voice. "I'm really OK. I told you on the phone, I wasn't hurt in the tsunami…"

She took a sharp intake of breath when I said the word as if I had blasphemed and she shook her head.

"We are all OK," I waved at everyone sitting around the table, "and I'm not coming home. I don't want to come home. I haven't finished my trip."

I looked at Jess who was shooting glances from behind her glasses at Tuna. He was watching the scene with my mum and dad with an amused smile.

"What do you mean new home in Spain?" I hissed at Jess across the table, trying to distract her from Tuna whilst feeling a stab of jealousy. She tore her eyes away from him and grinned again.

"Well, you know Dad ran off to Spain? Well, mam realised that really she loved 'im and…"

"Jessica, I don't want my dirty laundry aired in public thank you," Mum said abruptly.

Jess made a face at her when she turned back to me.

"We'll tell you all about it when we get you back to the hotel and you can have a nice hot bath," Mum said, taking my arm again.

I held my ground.

"I don't want to go back to the hotel."

"But we've got a lovely surprise there for you," Mum said, looking disappointed.

"It's OK," Jess said tottering away, "I'll go and get it for her mam. Get me a *Bacardi Breezer* while I'm gone, will you, Dad? There's a good man. Pineapple."

"It's ten o'clock in the morning!" Mum called after her but Jess had disappeared around a palm tree, heels clacking, and hair bouncing.

"Do you mind if we pull up a chair *bach*?" Dad asked pulling up two chairs anyway. I shook my head and sat down, and sulkily made introductions around the table. Mum nodded at them all, and then in old-mum style, grilled each one of them about their jobs. She had finally reached Dazzer who was looking terrified and kept fidgeting and squirming in his chair when I heard Jess's heels clicking on the path.

Mum smiled and patted my knee.

"You're going to change your mind about coming home when you see this," she smiled smugly.

Jess appeared around the corner with my surprise and the wind was knocked clean from my body as I stared at it. My surprise was Rich.

"Fookin' 'ell!" Dazzer jumped up from his seat. "What are you doin' 'ere? I thought you was still in Pai?"

Rich shot Dazzer a warning look.

"…oh yeah …sorry…" Dazzer mumbled.

Rich's eyes turned back to me along with everyone else's, apart from Tom who was watching Tuna with a wary expression. Mum's face was smiling and expectant; Dad's was a bit bewildered; Steph and Lata were wide-eyed and horrified; Tuna's expression was inscrutable. My eyes met his briefly. His jaw was clenched but his eyes were soft and he held my eyes steadily. I looked back at Rich. I couldn't believe he was standing right there in front of me.

"Hi babe," he said finally moving towards me and smiling softly.

Mum coughed and made meaningful faces at all the others around the table and they buried their heads in their breakfast again, or started talking about the weather, all the while watching us from the corner of their eyes.

"So did you see the cricket…?" I heard Dad asking Tuna.

"How's Tim?" Jess asked Lata slyly.

"Can we talk?" Rich said leaning down to where I was sitting, "Alone?"

"Why?" I asked abruptly.

Mum glanced at me sharply.

"Because we've a lot to talk about," he said quietly, "and I'd rather not have everyone and their dog listening in."

His twinkly brown eyes were smiling at me, his lips were pursed in his old charming smile, his black hair was flopping down over his eyes. I noticed he'd lost more weight. I could smell his old familiar smell, and my stomach flipped.

Memories, like pages of a photo album flicked through my mind. My mouth was dry. I couldn't believe he was here. I felt angry at myself that he still seemed to have an effect on me.

I nodded and stood up.

"OK."

As we walked away from the table, I glanced at Tuna. He gave me a small smile and nodded his head slightly. As we rounded the palm tree, I heard Mum saying to all that would listen, "Her first true love. She'll come home now he's come to get her. I think we may have a wedding on the cards you know…"

***

We walked along the sand not touching each other. I looked out at the sea, determined not to look into those eyes I knew so well.

"So how have you been?" he asked me eventually.

I shrugged.

"OK," I said shortly, "as well as someone *can* be when they've been dumped and humiliated and left alone in a strange country."

His shoulders hunched forward and he buried his hands in his pockets. From the corner of my eye he looked like a little boy.

"I want you to come home with me Ruby."

I laughed bitterly.

"Well, I'm not going to."

"I made a stupid, childish, awful mistake," he carried on nonetheless, "and I wish with all my heart I could take it back."

"Well, you can't."

He nodded.

"I know. But I want to try and make it up to you," I felt him studying my profile, "I want us to go back to our old life Ruby. You and me, in our flat, with Moggy…"

I felt a lump rise in my throat. I thought of the flat, of being curled up on the sofa that we had shopped for in Ikea, with Moggy sleeping on my lap. I thought of mornings lying in bed with the rain pattering against the window and feeling warm and safe and cosy…And then I thought of the sun on my face, the wind in my hair, and my arms wrapped around a slim waist, my face resting against a muscled back.

I shook my head.

"Not gonna happen."

He reached out, caught my arm and spun me to face him. I pulled my arm away.

"Look," he said, giving me his killer look, his little-boy-lost look that had always won me over, "I knew after you left that I had made the biggest mistake ever. I thought you must have gone home. I finally realised I had to come after you. But when I got back you weren't there and your folks didn't even know we'd broken up. I was frantic with worry. And then the tsunami hit and…"

His dark eyes filled with tears.

"I was so scared I'd lost you," he said his voice breaking, "I was so scared that I wouldn't see you again. And that you'd died not knowing that I love you. I love you so much Ruby."

He sniffed and wiped at his eyes with the palms of his hands. I felt the ice that gripped my heart beginning to thaw a little. He reached forward and took my hands in his.

"I want to try again Ruby, and *this* time I won't screw it up," he said earnestly. "You're my life, my reason for living."

He waved an arm in the air.

"This has all been a dream, an adventure," he said dramatically – I began to think he had been taken over by a Stepford Wife robot too – "and now it's time to get back to reality, to what's important. To you and me and our future together, our life at home. Imagine how happy your family and my family would be. We can go back and do all those things to the flat we'd been planning, I'll support you in whatever you want to do, just like you supported me with the travelling; we'll put together some money for a bigger place."

And then he served the killer blow. His eyes glinted and he took a deep breath.

"I want to marry you, Ruby," he said grinning, "I want to have children with you. As soon as we can. I want to spend the rest of my life with you."

I stared at him open-mouthed. I had never thought I would ever hear those words from Rich; words that I had waited for for so long. And he was there in the flesh. My Rich. The man I had been in love with and planned a whole future with. He'd come back for me just as I'd yearned for when the whole Nicole nightmare had begun.

I shook my head, feeling confused and bewildered.

"This is all," I struggled to find the words, "a bit too much, Rich. I need some time to think."

"Anything, sweetheart, anything," he gushed pulling me into his arms for a hug. My arms hung down by my side as I stood there woodenly.

"Tell Mum and Dad that I've gone for a walk, will you? I'll see you all back at your hotel. Which one is it?"

"The Golden Palm."

Of course, only the best for Mum. I had seen the five star Golden Palm – you couldn't miss it with its immaculate lawns, huge swimming pool with tumbling waterfalls, and ivory, pillared reception beckoning through an alley of statuesque palm trees.

"OK," I nodded and turned away. I walked along the shore, letting the waves lap over my toes. I felt Rich's eyes on me for a while, until finally, when I glanced over my shoulder for the fourth time, he had disappeared into the trees.

I couldn't believe this was happening. All that I had wanted to happen had happened. I leaned down and picked up a spiral shell and stroked its hard smoothness. I felt a little surge of excitement flutter in my stomach as I thought of going home; of winter evening shopping trips together; of romantic nights in our flat with Rich cooking for me, and me sipping a big glass of wine. I thought of him picking me up from work, smiling as I got into the car; of wandering the streets of London, lit by Christmas lights, Christmas presents in our hands. I thought of Sunday mornings reading the papers together and sipping orange juice. I thought of walking into a bar and smiling smugly and safely knowing my man was with me, right behind me.

And then I thought of Tuna. What future did we have together? We couldn't just keep travelling forever, could we? And then at the end of it what would happen? He would go back to Australia, and I would go back to the UK. That would be one hell of a *long* distance relationship.

Going back with Rich made so much sense. I went and leaned against my palm tree, and sat there until the afternoon sun was coming down low over the sand.

***

I found my way to the Golden Palms and to my gob-smacked surprise, found the various members of my family, lifting and moving rubbish and debris from the beach along with other helpers. Mum was wearing what I can only imagine was her 'Aid-worker' outfit – beige combat trousers, a khaki green vest, her hair held back in a khaki green scarf, her make-up and jewellery minimal but meticulously applied and khaki green trainers on her feet that looked like they had never been worn. Dad was still in his beige shorts/long socks/sandals combo, but with a different coloured Hawaiian shirt tucked into his chest-high waistband. Jess was also getting into the mood of it, with a pair of tiny camouflage-patterned shorts. She had even made a concession to comfort and donned a pair of pink trainers instead of her usual high-heel affairs. She was screwing up her nose into a wrinkled look of distaste, as she picked up an unidentifiable piece of material and carried it with an extended arm over to the skip that was steadily being filled. Then she sat on the sand for a quick break, obviously exhausted from displaying so much good will. Rich was also digging in, clearly trying to impress my family, made obvious by the way he grunted loudly when he picked up any heavy items and shot them a look every six seconds. Steph and Dazzer were managing to dig and pick things up without taking their love-sick eyes off each other. Lata was silent and sullen as she worked alongside Tuna and Tom. Tuna straightened up and wiped his arm across his forehead. He didn't have a top on, and his torso was brown and covered in a fine layer of sweat. He caught my eye but didn't smile when he saw me; his eyes were like shutters, closed to the world. I didn't know what he was thinking. I felt a twist in my chest and looked away from him. I walked over to Jess and helped her to her feet.

"You had a thing with Tuna, didn't you?" She hissed at me. I looked at her startled.

"How did you know?"

"Oh, I've seen the *looks*, and he hasn't said a word to Rich, even when Rich has tried to chat to him," she looked at me for a second and then sighed as I narrowed my eyes at her. "Oh alright, Tom told me the whole thing earlier. You lucky cow. He's *lush.*"

I nodded and let my eyes flicker over to him again. He was bent over, collecting together wood and tangled palm leaves.

"So what are you going to do?" she asked.

I shrugged. Except I already knew what I was going to do. Ruby the traveller was already becoming taken over by Ruby the well-behaved, twenty-something, sensible woman. I walked over to a portly middle-aged man who seemed to be in charge of the clean-up effort. He turned green, empty eyes on me.

"Can I help?" I asked. He nodded.

"Yeah, of course," he said and then added, "every extra pair of hands helps."

He handed me a shovel.

"We've got to get this sand all up," he said in a Canadian accent, waving a hand over a huge dune of muddy sand that was blocking the path outside the row of hotels.

"I have to warn you," he added in a low voice, "there are still a few local people missing. We haven't found their bodies."

I felt instantly cold.

"I understand."

His face was tired and worn. I wondered if he lived here or if he was just on holiday.

"We already found my wife two days ago," he added in a thin voice. I stared at him horrified as he turned back to digging.

"Why don't you go home?" I asked him quietly, "You should be with your family."

He glanced over his shoulder at me.

"This is my home," he said, his eyes looking at me blankly. "My wife was Thai. My family is Thai."

He turned back to his work, sweat trickling down his wide neck and making the grey hair at the back of his neck curl.

I turned to look at my dad, his fuzzy hair slick to his scalp from sweat. He dabbed at his forehead with his handkerchief. Then I looked at Mum, working alongside him, not caring about her manicured nails getting broken. And then at Jess who was smiling at a young, handsome Thai man who walked past without a top on, grinning at her broadly. I turned my head to find Rich watching me. He winked and smiled. It could all go back to normal, I told myself. Well, sort of normal now that Mum and Dad and Jess were moving to Spain – I still hadn't had the full story. Lost in my own thoughts I began to shovel.

***

Later that evening, we all stood at the bar of the hotel, sweaty and dirty from the day's work, covered in sand, and nursing sore hands and feet. But a lot of work had been done, a lot of rubbish and debris cleared so that the locals could begin to rebuild their lives. Life was going on as normal; they were picking up their lives from where they had been so dramatically interrupted.

My dad bought a round of drinks for everyone and we all perched on stools along the bar. Tuna was at the end as far away from me as possible, looking down into his drink. I wanted so much to go to him and put my arm around him. I wanted to see that smile again.

An arm slipped around my waist and I looked with surprise into a pair of brown eyes.

Rich grinned.

"So everyone," he said loudly, "Ruby and I had a chat today and well, she has decided to forgive me. We're going to go home and try again."

I stared at him. Mum beamed, her eyes shining. Jess looked at me with narrowed eyes and then glanced at Tuna who stayed perfectly still, not raising his eyes from his drink.

"Uh…well done," Dazzer half-heartedly mumbled, while his eyes darted nervously back and fore from Tuna to Rich.

Dad leaned forward and kissed my cheek, and whispered something into Rich's ear, which made the smile on his face falter slightly. But he flashed it back up to full-force and turned it back on me.

"And I *think* that this might be a good time to announce that we're going to get married."

Say something! I kept thinking to myself, but the words just stuck in my throat. It was happening again; the power that Rich used to have over me had managed to engulf me like an invisible cloak.

"I...uh..." I looked wildly round at the faces, and kept coming back to the same one, to Tuna's profile as he stared and stared into that bottle.

"Oh, Ruby darling," Mum gave me a hug, "that's just wonderful news. I knew you would come to your senses. It's time for you to come home now."

I felt like it was all surreal and that my life wasn't really being steam-rolled in a direction that I wasn't sure I wanted it to take.

Suddenly, Jess stood up from her barstool.

"Ruby," she said, with a quick glance at Tuna.

I looked at her and for some reason, something in her voice made everyone stop talking.

"Is this what you want?" she asked me, looking straight into my eyes, "Really what you want?"

I stared at this girl, this mirror image of me. This girl that I had shared everything with, this girl that knew me so well. There was a warning in her eyes, something she was trying to tell me. And then I realised what it was. *This is it; this is your chance to get out now, if that's what you want.* She had given me that chance.

I looked at Steph, her big round eyes sympathetic as she clutched Dazzer's hand; Lata's eyes were as intent on me as Jess', urging to me to be honest; Dad's eyes were caring and supportive; Mum's were wide with worry. And then I looked at Rich, and looked into those eyes I knew so well, the smooth one-toned chocolate colour of the irises, not flecked like Tuna's with silver and grey. Those eyes smiled at me and offered me a security, a safety that I had thought wouldn't be mine again after Pai.

"Yes. It is."

Finally, I looked at Tuna. He looked up from his beer and met my eyes. His were tired and red, his mouth was clenched, and a muscle twitched in his jaw. I hoped I could convey my helplessness to him, as I nodded my head. Mum raised her glass and made a toast. Jess met my eyes and shook her head before sitting down again. Everyone started chattering at once, Rich hugged me tightly, and Dad put a drink in my hand and so it was a few moments before I realised that Tuna had gone. His untouched beer was left where it was on the bar on its own.

That night, I lay next to Rich, hearing his familiar breathing, and stared up at the ceiling fan spinning round and round tirelessly. When he had tried to make love to me, I had been overwhelmed by the familiarity of it all. His lips on my lips had felt the same, his hands moved over me in the same way, he was soft and warm and our bodies fitted back into their old slots. But I had felt strangely detached, like it was all happening to someone else and I pushed him off me.

"It's OK," he murmured, "I understand. It'll take time."

He gave me a kiss on the cheek, turned over and went to sleep. I had lain still ever since, watching the fan going round and round and round on its pre-ordained course.

***

The next morning, I left Rich snoring in bed and walked down from The Golden Palms and over to the hotel that Tuna had booked into. I thought that if I could just talk to him, explain my decision and tell him that I had no choice, then maybe he would understand. But when I asked the girl on the desk to call his room – the same girl that had checked us in – she told me he had checked out the night before.

I felt sick.

"Checked out?" I stared at her. "Where did he go?"

"He no say, miss," she smiled sympathetically, "I'm very sorry."

I ran out of the lobby and down the beach towards my old guesthouse; the one that the others were all staying in. I ran into Lata and Steph's room breathlessly, only to be met by the sight of Dazzer's bum humping away on top of Steph, with his shorts round his ankles.

"Fook me Ruby!" he shouted, tumbling off her and grabbing the nearest thing to cover his privates – which happened to be a walking boot. Steph hurriedly pulled a beach towel over her.

"Shit! Sorry, sorry!" I blurted, putting hands over my eyes and turning round ineffectually in circles. "I'm looking for Tuna. Do you know where he is? Have you seen him?"

"No, we haven't seen him since last night," Dazzer grumbled, "And I doubt he wants to see you anyway."

I ran out of the door and knocked on Tom's door, not wanting to interrupt anything else embarrassing. He answered the door looking sleepy, his hair sticking up, and he was yawning.

"Alright Rube…"

"Have you seen Tuna?" I asked quickly. He shook his head. I sped away from him as he stood there rubbing his eyes. I ran to the front desk and threw myself across it. Praya was standing behind it with a sweeping brush and he looked startled.

"Hello Miss Ruby," he said smiling.

"Have you seen Mr Tuna, Praya? The tall man I was with? With blonde hair?"

He shook his head and frowned.

"He no stay here, Miss Ruby," he said, "but nice Mr Tom. He is here. He is good nice man. He in room five."

He winked at me. I shook my head in exasperation.

Where was he? I was frantic. I ran back to the Golden Palm looking into every bungalow, shop or café that I passed. I looked behind trees and wandered along the jetty where all the boats left from. Finally, I got back to The Golden Palm, defeated, and found Jess tanning herself by the pool. She was taking great pleasure in languorously rubbing suntan oil into her chest and legs while two male hotel employees watched her avidly. They were both so mesmerised that one was raking the pool, while the other was emptying the bin into the laundry basket.

"Whassup sis?" she asked as I flopped down next to her on a sun bed, my head in my hands.

"It's Tuna," I said miserably, "I can't find him."

"But he's gone," she said matter-of-factly.

"What?" I looked at her in astonishment.

She nodded.

"He left this morning on the first boat."
"But...but...how do *you* know?"
"He told me."
"*When*?"
"Last night," she said, "after you'd all gone to bed. I found him sitting on the beach when I went looking for a party. So we sat for ages and chatted."
"What did he say?" I asked quietly.
She shrugged.
"I'm sure you don't want to know that," she said leaning her head back on her bed, "You made your choice."
I glared at her.
"But *where* has he gone?"
She shrugged.
"Dunno."
"Come on Jess, tell me what he said!"
She sighed.
"Well, he was devastated obviously but he said he respected your choice and he needed to get away from you."
She raised her head and lifted her sunglasses up onto his hair. Her eyes narrowed to small slits.
"Why are you so interested anyway?" she asked, "What were you looking for him for?"
"To...tell him...to say I'm sorry!" I spluttered, "And to ask him for forgiveness, and....and... well, just to *see* him!"
Jess shook her head slowly.
"You complete idiot," she said realisation dawning on her face. "You made the wrong choice, didn't you? I knew you were making a mistake at the time. That's why I stood up and said what I did. He's such a lovely guy, Ruby, and he's crazy about you, and you publicly chose that cheating bastard over him."
I stared at her in horror as her words sunk in. I let out a loud sob to the consternation of an elderly Chinese man who was doing Thai Chi by the pool. He watched us closely, nearly falling off his one-legged pose and into the pool. Jess leaned forward and hugged me.
"What have I done, Jess?" I whispered into her hair which threatened to engulf me in a big, blonde, fragrant cloud.
"You were just scared, Ruby," she said softly, rubbing my back, "we all get scared."
But I knew that I had made my bed, and I was a coward so I would have to lie in it.
The next day we began packing for our return journey home. Mum and Dad had bought a ticket for me, a day earlier than Steph and Lata. Rich was whistling as he put clothes into his new hardback suitcase. As I dragged my rucksack out from under the bed, he snorted.
"God, I hate the sight of those things," he said laughing, "I'm glad I don't have to lug a bloody rucksack around anymore. I chucked mine as soon as I got home. *This* is the new state-of-the-art suitcase, bullet-proof, a variety of different handle-types, three hidden compartments no-less, *and* an alarm if anyone tries to break the lock."

I looked down at my raggedy red rucksack and remembered how clean and new it had been when I'd bought it. Its dirt told a million different stories, its rips and tears held a thousand different memories. It looked sad and forlorn sitting there on the floor next to Rich's super-duper fancy suitcase. I thought of where that backpack had been with me, what it had seen and what it had been through.

I looked at Rich laying his perfectly folded, brand new Calvin Klein shirts into his case, humming to himself. He glanced at me and looked me up and down, in my greying white vest and my floaty blue and white skirt that I had bought in Chiang Mai with him and that was looking decidedly threadbare.

"What are you going to wear for the journey, Rube? I mean you want to arrive in London looking your best, don't you?" he said, raising his eyebrows. I suddenly had a flash of my life at home – Rich telling me what to wear, what to do, how to act. And in that moment, it all became clear, like a fog lifting from my brain; I didn't want my old life back. I couldn't go back. *There was no going back.*

I threw my clothes into my backpack frantically, in no particular order, forcing them in hurriedly. Rich watched me, frowning.

"They'll get creased like that, Rube," he said worriedly.

I looked at him as I rammed flip-flops into the side pockets.

"I'm not going to London."

He lay another shirt into his case.

"And where are you going then?" He asked in an amused voice. "We're going home, and you may have forgotten that our home is in London. And unfortunately we have to fly into London to get there."

I shook my head.

"I'm not going home."

He stopped folding the sleeve of a shirt and looked at me, his eyes suddenly cold.

"What do you mean," he said in a low voice, "you're not going home?"

I held my chin up in defiance.

"Just what I said. I'm not going home."

"But...but...you said you forgave me and I thought we'd decided to get married..."

"*You* said I had forgiven you and *you* decided that we should get married," I felt a sudden anger and exhilaration rising up inside me. "You've always bullied me Rich, you've always controlled me, and told me what to do, how to dress, and how to live. And I don't want to go back to that."

"This is about Nicky, isn't it?" he said with relief and smiling gently.

"Nicky?"

He gave me a sad look.

"Sorry. I meant Nicole."

I laughed.

"God no. I mean it *was*. You hurt me, beyond belief, Rich. You left me alone, in the middle of a country I didn't even want to be in. You didn't give a shit about my feelings or what happened to me. I was *so* scared; you have no idea!" My voice was rising. "And I got on with things without you. And I learned to live without you. And I made my own friends, and my own life. And so yes, while it was once about Nicole, it's not anymore; it's about *you.* I don't give a damn about Nicole. In fact I would like to thank Nicole! She did me a favour!"

Rich raised his hands to try and calm me.

"Sh now baby," he said in a soothing voice, "this is normal. You're going to be angry."

I shook my head at him.

"You don't get it Rich, do you?" I said in a quiet voice, "I don't want to marry you; I don't want to come back with you or live with you or have your babies. I don't *want* my, or your, old life back. I have a lot more travelling to do before *I* decide where *I* am going to settle down."

For the first time, Rich began to look worried.

"Look, you've been through a lot. The tsunami…"

I shook my head.

"The reason I want to thank Nicole is because she forced me out of my comfort zone. She forced me to learn to stand on my own two feet. And she forced me to learn that you aren't the be-all-and-end-all. And because of her, I learned to fall out of love with you and into love with someone else."

Rich looked like I had slapped him across his face.

"What do you mean? With who?" He asked, suddenly angry. "Who the fuck is he?"

"He is a caring, sensitive, funny, intelligent, free-thinking, wonderful person," I said over the top of his rising voice, "and I was blind to have even considered *thinking* of coming back with you when I had a man like him right there in front of me."

Rich was finally silenced and his eyes were flashing furiously.

"If this is just to get back at me…" he said after a few moments loaded with tension.

"It's not Rich," I said softly, "I didn't intend to hurt you. I was just bowled over by you and my family turning up and insisting I go home. I thought about how much I wanted to hear you say those words when I was alone in Laos, and I thought I had to take the opportunity, take the safe route, and let everything go back to the way it was."

He was glaring at me, his mouth twitching in rage, his hands clenched.

"You see, Rich, my love for you is – was – like a cosy fire on a cold winter evening, somewhere I could curl up and feel safe and not be challenged and not have to face any change, or anything frightening. But Tuna opened the door to that room, and showed me the world outside, and it's scary. When you offered me the fire again, it was so tempting to close that door and stay safe and warm."

I was smiling as the image filled my mind.

"But I realise now that once I stepped through that door, along with the fear came the exhilaration of a fresh, crisp morning, or a cool refreshing breeze washing over me. That's what Tuna's love is like. It has opened my mind to the world, and instead of being frightening, it's like being awoken from a deep, fuggy, sleep, and no matter how much you try, you can never go back to being asleep again."

Rich stared at me.

"I don't know what the bloody hell you're talking about, but this bloke," he spat out the words, "this other guy, is *Tuna*?!"

I sighed, knowing how everything I had just said had been lost on him.

"I'll kill him," he said, punching the wall and then clutching his hand in agony.

"He's gone," I said.

"Ha," he laughed bitterly, "yeah because you chose me over him. He'll never forgive you; you know. Not now."

I looked down at the floor.

"Well, I won't know until I find him."

"Find him? *Find him?!* You can't be serious. You're coming home with us. Your mum and dad'll never let you stay..."

"They won't have a choice," I said doing up my bag.

Rich suddenly grabbed my arms.

"Please, Ruby," he begged, his voice wheedling, "don't do this. I'm sorry. You've paid me back now. Come home with me. We can have our old life back..."

I shook my head and looked at him sadly.

"No, Rich."

He let go of me suddenly.

"I don't want you anyway," he spat, his mouth curled in a sneer, "Nicole was much fitter than you, and there's loads of other girls I can have back home; in fact, there are a couple I *was* having behind your back anyway. I just thought you would make good 'wife material'. You know boring, faithful, stay-at-home while I go out and have fun."

I looked at him sadly, at his red, angry face. I tried to remember how much I had loved him, but I just couldn't understand how I had. It had blown away on the breeze coming through that open door.

"Bye, Rich."

I heaved my rucksack onto my back and headed out the door.

"You'll regret this!" he shouted after me. I felt like I was in a Mafia movie; I half expected him to threaten to cut of Moggy's head and put it in my bed.

As I walked down the stairs and out into the bright sunshine, I felt wonderfully light. I felt free.

Chapter Thirty-Two

Against all odds, my parents had become best of friends with my little group of mates, and I found them all chattering around breakfast at The Golden Palm, which my dad was treating them to as goodbye present. It was a buffet breakfast and consequently Dazzer and Tom in true backpacker style had piled their plates with everything they could get their hands on – after all they didn't know when they would get a decent meal again. Dazzer had even taken one of the carrots that had been carved into a flower as a table decoration.

"Well, I think that Steph's mother will just fall in love with you," Mum was saying unconvincingly to Dazzer, peering over his pile of food at him.

"Yes she will," Steph gushed.

I thought of Steph's battleaxe mother and felt immensely sorry for Dazzer. And then it struck me – Dazzer meeting Step's mum? They'd only known each other for about half an hour! I sighed and shook my head as I walked towards them.

"Well, you see, you've just got to follow your dreams," Dad was saying to Tom who was nodding seriously, "I mean I did. I went off to Spain because I had just had enough of the drudgery of everyday life in the grey old U of K. And I was depressed – that's what it was, *depressed.* And so I thought my wife didn't love me anymore. Luckily," he patted my mum's knee and they smiled at each other, "Donna here came after me and made me see sense. And she decided to follow my dream too, and join me in the restaurant business."

"He needs somebody with a business head out there," my mum said fondly. And to my complete and utter astonishment they leaned their heads together and kissed each other. A full-on passionate kiss – no tongues because it was breakfast after all. Jess had a look of horror on her face but all the others looked at each other with soppy looks on their faces, as if they had witnessed true love.

"You two are just like my heroes," Tom said shaking his head in admiration at my Dad, "you're like the perfect couple."

"Ahem," I coughed from behind my dad and they all noticed me for the first time. Mum clocked the backpack on my back.

"Oh good you've packed," she said smiling, "But you could have left your bag in your room you know?"

I shook my head.

"I'm not coming with you, Mum."

She frowned through her smile and cocked her head to one side.

"But we've bought you your ticket," she said, "and Rich is taking you home and…"

I sighed. And then I heard footsteps behind me and Rich came running up, all flustered.

"She's leaving Mrs Jones," he said gasping, "she's going after Tuna."

"Tuna?" Dad asked frowning, "That quiet young chap that left a few days ago? Nice boy. But what on earth does he have to do with you?"
"She's sleeping with him!" Rich blurted out. "She's confused and she thinks she wants to go after him. She wants revenge on me see..."

"Revenge?" Mum asked looking from me to Rich and back again.

"Uh...um...I mean..." Rich stammered, shifting his eyes back and fore nervously.

"Why on earth would you want revenge young lady?" Mum said sternly to me. "You've put this boy through quite enough already! Running off like that with not a word to anyone, and leaving poor Rich all alone in the middle of nowhere in Thailand. Oh so he found comfort in the arms of a lovely French girl, but who could blame him after what you did? And yet he still found it in his heart to forgive you and to come and tell us, and ask us to help him to find you..."

"Rich didn't tell us the full story Mam," Jess piped up. I meanwhile, was staring open-mouthed at Rich. He was fidgeting nervously, his eyes darting back and fore between my mum, Jess and me.

"Well, I don't know what she told you Jess," he said indignantly, "but that's what happened..."

"How could you?" I asked him under my breath.

"*He* went off with the French girl first which was why Ruby did a runner," Jess said, smiling at Rich spitefully, "not the other way round."

"Oh and how would *you* know?!" Rich spat at her.

"Tuna told me, the night he left. He told me all about it, about how he had to look after Ruby through all those nights where her heart was breaking. About how it was *he* that held her as she cried, and brought her food and drink, and blankets, while you were off running about with *Nicole*," she said Nicole with a French accent, and Tom couldn't help mumbling "Papa?" in reply before muttering "sorry, sorry" and shaking his head.

"Well, of course Tuna's going to say that," Rich ranted, waving his arms in the air, "he was in love with Ruby, and she chose me instead of him! So he's going to make up rubbish like that to get you all to turn against me."

"Uh, actually Tuna's not a liar mate," Dazzer spoke up, and then sort of shrivelled in his chair as Rich glared at him.

Dad looked at me, his eyes questioning.

"Is this true Ruby love?"

I looked into his wide hazel eyes, the eyes that Jess and I had inherited and I didn't even have to nod. He got to his feet, and strode over to Rich. He grasped him by the collar.

"I think you and I need to have a chat boyo," he said marching him out of the restaurant to the curious stares of the other diners.

Mum stood up and immediately threw her arms around me. I was beginning to miss the old mum, the one who only hugged on birthdays and Christmas; these dramatic displays of affection were becoming a bit tedious.

"I'm so sorry my darling," she said, sobbing (again) loudly, "when Rich turned up looking all forlorn, we just took his word for what had happened. We thought you had had a funny blip or something from taking too many drugs..."

"Mum! I don't take drugs," I burst out, disentangling myself from her arms, and looked shiftily at Tom and Dazzer who grinned back at me.

"Well, you know, I thought it was like *The Beach*, you know with Leonardo Dicaprio, with big fields of marijuana and opium," she pronounced the 'j' in marijuana with distaste, "and that you had run off to be wild and hippyish and sow your wild oats and had left poor Rich behind. And he seemed so ready to forgive you we thought we should help him to find you. And all along you must have thought we were so heartless trying to force you to get back with him when he did that to you."

"OK, Mum," I said sternly, "that's quite enough."

I forced her down into her chair, and made her take a sip of water, as she flapped her face with her hands, trying not to cry.

"It's OK, I don't blame you," I softened my voice, "But I am in a rush and there's something I need to do."

I looked at Tom.

"Do you know where he is?" I asked him.

"I'm not sure, because I haven't heard from him, but I do know where he was planning to go before heading back to Australia," he said.

"Where?" I gasped.

Everyone was leaning forward in their seats and hanging onto our every word.

"The Gili Islands."

I nodded.

"He told me about them."

"Gili Trewangan," he said, "that's his favourite. But I don't know where he stays."

I grinned at him.

"That's OK," I felt like I was going to burst with happiness, "I'll find him."

Steph clapped her hands together in delight, and my mum started sobbing into her hanky again.

"I really liked that young man Tuna you know," she was murmuring while Tom rubbed her back soothingly.

Lata meanwhile was staring blankly passed my head with a look of wonder on her face as if she had seen a ghost. I turned around, my heart lifting; maybe Tuna had come back? But I was met by an equally shocking sight. Tim was walking towards us, sunglasses on, a bag slung over his shoulder. Steph clapped a hand over her mouth and gave a little scream. He grinned at Lata as he strode towards her.

"I was thinking," he said to her, as he got down on one knee at her feet and took off his sunglasses to reveal those startling blue eyes that were shining and full of love, "a Thai wedding would be lovely."

Lata threw her arms around his neck and they held each other tightly, laughing. Of course Mum by now was sobbing hysterically; I wondered if all the water would short circuit her robot wires.

While everyone was preoccupied with Lata and Tim – and Dazzer was tucking into his second plate of breakfast – I decided to slip away. I hated big goodbyes and I was getting pretty good at this disappearing lark. But as I made it through the double doors, I felt a hand grab my wrist. I turned to look into my own eyes. Jess was smiling at me.

"I thought you needed a bit of help back there," she said.

I grinned.

"Well, we always did work as a team, didn't we?"

"After talking to Tuna, I felt so bad that we had believed Rich, and had come over here and steam-rolled you into getting back with him."

I shook my head.

"You were just doing what families do."

She nodded.

"And there was no way I was going to allow you to let that one get away," she said smiling mischievously, "do you know if Tuna is into twin fantasies?"

"I don't know, but I am certainly *not* going to indulge him if he is!" I said, screwing up my face.

"I got off with Taylor once," she said thoughtfully, "it was a bit strange but it wasn't as bad as you might think."

"Jess! No!"

She smiled and shrugged her shoulders.

"You've got to try everything once," she said. "But I realised I still need cock."

"Oh God, Jess," I said glancing around at the startled business man who was wandering past. "Look I have to go."

"Yes you do," she said giving me a quick hug. "Go on. Go!"

I ran out of the lobby, down the steps and bumped straight into Dad who was rubbing his hands together as if he was brushing sand off his hands.

"Ruby love," he smiled, "where are you off to?"

"I'm going to find Tuna, Dad."

He nodded.

"Good girl. Follow your dream."

"You didn't hit Rich, did you, Dad?"

He shook his head.

"No, no. I'm an older man; can't go round clocking young men on the head now can I? Got to be the mature one – not that I didn't want to mind!" He glanced around and then leaned in closer. "I just marched him up to the room, made him grab his things and then marched him right out of the hotel, and down to the jetty, where I uh…helped him onto a boat to the mainland. So you won't be seeing him again."

I grinned.

"Thanks Dad."

"We'll probably see him on the plane later mind, but that's no bad thing. We can make his journey particularly uncomfortable. I'm sure Jess will accidentally tip her coffee on him or something," he winked at me. I gave him a hug.

"Now listen," he said putting his hands on my shoulders, "you're a grown woman so I can't be worrying about you going off. But you be careful. And if things don't work out, with you and this Turbot guy…"

"Tuna."

"Yes, that's what I said, Tuna…well you know you can come home anytime," he said gently, "even though home is now in Spain of course!"

I nodded, and he pushed me away gently.

"Off you go now," he said, "And make sure you send us one of those emails. I'm getting quite a dab-hand at it now!"

I ran down to the jetty and clambered onto the waiting taxi boat. I was alone again, on a boat setting off on an adventure. But this time I wasn't scared or lonely. I was brimming with excitement and happiness and I revelled in the refreshing air coming through that open door.

Part Five

The Gili Isles

Chapter Thirty-Three

The coast of Bali came into view through my window as the plane began to descend. I felt thrilled to see the verdant land meeting the bright blue sea. The landing quickly became terrifying as we flew lower and lower over the sea until I could see fish leaping from the waves; I became convinced that we were crashing into the water, and the pilot had decided not to tell us so as not to make the last moments of our lives hellish. But I finally felt the welcome bump as we hit the tarmac of the runway and we sailed into the prettiest airport I had ever seen. It looked more like a temple than an airport and beautiful Balinese women in bright sarongs met us off the plane. The customs officer told me that he loved me before proposing to me, and so I entered Bali with a smile, amazed by the first customs officer that I had ever met that hadn't taken an instant dislike to me.

I marvelled at the astonishing multi-coloured beauty of Bali as I travelled via taxi: the juicy greens of the lush virginal landscape; the passionate pinks and reds of tumbling flowers spilling onto the roads; the glistening gold of the ubiquitous pagodas; the cerulean sarongs worn by women carrying baskets of ripe fruit on their heads. I drank in the sounds of the hooting traffic; the bells on the oxen harnesses; the shouts of street sellers. I tasted the smells of incense wafting from the tiny Hindu offerings placed everywhere: on temple steps; outside houses; on the roadsides. I became heady from the smiles of the Balinese people, with their flashing eyes and effervescent pride in their country. And so I had driven through Bali on a tide of optimism.

Then I had to get a boat across to Lombok, which was twelve hours away. And it all went downhill from there. At the pretty ferry port of Padangbai, touts immediately descended upon me. My backpack was forcibly whipped from my hands and thrown onto someone's back and I ran onto the ferry, noticing with some alarm that it was listing heavily to one side whilst trying to keep hold of the strap of my backpack and desperately hoping the wiry young man beneath it wouldn't disappear with it. Then about ten touts stood around me on deck and tried to force me into giving them a ridiculous tip. Because I refused to give them more than the typical rate, they shouted and ranted and raved and then tried to drag my rucksack off the boat again, so I had to actually sit astride it in order to stop it going anywhere. Eventually they spotted some very green and innocent-looking Scandinavian girls who were smiling at everyone and gazing around in awe, and they raced after them instead.

I felt a bit jittery, and bit incredulous that I was doing this alone, but I felt proud of myself and looked around defiantly at anyone that tried to make me move from the aisle, where I was perched on my rucksack. Eventually a young man approached me and offered me some of his rice. I shook my head gratefully and he sat on the seat closest to me as I wobbled about in the aisle.

"I must apologise for my countrymen," he indicated the group of men who were crowding around the girls and shouting at them, while the girls stared back at them terrified and goggle-eyed. "These men are from Lombok as am I. They are not nice men. But we are not all like this."

I nodded.

"It's OK. There are some horrid people in my country too," I smiled.

***

Twelve hours later, I gratefully stepped off the boat onto Lombok, gasping clear fresh air after being engulfed by cigarette smoke for most of the journey. From there it was a bus ride, where I was crammed onto a mini-bus along with about fifty seven other people and a couple of chickens, and we were thrown around from side to side as the bus hurtled along winding roads that twisted along the palm-lined coastline. The bus driver finally screeched to a sudden halt at a small town and announced that he went no further. I stood in the dust for a while waiting for onward transport. After driving at one hundred and ninety kilometres per hour in the bus it was with some frustration that I found myself on a donkey and cart plodding along for the last five kilometres to the beach from where boats left for the Gili Islands. Once at the beach, yet more touts tried to extort money from me for carrying my bag the ten metres down the beach to the waiting wooden boat. By now exhaustion and irritation had dissolved my optimistic mood and I began to worry that I might not find Tuna; I would have come all this way and he might not be there. Worse still I might find him and he might tell me where to go. I wouldn't blame him. Well, I decided, I would just lie on the floor and hang onto his ankle until he changed his mind. I sat on the small wooden boat along with other backpackers clutching their rucksacks and local women wearing headscarves and carrying baskets of vegetables and surprisingly calm chickens trussed up by the ankle and being carried over a shoulder. The water was silvery-blue, and the late morning sun was getting hot.

Finally, the hazy coastline of Gili Trewangan came into view and my heart lurched into my mouth. My future lay on these islands.

I jumped down into the water, lugged my rucksack onto the beach and looked around. Tuna was right. This place really was a little slice of paradise. Drooping palms shaded a long white sandy beach; local children played on the beach throwing coconuts at each other; painted fishing boats bobbed in the surf. The main road – the only road on the island – was cobbled for a stretch of about half a kilometre and then it petered out into a sand track. Along the cobbled stretch of road was a collection of upmarket hotels, alongside beautifully decorated open-air restaurants. On either side, these were lined by smaller, backpacker establishments, laid-back cafés and second-hand bookshops or knick-knack stalls. Fresh fish was sold everywhere and people asked me to stop for lunch as I strolled along. The only traffic on the road were donkeys and carts. I beamed as I walked along. I loved it. But as I looked around and realised that smaller lanes ran off behind the hotels leading to a maze of streets and other hotels, I didn't know where I was going to start.

And then I remembered Tuna telling me about where he stayed; it was along a sandy track, and it consisted of huts dotted amongst the palm trees and meadows of flowers. It was opposite the beach: he'd said he could see the sand through his small window and there was nothing else around, just the huts in the trees, so he could hear the sea.

The problem was which way down the road was it? Left or right? Both ends became a sandy track that went off around the coast. I just had to choose, and I picked left. I trekked off with my rucksack weighing me down and making me sweat in the hot midday sun. Eventually the sounds from the main strip faded away as I rounded the coast. There was nothing ahead, just the sandy track running along the beach and disappearing into the trees. I heard the soft clip-clop of some hooves that were padding through the sand and turned to see a donkey dragging along a cart. The driver was a young boy of about twelve. He waved at me, pulled the donkey to a stop alongside me and he indicated for me to get onto the cart. We plodded along. After ten minutes of nothing but palm trees, I began to worry I had made the wrong choice and was thinking about hopping off the cart and heading back the way we came. But then I saw a wooden sign nailed to a tree.

"Sunshine Guesthouse," it said. My heart pounded as I glimpsed to the right of me small bungalows on stilts dotted through the trees and surrounded by small white and pink flowers. I glanced to my left to see the powdery beach through the palms, the gentle waves lapping the shore.

I jumped off the cart, giving the boy some money and waved at him as he drove away. Hurrying down the path leading to the guesthouse, I was met by a young, man who was clutching coconuts that he had just knocked out of a tree.

"Hello! Hello! You wan' room? You wan' bungalow?"

He beamed at me, a broad handsome smile.

"I'm looking for someone," I said. "His name is Tuna. He is tall with blonde hair and blue eyes."

He frowned and shook his head.

"No, no Toonah here," he smiled again. "But nice bungalow, nice, nice room. Come, see."

He urged me to follow him, jerking his head towards the nearest hut. It was very quaint, with wooden beds, a basic bathroom, and small wooden windows that opened to look out towards the beach. I was exhausted and I just wanted to get my backpack off my back. I nodded at him and he ran away happily to get me a key. He returned with a coconut with the top cut off and a straw sticking out of it.

"For you, lovely lady," he said. "Any time you wan' more coconut you tell me. I get for you."

He nodded and backed away down the steps from my little veranda smiling.

I had a shower, put on my white sundress and then sat on the cane chairs sipping my coconut juice and wondering how on earth I had got to this little pocket of paradise. Slowly my mood darkened as I began to realise that it was probably likely that Tuna wasn't even here, and it had all been a wasted trip.

I wandered down the path to the beach and stood amongst the trees, looking out to sea. There were red and white sails of fishing boats far out on the waves, and the sea was mottled with bright green and dark navy where coral reefs circled the island. I thought of how Tuna had promised to teach me to dive. I had never felt more lonely in my life than on that perfect beach.

And it was at that moment that I turned my head and I saw a figure further off along the sand, sitting under the shade of a palm tree on a bit of driftwood, reading a book. My mouth was suddenly dry. It was him.

I walked slowly along the sand until I was standing just behind him.

"I don't know if you can help me," I said softly. "I'm looking for someone."

He didn't make any obvious physical reaction, and he didn't turn to face me. It was almost as if I hadn't spoken. He just stayed sitting very still.

"You see," I carried on, "I really hurt this person. I got confused and made a really stupid mistake."

Still no reaction.

"I was scared, because I had been hurt badly myself," my eyes bored into his back willing him to turn around, "and I took the easy option. But I realised very quickly that it wasn't what I wanted."

He put his book down on the sand but still didn't turn around.

"I realised what I wanted was him. And I've been looking for him for days, hoping that he would forgive me."

"And what if he won't forgive you?" He asked finally, his voice cold.

I felt a sob catch in my throat and I battled to hold it down.

"Well, that's a shame because I won't ever find anyone that makes me feel the way he does. You see this man is wonderful, and sweet and kind and gorgeous and I have never had such amazing sex in my entire life," I paused, "and well he wouldn't have much choice but to forgive me, because I would just follow him around the world, until he got so sick of me stalking him that he would have to forgive me."

I could tell he was smiling; just by the way he moved his head and looked down. I could see the dimple in his cheek.

"You see I love him."

He turned suddenly and looked straight into my eyes. He raised his eyebrows in question.

I nodded.

"I love you," I said again, wanting to fall into the swirl of his silver eyes.

He stood up and stepped towards me.

"I love you Tuna and…"

"Oh shut up," he stopped my words with his mouth. I kissed his mouth and his chin and his nose and his cheeks and his eyes, and then he hugged me so tightly that he lifted me off the sand.

"But what about going home with Rich and your family and all that?" he asked finally.

I smiled shyly.

"Well, I was kind of thinking, I always wondered what it would be like to live in Australia. I mean I watch *Neighbours* avidly, and I could grow a mullet, and I'm sure AFL isn't *that* much different to rugby, and I could learn to say things like 'G'day, you great gallah'."

Tuna threw his head back and laughed loudly.

"You crazy girl," he said, "I love you."

"Do you?" I asked.

He nodded.

"Ever since you walked into that shitty hostel in Bangkok, acting like Lady Muck and looking at me like I was a cockroach," his eyes flashed. "And look at you now Lady Muck, you just can't wait for me to get you back to my dollar-a-night hut and have my wicked way with you."

"You got it," I said laughing and dragging him along the beach.

When we got to Sunshine Guesthouse, the owner gave us a big smile.

"You said he wasn't staying here!" I said to him accusingly, pointing at Tuna. He frowned and shook his head.

"No you asked for Toonah, not Mr Tuna," he pronounced it Tewna.

I shook my head and rolled my eyes at Tuna, and we ran quickly down the path and into his bungalow where we locked the door and didn't emerge for a very long time.

Epilogue

I have had to talk Steph out of calling her future son Bazzer. He is due in a month. She was a blooming bride because she was six months pregnant. Dazzer was unrecognisable with his short hair and smart suit. He's working in investment banking now, has finally grown out of his sexist/racist/offensive comments, and is actually a very nice, respectable young man. I managed to go home to the UK to the wedding but I missed Lata's wedding because she and Tim did it that week after he showed up in Railay. Steph was bridesmaid, and Tom gave Lata away, and they all wore bikinis, sarongs or board shorts. Lata's mum was horrified though and so they had to have the whole big shebang again in London when they got home.

Mum and Dad's bistro is flourishing now Mum is running the business side of things, and I've never known them to be happier. Mum has embraced her role as a Spanish matriarch and has huge dinners with all her neighbours and their families, who are all a bit bewildered by this glamorous woman who has landed in their midst. Jess has also embraced the Spanish lifestyle with gusto – well the partying and showing around good-looking tourists anyway. But I recently had an email from her saying the following:

Dear Kylie (my new nickname according to all my British friends)

How's Down Under? And how's my gorgeous future brother-in-law?

Espanya is still fuckin' fantastic, especially since a guy walked into the bistro last week. Said his name was Charlie and that you'd given him our address and said he should look us up if he ever got to travelling round Europe.

Well, sis, all I can say is thank fuckin' you! We are engaged! Yes! Honestly! Mum had a fit when I told her, you can imagine. But I am head over heels in love with him! He's gorgeous! Although I'm working on getting him to shave off his manky dreads.

Jess x

After buying a camper van and travelling around Australia for six months, Tuna and I finally settled in the beautiful little town of Coral Bay in Western Australia. I'm training for my dive master qualification now, after getting my open water licence through Tuna's school. Tuna's diving school is flourishing, and I run a small guesthouse and café alongside it, where I get to meet travellers from all over the world. I have taken up pottery again and have even sold a few of my products, so the café is being converted into a shop as well. Tom came to visit us recently after he broke up with Mali. We travelled over to Port Douglas to visit Trish and Tammy, and Tom and Trish got pretty friendly. She's visiting him in the UK at the moment so I think we're going to be seeing a lot more of Tom in the future.

As for Tuna and I, we have had to put our plans for our next big trip to America on hold because I am six months pregnant. But once she's born, we're strapping her into one of those baby carrier rucksacks (Tuna will carry it) and taking her with us. I have that cosy fire with Tuna now. But every now and then we still remember to open that door and step out into the bright sunlight and the cool refreshing breeze.